...er, but some of us are ... the stars."

— Oscar Wilde, *Lady Windermere's Fan*

Author Bio

CAROLANN COPLAND is the founder of *Carousel Creates*, a writers' centre in the Dublin Mountains.

She has a Bachelor of Education in English and Drama and has been a teacher for fourteen years.

Although she writes mostly novels; Carolann loves to dabble with short stories, plays and poetry; writing between Dublin and Andalucia in the South of Spain. Discovering her love of writing a little later than others has meant that she has let it become a major part of her life and she means to enjoy every moment. She wakes up each morning on fire with a desire to write. Walking in the woods or along the beach in all weathers is where she likes to concoct her extraordinary plots but most of her ideas come from polishing the ordinary things in life and making them shine.

From Dublin, Ireland, Carolann has also lived in the Middle East and the United Kingdom. She is married to Neil and is a mother of three children aged ten to twenty-two.

Through mentoring writers of all ages; from all walks of life; Carolann is happiest when she is sharing her passion for writing. She is a member of two writing groups and works to promote other writing groups in Dublin.

Having spent all her life engrossed in reading stories, Carolann now looks forward to sharing her fictional world with other readers.

Summer
Triangle

by
Carolann Copland

October 2013

Summer Triangle
2013

Published by Emu Ink Ltd
www.emuink.ie

F115, 515
£10.00

© Carolann Copland

Cover Design by Gwen Taylour

ISBN: 978 - 1 - 909684 - 25 - 6

Acknowledgements...

SUMMER TRIANGLE is dedicated to my writer friend, Kieran O'Kelly, who died earlier this year. Kieran was the first editor of this book and an excellent critic. Keep guiding my pen, Kieran. We miss you.

No book is an island. There are so many people to thank for surrounding me with support...

...To my parents; Joe and Bridie Maher. They have been incredibly encouraging in pushing me along on my writing journey. My mother urged me to get writing. She knew it would make my life complete and it does. My parents give over their house to Carousel Writers; my father's beautiful gardens making sure that we have the most inspiring venue possible in which to be creative.

...To Neil. My mother told me to marry him. She liked that he made me smile and that he encouraged me to do all the things that were important to me. Twenty-five years later, he still makes me happy.

...To my siblings; Doreen, Joe, Siobhán, Colum and Lorcan. They have nurtured my confidence, feeding me titbits of just enough praise and criticism.

...To my children; David, Katy-Anna and Aoife. Thank you for being patient when Mammy's hiding away in her writing room. They are to blame for the sign on my door that reads *A clean house is a sign of a broken computer*.

...To all the writing groups that have sailed with this book.

Especially to Tara Sparling, Bernadette Kearns, Joan Brady, Orna Ross, Elizabeth Hutcheson, Conor Kostik and Siobhán Parkinson. I am in awe of their talent and have used it and abused it while they shaped my novel into being.

…To the writers at Carousel Writers' Centre; above all Annmarie Miles, Kathryn Crowley, Fatima Jaber, Catherine Brophy and Annette Bryan. They pushed the novel that last inch in the publishing direction.

…To the Irish Crime Writers' Association; especially Laurence O' Bryan. They gave my Summer Triangle the polish it needed to make it shine.

…To those I have never met but keep me going on Facebook and Twitter with their constant encouragement.

…To my teacher friends who listen to me constantly prattling on about my writing life and never tell me to shut up.

…To Margaret Birmingham for peace of mind.

…To the Gardaí. Particularly Alan Greally, Tara Mc Manus and Orla Darcy. Your knowledge fed the authenticity of the crime scenes.

…To Emer Cleary and her team at Emu Ink Publishing for their brilliant shaping of the end product. You have not only made the publishing process seamless, but brought me on an immensely enjoyable passage from writer to published author.

…To my best friends for being there, cajoling and encouraging. Thank you Jackie Murphy, Louise Williamson and all my Knocklyoners.

…Finally to Louise Phillips who has inspired confidence in so many writers, including myself. Her enormous generosity of time and wisdom is deeply appreciated, and I take pleasure in counting her among my friends.

And so… I present to you Summer Triangle. Thank you for giving me the utmost compliment by reading my book.

Chapter one

I COULD not be happier than I am at this moment. I watch the carousel build up speed and Shadia holding on with both hands. Her hijab flapping behind her falls back from her head, allowing me to see more of her laughing eyes each time she circles past me. Rising and falling on her golden horse, with the flashing green lights brightening the dark around her – the freedom of this special night tells on her beautiful face. I know from her look that she's thinking of our first, sneaked kiss from earlier. My mouth still melts from the taste of her.

I'm standing at the foot of the steps and can hear her calling to her friend now, above the noise of the crowds and the music chimes.

'Maeve! What a perfect night!' Her voice. So happy.

She lets go with one hand and reaches out to hold Maeve's as they go around and around together. I close my eyes for a moment, enjoying the breeze the carousel movement creates, cooling the Riyadh spring heat. It's almost midnight but I'm still sweating under the white cotton of my clothes. I remove my glasses to rub the sweat from my forehead with my sleeve. My mouth is watering from the smell of chicken shawarmas in the tent behind me and I make a move to join the bustling queue for food.

'We should go soon.' Omar taps my shoulder to get my attention.

I shrug and put my glasses back on. 'Yeah. Soon, Omar.'

'Shadia's parents said to be home by 10pm.' Omar's worrying about his job. Late home means he'll be in trouble for neglecting his duties as our driver and chaperone. 'You took a week to persuade them to give in and let her come out with you, Majid. I can't ignore their calls anymore and you've all to be in school at...'

'Hah... school! I feel a sore throat coming on tomorrow... It's okay, Omar. Reee...lax. I'll take all the blame when we get home. The girls are having a good time. Let them have one more spin around and then we'll go. Okay?' I smile at him to ease his worry. We're in so much trouble already that another few minutes won't matter. The wariness of our parents about us going out with Shadia's Western friend screams out from the missed calls on my mobile, so we might as well make the rage worthy of the crime.

Omar nods and the creases on his forehead smooth over a little. The horses are slowing now and I wave to Shadia and Maeve to stay on for one more go. Their girly shrieks make us smile as they swap their horses and climb into a golden carriage. Princesses.

I sit down on the bench and Omar shifts over to make room. 'So sky gazer,' I say, eager to talk about something else. 'Three stunning stars.' I point upwards. Omar has been guiding me through the constellations since I was a baby. Nothing gives him greater pleasure and I'm rewarded by his animated face.

'*The Summer Triangle*, Majid,' he says. 'Made up of Vega, Deneb and Altair. Good Islamic names for stars that guide us on the right path.'

'Summer? It's only March 17th.'

'You can see it first in the spring here in the East, then it gradually becomes apparent in the summer in the West.'

I nod. Omar looks up at the carousel starting again and then at his watch.

'They'll get over it, Omar. Shadia's parents,' I say with mock confidence.

Omar smiles another half-smile and raises his eyebrows at me.

'Okay. I know,' I sigh, 'but there's no harm done. Shadia's never allowed out. She's really enjoying herself tonight and she might not get another chance for a while.'

Omar nods and stands up. 'Okay, Majid but there'll be spit and venom when we get back. I'll go and bring the car to the gate and wait for you there.'

Watching him heading out past the sign for the *Riyadh Irish Festival*, I feel the tension of the journey home building already.

'Ten minutes, Omar,' I call. 'We'll...'

Without warning, the lights go out all over the park. The rides slow and the music fades. A few women screech excitedly and we wait to see what might happen next. Midnight is drawing closer.

There's silence and after what seems like minutes, excited giggles turn nervous and heckles begin to pepper the atmosphere. I look expectantly towards the starlit sky for fireworks or something equally fantastic, but there's nothing. I can just about make out the shadowy figures of Shadia and Maeve, standing up now and feeling their way through the darkness on the still carousel.

An explosion rips through the air and I find myself face down on the ground with nothing but ringing in my ears and a tremendous heat rising behind me. I'm acutely aware of my racing heartbeat and my mind is whirring as beads of perspiration, from both the intense heat and fear, drip down my back and forehead. I twist around and the fire pouring from the horses' heads on the previously picturesque carousel fills me with dread.

Shadia.

I roll over and try to stand up. I can see Maeve now lying sprawled along the edge of the carousel staircase. The light from the blaze dances in her wide open eyes, staring, lifeless now, in the direction of the smoke-filled sky. The flames from the carousel creep down towards her feet, eating at the wooden steps and a long piece of gold, spiral steel is embedded in her front.

'Omar! Omar!' I scream as people race into my path from every direction. The fear of another bomb to follow the one now tearing their worlds apart is apparent on their faces; their mouths silently shrieking.

The dead and injured, mostly women, hang from painted animals and plastic cars; their fallen hijabs exposing their black, blonde or red hair – all with pale faces. Omar is here, pushing back through the crowds to get to the carousel... to me... to Shadia...

3

Then I see her.

Crawling out from behind the burning horses she struggles down the steps. I stand still, staring at the mass of flames writhing just a few metres away. Her eyes, wild with pain, search mine, beseeching. Her abaya is almost burnt away. She is lit up from head to toe. Staggering towards her I feel the vibrations of a roar deep in my throat, but I am pulled back by Omar's strong arms before I can reach her.

I snarl, kicking and elbowing at the cage around my middle, preventing me from getting to her as she falls in a heap. The smell of her burning flesh fills me with rage.

She lies still.

The only movement around her now are those licking flames and my desperate arms struggling to reach her.

Chapter two

SITTING up in bed at 7am, still fully clothed in her tracksuit bottoms and hoodie, Shona reached down and ran her hands over her swollen tummy. It was actually moving inside her.

'Jesus,' she whispered, and the tears came again.

She hugged her legs and hung her head. When she eventually looked back up, her mother was standing over her.

'Where were you until 3.30am, Shona Moran?' Norah's arms were folded across the lace of her long nightdress. 'You have to leave for school in an hour. Look at the state of you!'

Shona turned and glared at her mother. Let her think that she'd been out drinking half the night. It was better than the truth. She ignored the rant that followed. How could she say where she really was until that time? She couldn't explain that she had been walking a Dublin beach in the rain until all hours, trying to ward off the idea that the waves had looked more inviting than the last bus home.

Shona noticed her mum staring at her chest, her forehead creased in puzzlement. Surely she was over the floral tattoo that ribboned its way along her neck and the top of her breast. Another thing to row about, as if she needed more. She flicked her black curls away to show it at its best and huffed.

'Go away, Mum.'

'What is it, Shona?'

'What? My tattoo? It's Fuchsia. The flowers that…'

'No! Not your bloody tattoo! I mean what's going on with you? You're acting strange.'

Shona slouched further down under the duvet.

'Yeah, right! If I breathe you think I'm acting weird. I'd be

5

worried about myself if you started to think I was normal. Five minutes more and I'm up. Okay?'

Shona closed her eyes and waited for her mother to back off. There was no movement and she jumped when Norah suddenly pulled back the duvet and pushed up the front of her top.

Her mouth dropped open as she stared, disbelieving, at her daughter's bump. Neat and compact, but undeniable. She looked back up at Shona, her face now as white as her nightdress, the sudden realisation beginning to register. Silence exploded around them for a moment as Shona stared back defiantly.

'So. Now you know.' Shona waited for the shouting but nothing came.

Norah shook her head slowly, put her hands to her face and backed out of the door.

*

A few hours later Shona sat in the stuffy classroom feeling as though she might keel over. That made her smile. Imagine Mr Cannon's face if he had to deal with a fainting attack. When she came to, she could very calmly say... *it's alright Mr Cannon. No need for alarm. I'm only six months pregnant.* The poor man would die. Shona looked around her at the other girls intent on their sample exam papers. Friends? Not exactly. A few drinking partners. Shona Moran was a great one to call up if you wanted a piss up, because she could drink everyone under the table, even the lads. The teachers, however, condemned her for wasting her private education. Her weekend job in the pub suited her. Every other night was for life's long parties. Or at least they used to be.

Time flew by interspersed with attacks of dizziness and she was racing towards the end of the last question when the familiar woozy feeling hit her stomach again. She wondered why people called it morning sickness. It was morning, noon and night sickness. Everything she had read told her that she'd be sick for the first three months but here she was, six months in and it was still puke city. She would try to get through this comprehension before going out to the loo. No. She wasn't going to last. To hell with it anyway. She'd have to leg it if she wanted to get there in time. She pushed her chair back noisily and tripped over the desk in front of her.

'Shite!' Every pair of eyes in the room bored into her.

'Shona Moran! What are you up to now?' Mr Cannon was up and marching towards her.

Shona pulled herself off the floor and pushed past the startled man.

'Gotta go to the toilet, Mr Cannon.' She was running now.

'There's only ten minutes left, Shona. Surely you can wait.' But she was out the door and racing, just making it into the cubicle in time. When she was finished, Shona lowered the seat and sat and cried. Her father would tell her that there were worse things that could happen. They had prayed at assembly that morning for the families of the Irish women who had been killed in that bomb in Saudi Arabia. That was awful, but this was happening to her.

Ten minutes later Shona heard a light tap on the door.

'Shona Moran. Are you still in there?' The unmistakable clipped tones of her school principal.

Shona didn't answer. Mrs Brogan could go to hell. They all could. For six years Mrs B had been telling her where she was going wrong with everything and how if she would only try a little bit harder she could do great things with her life. Well Old Broggers couldn't even try to tell her how to fix this. Shona Moran was seventeen years old and she was having a baby.

'Shona... Open the door please.'

Nothing.

'Shona. Mr Cannon has informed me that you upset all the other students with the commotion of leaving the exam room. I hope you have a very good explanation young lady. I'm waiting here until you come out and if I find out that you have notes in there with you during these practise examinations, I promise you that you'll face the full consequences.'

Shona started to laugh. Broggers thought that she'd been cogging. If only her problem was that small.

7

'It's not funny, Shona. I'm going to climb over the wall into the toilet and open the door myself if you don't come out right now!'

This made Shona laugh even louder. The very thought of the ancient principal, trying to climb over the wall from the next toilet, made her howl.

'Fine! Have it your way!'

Shona stopped when she heard noises from the other toilet, where Mrs Brogan was indeed trying to climb her way into the cubicle. Jesus.

'Okay, okay. I'm coming out.' She heard the sound of the old woman retreating and pulled the lock slowly. She moved out into the sink area and the principal walked past her. Shona watched as the woman began to search the area, lifting the lid of the cistern to make a thorough search.

'You won't find any notes belonging to me, Mrs Brogan.' The woman ignored her and kept up the search. Then she turned and stared at Shona.

'There's a terrible smell in here, Shona. Were you sick?' The principal kept looking at her and Shona saw the light come on as the woman realised why Shona Moran had had to race to the bathroom ten minutes from finishing the Spanish exam, and why her eyes were red from crying. Mrs Brogan's eyes dropped to Shona's middle and took in the large jumper that looked odd on her tiny body, and couldn't hide her secret anymore. Shona waited for her to shriek at her and demand that she go straight to her office immediately, where Mrs Brogan would give her a final dressing down – the last of so many and this time for the ultimate sin. She was trying to stare her out but the woman was looking at her strangely. A look that made Shona want to cry, instead of giving in to the defiance she was trying to hold on to. But the tears won and next thing she knew she was in Mrs Brogan's arms crying her heart out.

Chapter three

I SIT rigid in the passenger seat beside Omar. He's chatting about his day; waffling on about the latest football results. He continues his one-sided discussion about his wife Karima and her constant nagging; subjects that I used to join in with; laugh at even but that was the old me who loved Omar. This is the man who taught me how to play football and who is cool enough to know all the latest computer games. My driver has known me since I was a baby and I've respected him all my life. But here I am, clutching the seat, clenching my teeth, pushing my feet into the floor to try to quell my temper, and what my mother would call a seventeen-year-old rage gets the better of me as the words fly out like bullets.

'Shut your mouth you stupid, ignorant servant!' I yell. 'Know where your place is when nobody wants to listen to your constant prattling. Drive me home and leave me in peace. I'm not a child anymore. Speak to me as you do my father. Now, shut up and drive!' I want to stop, to swallow my words back down again. I can't believe what I'm saying. I'm so angry. Will it ever stop?

Speeding along the road for the next ten minutes in silence, Omar's eyes are staring hard, his knuckles white against the wheel. He pulls into the car park outside our house and makes a big gesture of walking around to let me out of the car, glaring at me as he makes a sweeping bow in my direction.

I feel his patience thinning as he slams the door of my father's red Mercedes. I'm closing off his friendship. Soon there'll be no one to talk to. Maybe that's a good thing. What is there to talk about anyway?

There it is. The muzzein call to prayer. Once more Allah's giving me a place to run to. A sanctuary. I need no one else.

Dropping my school books on the floor inside the door, I walk in the direction of the mosque. Five times a day I'm at peace, magnetically drawn to Allah; my one constant. I'll try to speak to the Imam after prayer. My teacher is the only person who makes sense. He can guide me, help me on the right path; straight ahead to Allah.

But at the mosque there's no relief.

'Have you no studies to go home to Majid?' The Imam touches my shoulder as I finish the sentence of my Dua. I look up at my mentor and I watch him taking in my pained face. Praying isn't giving me the strength I need today.

'I feel bare, Imam. What will fill me?' I am pleading with him for an answer. 'My words are empty. Prayers pour out and drain my voice, but the thoughts that should match them are vacant.'

Imam Wassim crouches down on the floor to be near me before he speaks.

'The questions you want answers to are there for you in the Qur'an, as everything is, Majid. It is the book of life. You must read and read your book until the meaning is clear. Mohammed's writing is plain, peace be upon him, but we need to see it through focused eyes. Concentrate on the language and repeat the questions to yourself. Allah will give you the answers.'

I'm clinging to his every word.

'The rules by which we must live our lives are all there,' he tells me. 'It is with purposeful mind that we will interpret the word most accurately. When you read with eyes, and mind and heart wide open, and you ask your questions, the meaning will be clear and you will know what to do. Choose your interpretation wisely, young man, allow yourself to be filled with his knowledge, and follow one straight path to Allah.'

For a moment he has me enthralled and then he ruins it.

'Now go, Majid,' he says. 'Eat the food that your mother gives you, eh? Try to find it in your heart to forgive those who have read the Qur'an wrongly and taken Shadia away from us. Read your school books and allow your mind to grow. Then use your wisdom to find the answers to your questions. The peace of Allah be upon you.' His hands on my head are there to bless me but I just feel their weight, nothing more. We rise slowly and I follow him with my head hanging as together we walk out to the heat and glare of the sun.

Wassim turns towards me and pulls my chin upwards to face him. I force myself to look at him.

'I know it's only been a few weeks, Majid but you must try to forgive…'

I am angry again and this time with the Imam? I shout at him before he can say anymore.

'Forgive those who have taken Shadia away from us, Imam? Never. I know that the people who planted the bomb on the carousel were angry. I've read everything that has been written in the newspapers about these men. They say that they have *shown their voice against the Western influences contaminating our religion, our women and our culture.* Slowly over the last few weeks, I've come to realise that of course they were wrong to kill; but they are right in their belief that Western people who Godlessly populate Saudi Arabia *need* to be removed from our society.'

Wassim reaches out to touch my shoulder and I try not to wince. I half listen to him, ready to bite back.

'Need to be murdered, Majid? And take good Muslims like Shadia with them? They read the Qur'an wrongly, and the newspapers are written to hold Saudi people in a good light. Everything that has happened is wrong; caused by people with no real knowledge of the way that Allah works. They killed good people who were only here with their families, doing their job.'

I'm having none of his righteousness. I've read up on all of this. I know the way things are now and how wrong Shadia's friendship with the Irish girl was. I try to speak quietly now to allow him to see that I'm right.

'Shadia's friend Maeve argued with her about what she thought were the wrongs of Saudi law. Islamic law. She filled Shadia's head with this. Maeve was born in this country and was supposedly one of the Westerners more sympathetic to the Saudi ways…

So how bad must the others be and how much are they actually corrupting Saudi life?'

I take a deep breath and continue. 'You are the Imam. Aren't you looking deep into what has happened? Of all people, you should understand what drove these men to do what they did. I hate Shadia's killers, but more than that, I hate the *reason* behind their action.'

Wassim shakes his head and sighs. My fight is back.

'The Western people need to leave our country, Imam. They have no place here. Saudis are educated enough to do the jobs that the Westerners once held power with. We have no need for them now. Not them nor their women or children. We don't need their wickedness and Godlessness infiltrating our lives.'

'Majid, Majid…' I can feel his condescending manner. 'You are only seventeen. What do you know? Everyone can understand your anger and I know that the hurt you are feeling will take time to heal, but…'

'No!' My roar shocks even me and makes me stumble away from Wassim. 'Nobody can understand how it feels to lose Shadia. Her friendship with Maeve and her Irish family was wrong. They are the reason that Shadia is dead… and you know what? It's working. I hear her family are leaving to go back to Ireland. I hope that every Irish person in Saudi goes with them… and every Western piece of…'

'Majid! Enough. You are as poisoned as the men who committed this terror against you. Go home, Majid. Pray and rest. Come back to me this evening and we will talk about this more, but for now go home and calm down.'

What does he know, this old man? I rage at his lack of understanding and fall away from him. My steps become faster and I run the path to home.

The spicy smell of food wafts from the kitchen and I'm hungry but I don't want to eat or sit with them, and listen to their false cheerfulness. I reach for my school bag, still where I left it, but then I drop it. Who is Imam Wassim to tell me to concentrate on my studies? If he knew how obsessed my English teacher is about

American literature and Western poetry he would insist that we never go near him. I know I speak English with Americanisms because of his years spent living and teaching in New York. If he loves it all so much he should go back and stay there.

I turn to go to look for Omar. I hate the feelings building in my stomach since we spoke earlier. He'll be in his cabin at this time of day and I can eat with them. We can cry for Shadia together. Nearing the door which is slightly ajar, I hear voices inside.

'This time we should go together, Omar. We haven't visited Pakistan as a couple since we left there twenty years ago. First you go, then two years later I go. It's not natural.'

Karima's talking about Pakistan? Of course. It's coming up to four years since Omar's last visit. With everything that's happened, I've forgotten the thing that would normally fill me with dread.

'You know we can't do that. Firstly we have only saved enough money for one visit. Secondly, we couldn't leave the Al Faisals without both of us for two months. The whole house would fall apart.' Omar's voice is pragmatic.

'Bah! Let it fall. They might appreciate us a little more on our return. This family doesn't know how lucky it is with you and me running their lives, and us without a child to interfere with the demands of that pair. *Omar! Bring the car to the front. I need to meet my cousin at The Kingdom Shopping Centre!* As if her very life depended on it. And *Karima! Nazir has invited ten work colleagues to dinner tonight. We need to impress them, but at the same time make it look casual.* Let them run themselves for a while.'

Both of them? They would walk out now at this time? I push the door hard so it stands completely open, showing the picture of Omar and Karima sitting hand in hand at their tiny table. At first I am taken aback to see them in any position that isn't in line with their role within our household, but I recover my wits in time to shout.

'Go to Pakistan then! Both of you! Pretend, like my parents do, that nothing's happened! Shadia hasn't died. She wasn't burned to death, screaming. There's nothing wrong with the world. We'll carry on as normal and it'll all go away. Go! Nobody else cares what happened so why should you? Maybe it would be best if you both stayed in Pakistan and never came back!' I bark at Omar and feel the energy sap from me, just as the words of Mohammed drained from me earlier.

Omar and Karima stand at my interruption. Omar comes around to the front of the table and reaches out to me, but I slap his hand away and spit at his feet.

'I don't need you,' I hiss. 'I need nobody but Allah.'

I turn and grab the flimsy handle of their cabin door and slam it in my foster father's face.

Chapter four

TOMMY sat in the small kitchen, nursing a black coffee and waiting for the post. He and his pals had been celebrating his eighteenth birthday the night before and he was feeling the repercussions. He had dragged himself out of bed twenty minutes early so he could be ready to open his school report, with his mock exam results, himself. He didn't want to hang around and wait for his dad to tell him again how little he was impressed with his choice of college applications.

Tommy's mam had wanted to be a teacher. If she were here she'd give him a bit of encouragement. Tommy looked around the room that still captured the times when his mother had been alive. All those things in their terraced house that his mam and dad had chosen together; kept the way they had always been... but now jaded. Tommy's thoughts were interrupted by his rumbling stomach. He could murder a bacon sandwich but he couldn't shift himself in the direction of the grill. Maybe his dad would do the honours when he came in.

Rubbing his eyes Tommy resolved to steer clear of the pints for a while, or at least until his Leaving Certificate exams were over at the end of June. A couple of months. He pushed back his straight brown hair and rubbed his temples. The flutter of envelopes through the letterbox made him jump up and he rushed to pick up the mail.

Putting the *Northside People* newspaper and the bills addressed to his dad to the side; he picked up the envelope with *The parents of Thomas Farrell* written on it and wandered back towards the kitchen. He began to open the letter but stopped in his tracks as his mobile vibrated in his back pocket. He didn't recognise the number and answered it curiously.

'Eh, yeah?'

'Hiya, Tommy.'

'Who's this?'

'It's Shona, Tommy. Shona Moran.'

'Shona who?' Tommy scrunched up his face trying to place her. She sounded very nervous, and then he remembered. 'Oh, Shona from work?' Tommy was amazed to hear from her. They had little in common and hardly ever spoke to each other at their weekend job in the bar. Except for that awful night. The thought made him shiver.

'Yeah, that Shona. You know loads of Shonas?'

'No. I meant... never mind. What's up? You want to swap shifts at work?'

'Em, no, Tommy. You see, I know this is going to come as a shock to you and a telephone call's probably a terrible way to let you know this, but I suppose it's better than an email or text or something. I've tried to tell you a few times at work but I keep clamming up.'

The girl was ranting. Would she ever get on with it? Whatever it was.

'Shona, what is it?'

'Look, Tommy, we've kind of ignored the fact that we slept together the night of Mick's twenty-first birthday. I know I was out of it, we both were I suppose, but I do vaguely remember.'

'Some things are best forgotten about, Shona.' Shit. The girl was sniffing at the other end of the phone. She couldn't be crying over that night. 'Like you said, Shona, we were both out of it.'

'Yeah, well it seemed best at the time that we forgot about it. And, well, I know that we don't really know each other at all but... now that this has happened... we'll have to get to know each other a lot better.'

Tommy swallowed. She was definitely crying. What was he going to say to her? It wasn't as if Tommy was the kind of guy who slept around. This had simply been a mad drunken grope that had got out of hand, and it was months ago now. Ancient history.

He sat down on the nearest chair and stared at the envelope still half open in his hand. What was she on about?

Reluctantly he brought his mind back to waking up next to Shona the morning after Mick's birthday... What..? Six months ago? It had taken some time to figure out where he was. The overturned beer cans in the room, the half-eaten sausage rolls and the filthy ashtrays had made him realise that he'd crashed at the house where the party was held. He had eased himself out of the bed and had been amazed to find himself stark naked. Moving his eyes around the room looking for his clothes he had stopped when they landed on his jeans, sitting on top of a red dress. Nearby, a pair of black high heels, stockings and a red thong swiftly brought about the memory that he had slept with Shona Moran.

Now she was calling him and crying down the phone. Did she think they had something going? All this time later? He waited for her to catch her breath. He had to be firm with her. There was no way he was ever going to have anything to do with the girl again. He tore back the envelope in his hands a little more.

'Hardly anyone knows about this, Tommy and I'd appreciate it if we could keep it to ourselves for a little longer until we've made some plans.'

Plans? Tommy felt sick. With his left hand almost crumpling the top of the letter, he stared down at the list of five A's on the page. Then one B and a C. He would have to pull his socks up in maths and biology...
Wait a minute... Fucking hell. She couldn't mean...

'I'm pregnant.' Shona let out a huge sob. 'I'm already six months gone. I'm so scared Tommy. I don't know what to do. Please. Can we meet to talk about it?' Tommy said nothing.

'I'm only seventeen, Tommy. I can't believe this. I have to talk to you or I'll go mad. Everyone at work is always saying that you're a good guy, so I know you won't let me down. You won't, Tommy, will you? We're both working this Saturday night. Maybe we can talk after? Okay?' Her sobbing was reduced to sniffing again. Tommy still said nothing.

'Tommy? Are you alright? Tell me it's okay, Tommy. You'll talk to me. Won't you? On Saturday. Won't you?'

'Yeah. Yeah, sure.' What more could he say? He ended the call and put the phone down on the table. Tommy remembered looking back at her asleep in the bed before he'd high-tailed it out of the room. Her makeup had been streaked across her face, lipstick and mascara meeting each other somewhere in the middle. The bottle of beer on the locker beside her had upturned across her pillow and reduced her hair to a sticky mess. Tommy had been disgusted at himself as he left. When she was sober Shona was really gorgeous, but she was definitely ugly when she was drunk.

Tommy's mind started racing. How did he know that it was *his* anyway? This was Shona Moran. She couldn't remember who she was *talking* to half the time, never mind who she… Maybe she might want to have an … Too bloody late for that. Oh for fuck's sake.

Tommy sat at the kitchen table staring at his school results and then at the phone, willing the conversation away.

We'll have to get to know each other a lot better…

Who wanted to get to know Shona Moran, never mind have a baby with her?

Damn her and her… He would still go to college. This wasn't on. He had just turned eighteen for God's sake.

The key turned in the front door lock and Tommy saw his father's silhouette through the glass. He ran to the toilet clutching the letter. He'd take a few deep breaths…

'Tommy! Are you up?'

'In the loo, Da.' Tommy's voice came out as a squeak.

'I`ve been for the paper… So, did your results come?'

'Eh… The post came but there was nothin' for me.' Tommy scrunched up the letter from school and stuck it into the pocket of his jeans.

'That's strange. Maybe tomorrow, son. Sure, you know already that you did brilliantly.' His dad had obviously decided to be encouraging now. He must have realised how determined

Tommy was.

'Do you want a cup o' tea Tom?'

'No thanks, Da…Eh… I'm not feelin' very well… I think I'll go back to bed.' Tommy stood in the tiny toilet gripping the sink for support, trying to focus on the striped wallpaper reflected in the scratched mirror. The lines kept moving from left to right. Stale beer and bad news churned together in his stomach.

'What kind of hour did you come in this mornin' Tom?' Stephen raised his voice to carry down the hallway towards the toilet door and Tommy's unwilling ears. He didn't answer.

'At least you did come home this time.' Tommy heard his dad bang his mug on the sideboard.

Exhaling long and hard, Tommy hadn't realised he'd been holding his breath. His dad must be referring to the Shona night. His timing was perfect in bringing that one up again.

The lines in the mirror began to circle around him. Tommy heard the rustle of his father's paper and the clanging of the mug on the pine table. The usual morning routine. Coffee, paper, shower, tidy the house… Everything was normal… *Jesus Christ… Shona Moran's pregnant.*

'All the same, Tommy…' His dad was off again. '…You'll have to be a bit more responsible with the late nights and all if you want to become a teacher. You'll find out soon enough that lookin' after kids is feckin' hard work.'

Clutching the sink with one hand and the cistern with the other, Tommy reached over the toilet. His stomach heaved and he spewed the contents of last night's pint glasses into the bowl. When he was sure he was finished he flushed and watched his life spiralling downwards and disappearing from sight. He closed the seat, his legs refusing to hold him up any longer, and he sat with his head in his hands trying, in vain, to block it all out.

Chapter five

A NEVER-ENDING sunny day is how we Saudis have always spoken of life within *The Kingdom* and I agreed. Before.

But today, looking through the large picture window in our family sitting room, I'm watching the unexpected rain spatter angrily against its panes. Dark clouds have hung from the Riyadh skies for hours now, blocking out the sun's rays and covering the city's skyscrapers with a despondent gloom. They were built to reflect the sun and look wilted in the shade, like we're being invaded by Western skies.

I flick the remote control in the direction of the television. The old me would have immediately pressed a different switch if the news had shown up, but these days I'm very interested in what's happening in the world. I watch the pictures on the screen fill with the majestic presence of our Crown Prince, as his false smile welcomes the Irish ambassador to the palace, and the hairs rise on the back of my neck; the newsreader's voice grating with every word…

The Irish ambassador and His Royal Highness, discussed regional and international issues. Particular emphasis was placed on the recent bombing at Al Hokair Park, where most of the five casualties were Irish, and the subsequent emigration of Western workers from Saudi Arabia.

A dinner was hosted at the Yamamah Palace in the ambassador's honour and was attended by His Royal Highnesses Prince...

I listen in disgust to the litany of princes and ministers and dignitaries of The Kingdom of Saudi Arabia that have graced the dinner at the palace. I watch the scenes of opulence and falsity that surround the feast while the Irish man is fawned over by the

Saudi elite. I will him to choke on his roast baby camel.

'That's it! Lick his backside, why don't you?' I throw my hands in the air, knowing I am only speaking to the television screen, but not caring. 'This man comes here to Saudi Arabia as a Westerner sticking his nose in where it isn't wanted.' I stand and walk towards the screen; the discussion feels real to me as if I am sitting in the palace beside the Prince himself.

'You are Western so you don't belong here.'

I stare at the haughty, self-important look on this so-called honoured guest's face and feel my throat constrict with loathing for the man. For what he represents. For Ireland. For the West. I think back to the night that took Shadia on the 17th of March; the Irish national day. I see it still… the park decorated with Irish flags and lit up with green lights. Why did I give in to her pleas to go out that night, actually intervening with her father to allow her to go?

This man is responsible. Organising a celebration of something that should not be celebrated. Not here.

'This country doesn't need you.' I tell him. 'Go back to your own world and take all your Irish trash with you.'

I know my mother is hovering in the doorway now; unsure how to deal with my tantrums, as she calls them. I ignore her and continue to shout. I need to tell him… to get it out.

'The cream of our country waits on your every word. Our Prince, with his visiting British princes and his embracing and understanding of other religions. How dare he? How dare they all and how dare the Irish?!' I spit out the words. 'Get out! Get the Westerners out of The Kingdom! They bring nothing but trouble here!' I sink back into the sofa and push my black curls back with my sweating hands. 'Shadia', I sob. 'Shadia, Shadia…'

Some time passes before something on the coffee table catches my eye. I snatch the magazine up, looking around quickly to check that my mother has gone. It's open on an advertisement for the Riyadh Motor Show; another reminder of the people and places that I've been shutting out of my life. Every year, for as long as I can remember, Omar has taken me to the motor show. It was always just the two of us, our special day out. In the last few years my father has taken a lot of persuading to let his son spend a day out with a servant but he always relents in the end.

We rise early in the morning and after *Fajr* we head off to have breakfast with some of Omar's friends; always a noisy, happy affair. We spend the day going from car to car, sitting in some, gazing yearningly at others, taking in all their intricate details. The wonderful commotion of the all-male exhibition is something I dream about for months beforehand. I'm always a part of that important day, when Omar and I are allowed to choose the family car for the coming year.

I stare at the picture on the page. The amazing, red A Class Mercedes staring back at me. This year was to have been our finest hour. Since I turned about eleven, we've discussed what car I would have as my first; the turning point of my youth Omar calls it; the marking of the man I am to become. All my school friends are talking about the new cars they'll get when they graduate. We were going to show them all. We would buy the best. Black interior. Red exterior. Fast. It would drive like a dream.

But not now. Maybe not ever. Not with Omar anyway.

I think who might have left the magazine out on the table. Nobody else in this family is remotely interested in cars. Not my brother Abdul, with his one-track mind when it comes to horses and racing, the pride of our grandfather Mohammed Abdul. Not Mama; whose idea of cars doesn't extend beyond having Omar bring the car, any car, around to the front of the house and point it in the direction of The Kingdom Shopping Centre. Not Baba; who leaves the choosing and discarding of cars completely in the hands of people who work for him, extending his arms to sign on the bottom of the cheque. Not the sisters – both too young and neither of them serious about anything in life as yet.

It has to have been Omar. He must have been discussing this year's car with my father. Were they discussing me? Did my supposed new car come up in conversation? Do they think they can buy me back with a stupid old car?

Not a chance. I don't need their stupid funds to live my life. I have Allah. Wealth and material goods are a symbol of Western culture. Money is why the Irish are here.

I rip out the offending advertisement, ball it up and throw it across the room. It's coming to the time of the evening prayer and I will pray to Allah for the strength to resist their temptations. I leave the room, kicking the ball of red and black paper into the hall. I march through the door at the side of the house, *their* house, and slam it; leaving it and my mother, who had only retreated as far as the hall it seems, shaking.

At the front of the house, I stop short as I see the car parked showily across the front steps, the backdrop of the fountains lending it an extra arrogance, of which it has no need. This must be why the magazine was open... They've already bought it...

As it stands, gleaming in its newness despite the lack of sunshine, the unseasonal spots of rain lend it a touch of the exotic.

Red exterior.

Black interior.

A fast looking Mercedes. Not exactly the A class, but beautiful.

The keys dangling in the ignition invite me to sit in. I slide open the door and slip into the driver's seat, all thoughts of my earlier anger disappearing at the sight of this magnificent, enthralling machine. Within seconds I have turned the ignition on and am cruising out the gates. I can vaguely hear the muzzein call to prayer but let the words fade away behind me.

Forty minutes later, I am passing King Khaled International Airport. The rain has stopped and the sun is trying to come out. Riyadh is beginning to look a little bit more like itself. My thoughts during the drive have returned to my earlier anger and I allow it to revisit and take over the joy I had felt behind the alluring wheel of the Mercedes.

I round the airport and head for the famous red sand dunes behind, where Abdul, Baba and I have spent many weekends *wadi bashing* in our elaborate four-wheel drives over the years. The area is deserted today; the weather a deterrent to all part-time adventurers. I swerve as a few disgruntled camels edge across the road in my path. I know that the skill needed to drive up and over those dunes, and through the *wadis*, is something that has to be acquired. It's something that should only be attempted in a high-powered four-wheel drive on a dry sunny day. Any other car would be wrecked, ruined beyond recognition, if it was used for such an activity.

With this thought in my mind and a gleam in my eyes, I drive my new car towards the highest dune.

Chapter six

'WILL we sit here, Shona?'

'Yeah, Tommy. Grand.'

Shona and Tommy made a big deal of placing drinks, shedding coats and getting themselves settled in a quiet corner of the pub.

'So. How are you then?'

'Eh, you know. Brilliant!'

The reality of the situation was beginning to hit Tommy. At least Shona had had six months to get over it. All evening at work he had found himself staring at Shona's middle for signs of a bump. She was still wearing a baggy hoodie over her short skirt but now that he was looking he wondered how he hadn't noticed before.

Tommy's fingers were so tight around his untouched pint that the glass was in danger of breaking. It had been a long night at work and he wanted to be at home. But here he was, discussing shared parenthood with a girl he didn't even like.

'I know we're not exactly the best of friends, Shona. But, eh, I wanted to say that I'll support you… with whatever. I don't even know what that involves, but, sure, I'll do my best. You know?'

'It's okay Tommy. I don't suppose I'm that pushed about you either, but we'll struggle on. I told Mick that I wouldn't be working anymore after tonight. I'm hoping to still do my exams in June and it's all getting a bit too much.'

Tommy swallowed hard as he felt them size each other up through a stretched silence.

'Have you told them, like, at home yet?' He bit into the quiet.

'My mother copped this week and told my father. He keeps trying to talk to me but… Nobody's actually voiced it yet. Mum's still in shock. I'm amazed she hasn't lifted the roof over it. No doubt she's rising to the occasion. You?'

'No. Nothin' yet.'

Shona sipped her coke.

'This tastes like shit. It's flat.'

'Well. It wouldn't be your usual now would it?'

'Piss off!'

Oh how Tommy wished that he could *piss off*.

'Sorry.'

'Tommy. You know like... you said that you'd support me and all?'

'Yeah?'

'Well, would you come with me to talk to my parents about the baby?'

There. She'd said it. The baby. It was really fucking happening. Tommy reached for his pint and took a huge gulp.

'Jaysus.' He eased the glass back down on the table. 'What're they like?'

'Your worst nightmare. My mother'll hang you out to dry.'

'Yeah? Great. Can't wait.'

'We have to get it over with soon.' Shona stood up, pulling her skirt down an extra centimetre. This interview was obviously over and, Tommy realised, that he'd been given the job of a lifetime. Horrible clichés were flitting through his mind. A life sentence. A life for a life.

'I'll come over to yours as well if you like.' It was an afterthought for Shona as they headed towards the door.

Tommy looked her over. He was sure she meant well but he shivered at the thought of his father and Shona Moran in the same room together.

'No. Thanks. I'll be fine.'

'Suit yourself.'

Two days later Tommy was appalled to find himself perched on the edge of the sofa in Shona's immaculate sitting room. He wondered did anyone ever actually sit in the room or was it kept as a shrine to visitors. It was Monday evening and Mrs Moran was dressed in her Sunday best, like she'd recently come in from mass, and Mr Moran was sporting an uncomfortable look in a suit and tie. That sick feeling was still in the pit of Tommy's stomach as though he'd never quite recovered from the hangover of his birthday celebration. He wouldn't be celebrating anything for a while he thought, as Shona nudged him to pay attention.

'Mum. Dad. This is my em, boyfriend, Tommy.'

'Hello, Thomas.'

'Hiya, Tommy. Nice to meet you.'

'Mrs Moran. Mr Moran.'

On the bus ride home, Tommy couldn't quite figure out how he'd gotten from the conversational niceties, to agreeing to live with Shona Moran. In his wildest imaginings he couldn't picture her as his girlfriend. He couldn't even remember if she had been good in bed. And a responsible mother? Forget it!

She certainly was a forceful woman that Norah Moran and nothing anybody could have said to her would have changed her mind – but playing mammies and daddies at the age of eighteen had never been on Tommy's agenda. Sure how was he going to manage college? And he had to get through the Leaving Cert exams first...

Tommy was so lost in his own thoughts that he missed his bus stop and had to walk back to his house through the rain. Standing outside his front door, not wanting to go in and face his father he eventually reasoned with himself that it was best to get it over with. Shona's mother had asked for his home phone number. He needed to get to his da before she made minced meat of the whole situation.

In their very lived-in sitting room, his dad was slumped in a chair, holding his wife's photograph in one hand and a tumbler of whiskey in the other. On a Monday night? Tommy moved forward. He had to do this but it was so hard.

'Da... I need to talk to you.'

Stephen Farrell looked up and Tommy knew immediately,

from the look on his face, that the Morans had got there first.

The following day, Tommy's father skidded into their driveway, got out and slammed the car door. They were back from speaking to Des and Norah Moran. Well Stephen had done the speaking and Tommy had sat mutely by. He'd been in a kind of shock for days now, as if he'd been hit by a car and he wasn't sure, as yet, how badly he'd been hurt. His dad was livid.

'We won't get anywhere with that woman. She's decided that my son's goin' to stick by her daughter and nothin' anybody says is goin' to change things. She's an answer for everythin' and she's always right. And you and that girl's aul fella standin' there, with nothin' to say for yourselves.'

Tommy watched his father go into the sitting room and pour himself a whiskey. Two nights on the trot? He was beginning to see how bad things were alright. Down in one.

'I damn well needed that.' Stephen slammed the glass down on the table and poured another. Larger.

'There wasn't even a mention of a DNA test. Well I'll damn well insist on it. That bit o' skirt, 'cause let's face it a bit was all there was, has been around. No doubt about it. I can't believe you got messed up with somethin' like that.'

Stephen picked up the photo of his beautiful young wife, who had died in his arms along with their second baby. He carried it to the sofa and Tommy pained at the expression on his face.

'Like father like son?' he asked. He waited as always for the photograph of Sinéad to answer his questions. 'No comparison, Sinéad. So what if you were pregnant when we got married and yes, we were young but we loved each other. I was your first and last.'

Stephen Farrell was thirty-nine years old. Tommy had never known him to have a girlfriend again.

'There has to be a way out o' this. Jaysus, Mary and Joseph! Sure how're you goin' to manage college, Tommy?' Stephen got up and replaced the photo and poured himself another whiskey.

*

'Get your jacket on there, Des and look smart. We're going to see the estate agent. Come on Shona! For God's sake, what are you wearing? Get changed.' Shona noted her mother's busy voice. Norah Moran had some family planning to do. Not a minute to lose. She was all go.

'No grandchild of mine is going to be born into the wrong part of Dublin.' Norah pulled off her apron and her rubber gloves. 'I'll go and change my shoes and put on a bit of lipstick.'

'Oh yes! Let's set them up in a doll's house. That'll make everything alright. Let's give our only daughter all she's ever wanted in life. Sure, Tommy Farrell's what she's always dreamed of! The wet drip!' Shona's father never usually voiced his feelings to his wife. The fact that he was ranting and raving back at her made Shona aware of the gravity of her crime this time.

Norah stopped her rush and glared at her husband. He stared back defiantly but gave in easily and looked away.

'Where the hell's that jacket?' he mumbled. He would play the game too. He always did. No one was a match for Norah. Not her husband who liked an easy life and certainly not Tommy's dad who had screamed abuse at Shona's mother in this very room and got nowhere with her. Shona shivered as she remembered the way Stephen Farrell had looked at her. Like she was a trollop who had led his saintly son astray. As for the saintly son, he had stood in the corner and said nothing. Accepted his fate without question. Her father was right. He was a wet drip and her mother wanted her to live with him? The shiver came back and ran down to her toes.

'Are you still here? I told you to get changed!' Shona shot from the room at her mother's roar. Sitting in her bedroom with her mobile in her hand, she knew she should ring Tommy. God help him. She never thought that her mother would go that far. Why couldn't any of them stand up to her? Jesus she needed a drink. She ran to the loo. Spot on. Nature was an amazing thing. Even the thought of alcohol made her feel sick.

Shona considered the prospect of living with Tommy Farrell as she slipped into a long flowing dress that her mother had bought – no doubt Norah had hoped it would cover the tattoo. She had managed a whole six months off the gargle now. Early nights and healthy living. Saint Shona! She looked in her long mirror, rubbed her stomach and smiled.

'Hey, God. What were you thinking of? Sending me a baby...'

Shona knew it deserved two parents and a proper home. She was sure Tommy could be a good provider in the long run and sure if it didn't work out they could split up. It wasn't as if they were getting married or anything.

In fact she was surprised her mother hadn't mentioned the marriage thing. *Mother Mary Immaculate* she used to call her in front of her friends. Norah was always putting down other couples that *lived in sin* so why not her own daughter? Shona had no answer to that one as yet. She'd never been able to work out the reasoning behind any of her mother's actions. No more than her mother could hers, no doubt. For years now, most communications between them had resulted in rows. When Shona was supposedly preparing for her mock exams last week Norah had screamed at her for her lack of work. But the following day when Shona's mother had found out that Shona was pregnant; she'd simply taken a deep breath and taken control.

Shona wondered how her mum had felt when she was pregnant. Had she felt excitement? Joy? Maybe this would be the one thing that they'd have in common. Maybe this baby would make them close.

'What's keeping the pair of you up there?

In their haste, Shona and her father collided on the stairs and instinctively he reached over and gave her a hug.

'It'll be alright, sweetheart. At least it's out in the open now. I can't believe you managed to hide it this long.'

'I know, Dad. I kept putting it off. And now... I'm really not sure about this whole happy family thing with Tommy. You know?'

'Sure see how it goes, love. It can do no harm.'

'Get a move on!' The order from downstairs made them run.

Norah Moran had spoken.

Chapter seven

FAUSIA stood in the open doorway of her home willing her son to return; Shadia's mother Ranya by her side, helping her with her vigil. She heard the sound of a woman approaching her from behind. She knew it was Karima by the mixed smell of herbs and spices that always emanated from her clothes.

'Excuse me. I'm sorry to intrude. The food is spoiling in the kitchen. Shall I leave it or put it away?'

Fausia forced a smile, knowing how much trouble Karima had put into the day's cooking. She, like everyone in the household, knew the importance of getting Majid to pull out of his misery.

'Yes, Karima. Cover it and keep it for tomorrow. We will enjoy it all the more when your wonderful spices have had time to fuse even further. The smell from the kitchen is splendid. I'm sorry... you know... about...'

Karima reached out and touched the sleeve of her employer's *abaya* in a gesture of sympathy.

Fausia nodded, not trusting herself to respond. She turned towards the door as Karima moved away from her and as she did a piece of paper, rolled up in the corner of the hall, caught her eye. She bent under the table and pulled it towards her, unravelling it as she stood up.

'It is the advertisement for the motor show, Ranya. I had left it open on the table in the sitting room in the hope that he would want to accompany Omar, to think about buying his first car. I was trying to reach in and pull him from the depths to which he has sunk, but I have failed in this as in everything else with Majid. He isn't reachable anymore.'

'That's not true, Fausia. I am beginning to get through to my

Sa'eed now. These boys have been through so much with the loss of Shadia. They need time and patience from us. They'll be alright. Don't worry.' She linked her friend's arm. Their *abayas* rendered it awkward for them to get a proper hold but Fausia felt the warmth of the touch and forced a smile.

'Have you calmed down about your car, Ranya? I still can't believe that he would have taken it. To steal from another... I'm so surprised at him... It's very unlike him to do such a thing. I can't seem to understand anything he does these days. When your driver said it was Majid who had driven it away I hit out at him for lying.'

'Fausia, don't worry about it. I was livid at first. Of course I was... at the theft of a new car. A present from my doting husband, you know, to cheer me up. Such a waste considering that I will never be allowed to drive it, and I only screamed at Hamid because he had been so negligent; walking away and leaving the keys in the ignition.'

Fausia knew that, with night now approaching, Ranya wouldn't mind where her car had ended up. Like everyone else in the house, she had only thoughts for where its occupant had gone and whether or not he would come home. They walked back into the house, arms linked, their abayas swaying from side to side in their wake. Fausia and Ranya had a battle ahead of them and Fausia wasn't sure as yet what it was that she was fighting against. Whatever it was they would face it together though. The solidarity of women would always be a strong enough weapon.

*

It's been two days since the police discovered me, trapped in the car on the red sand dunes, no signal in my phone to call for help. I should be ashamed of my escort home, but I'm not. I'm not interested in them or their stupid car and I don't care what happens to me.

I take to my room and won't come out for anyone. My father

33

rages at me and my mother pleads with me. Ranya comes to tell me that she doesn't blame me for the car theft and that all is forgiven.

'I know how angry you are. You are grieving for my daughter as I am, Majid,' she says.

'Angry? You want angry?' I shout. I know it's wrong as I reach for it but I pick up the paperweight from my desk anyway and hurl it at her.

My father is furious. I overhear him fuming about me to Shadia's father.

'My son is lost to me. I don't recognise this monster living in my house. I watch my other children as they walk on eggshells in their own home, frightened of the time bomb ticking away in their brother's bedroom. Radwa has started wetting her bed. Something has to change. Majid's actions are holding us all to ransom.'

'I won't take any more of this!' He yells at my mother. 'As soon as he finishes his exams I am sending him to Al Jouf to spend time with my brother. I've had enough. We all have. Shadia is dead, and it's terrible, but we have to go on. Let him stay there away from his memories for a while and see if he can't come back and learn to cope. Allah, help us all!'

I sit up in bed. Al Jouf? To that uncle? I won't go. He knows how much I despise my cousins in Al Jouf. Anyway, I'm almost eighteen now. An adult. I'll leave. If that's what Baba wants then I'll go – but not to Al Jouf. I'll go anywhere but there. The world is out there waiting.... First I'll go to visit Shadia's grave. That's the only place where I can find peace. A place to think and make plans. I know she will help.

Chapter eight

'DID they not show you in the hospital how to do it, Shona?'

'Yeah. But it's easy to do it when there's a nurse standing beside you, and not an eejit like you! Go away, Tommy.'

'I'm sure you have it on the wrong way around.'

'So you're the expert in nappies now, are you?'

The doorbell rang. Twice.

'Ah Jaysus, it's your mother again!'

'No way. Don't answer it.'

'She can see us through the window, Shona. I have to let her in.'

'Do what you like.'

Tommy took a deep breath as he opened the door to Norah.

'How's my little angel today then? Oh dear. Exercising our four-day-old lungs this morning. What in the name of God are you trying to do to that child Shona? Here. Give me that nappy. Go and get dressed the pair of you. It's passed midday. Has she had her bottle?'

'No,' said Shona taking the stairs two at a time.

'There's one in the fridge ready to be heated,' followed Tommy, taking the stairs more slowly in his exhaustion, leaving his daughter's screams and her granny's mutterings behind him.

'I'm having forty winks.' A voice came from under the duvet as Tommy came into their bedroom.

'You were quick off the mark.'

'There's no need for three of us to mind one baby. You can have the next turn.'

'Yeah. When your mother's gone home no doubt. Thanks. She's not my mother. I'm stayin' up here too.'

'Suit yourself. Goodnight now.'

'Jaysus, Shona. We can't leave her there to mind Ruby on her own.' Tommy stormed into the bathroom, slamming the door.

He wanted to stay in the shower all day; let the strength of the water energise him but within minutes Norah was calling up the stairs.

'I've put the kettle on. I'll make us a bite to eat for lunch. Okay?'
Norah's grandiose offer was met with silence.

'I'll take that as a *thank you. That would be lovely.* Will I?'
Tommy tumbled out of the shower and, wrapped in a towel cursing Shona and her mother to hell and back, dripped his way out of the bathroom door before shouting over the banisters.

'Lovely Norah. Thanks.'

He then stomped back into his bedroom holding the towel at his waist as if it offered any protection from these distressing women.

'Did you hear that Shona? She's stayin' for lunch. She'll be here all day. Shona?'

Tommy looked over in disgust at the sleeping girl. Breathing soundly. Not a care in the world.

'What I wouldn't give for a few hours shuteye,' he mumbled.

Dressed and downstairs he was not enjoying the conversation. At least baby Ruby was asleep. Like mother like daughter. The smell of soup and toasted sandwiches was too much for Tommy's fragile state, but against his better judgement, he gushed all over the new granny anyway.

'That smells wonderful, Norah.'

'Doesn't it? Now, I bet you feel like a new man, all washed and dressed and sure you might get a chance to shave when you finish your lunch. Or is it your breakfast?'

Tommy pulled at the bit of stubble on his eighteen-year-old chin and took another deep breath. If it weren't for his desperate need to eat, he would have turned the soup over her head. How had she changed and dressed Ruby, fed her a bottle and made tea and food in that short time? Bloody wonder woman!

'Is she coming behind you? It's gone very quiet up there.'

Tommy was now angrier with Norah than he was with Shona, so he made excuses.

'Eh, Shona? Well. I came out of the shower and she'd fallen asleep. She was only lyin' down while she was waitin' for the shower, but she's so tired. I didn't have the heart to wake her.'

'Well she'll have to get up soon. I've put a wash on and tidied up a bit but I can't stay very long. Certainly not long enough to rewind this house to its pre-bombed out state.'

Norah put the dustpan and brush back to where she no doubt thought should be its rightful place.

'My God! You'd think you'd had triplets.'

Tommy tried not to concentrate on the noise of the scraping of knives and forks and the clanging of cups but maybe it would drown out the screaming in his head. How was he not going to kill the interfering old bat?

Norah and her husband hadn't been near them in weeks. Not since they'd got together with Tommy's dad and the three of them had set himself and Shona up in this play house. But now that there was a baby around, a few weeks earlier than anticipated, Norah wouldn't leave them alone for five minutes. He couldn't take this crap. Tommy took a big breath and dived in.

'Norah. We're really tryin' hard here.'

'I never said you weren't Thomas. It's just that you both have to realise that babies need a lot of care. They know when you're feeling stressed so they cry. They need to be comfortable. Now, Ruby had a sore bottom when I changed her, so you need to be more careful when you're cleaning her and in this cold weather, you have to do it quickly before she gets a chill. And the house. Well. Babies need to be in a hygienically clean environment and...'

'Okay, Norah.' Tommy was raging. 'So when you were a mother you were perfect! Four days after you had given birth to Shona you had the house spotless. She had all her bottles on time. All the laundry was up to date. You and Des ate all your meals at a set table and your baby never had a sore arse! Weren't you absolutely, bleedin' wonderful?!'

37

'How dare you, Thomas? I just was trying to help you!'

Tommy noted the distress on Norah's face but there was no stopping him now. A few nights with no sleep meant that he had plenty more to say.

'Help us? You've been givin' us an earful ever since we got back from the hospital and you're tellin' me you're tryin' to help us? Well I've got news for you Norah Moran! Your daughter's not as perfect as her mother. Okay? A few genes misplaced along the way, was there?'

'Thomas, for God's sake... Don't be so cruel!' Norah sat down at the table looking shocked.

Tommy stood and stared at the crumpled wreck that she was but continued to drive his bulldozer through.

'Me? Cruel? You're the one tryin' to make your daughter into some kind of replica of yourself. Now that would be cruel.'

Norah was in tears now. Her face was crushed. Tommy knew that she was falling to pieces before she even spoke but he was too angry to stop her.

'How could you understand?' Norah spat at him. 'One shag and you had Shona pregnant. A baby neither of you even wanted!'

Tommy was amazed at Norah's uncharacteristic use of language. Where was all this going? She was ranting now.

'It took Des and myself ten years to work out that we couldn't have children. Ten years of trying, losing and trying again – each time ending in heartbreak. Shona was a year old before I ever set eyes on her. I have no idea what it's like to hold my own newborn baby. Not a clue what it feels like to give birth to a beautiful baby daughter.'

Norah's arms were wrapped around her shoulders; her words coming in gulps now, barely audible. But Shona, standing in the doorway, woken by the shouting, was able to grasp the essence of what she was mumbling. Even while the baby woke and tried to drown out the confession, Shona was able to hear the words 'adopted' and 'someone else's daughter' loud and clear.

Chapter nine

I CAN see Omar as soon as I run out of the school door and bound down the steps towards him. There is no mistaking the surprise in his eyes and I can't say I blame him – he hasn't seen sight of the old me for a long time now, but today will be different.

Jumping into the passenger seat beside him, instead of the back seat where I had remained for weeks now, aloof, we sit in silence for a few minutes as Omar pushes though the evening traffic. Eventually he looks over at me, a nervous smile on his face. I reward him with a confident smile in return.

I can hear him take a deep breath before he starts.

'Majid. Karima and I… we must go away to Pakistan for two months to see our families. It's been a long time. Please try to understand.'

I look over at him and nod in recognition.

'Majid… will you be alright? While we are gone? Your father says that you are going to Al Jouf to stay with your uncle for a while?'

That gets more of my attention. 'No!' I bark. 'There is no way that I'm going to that place.'

Omar smiles a little.

'So what will you do for the summer, young man? Your exams finish tomorrow. Your father has his mind set on you going to your uncle's. University is three long months away…'

'You're right, Omar, but don't worry about me. I'll be fine. When are you travelling to Pakistan?'

'On Saturday. Five days' time.'

I look at him curiously.

'So how do you get from here to Pakistan, Omar? Is there an

airport near your home?'

Omar smiles again and shakes his head. 'No, Majid. I have never been on a plane. We go by bus to Dammam and we sail from there to Gwadar. It is a long journey, but an enjoyable one with a wonderful destination. I hope to leave straight after *fajr* on Saturday morning and catch the ferry that evening.'

I look at him intensely as the traffic lifts and he moves swiftly towards the motorway. He is worried once more, I can tell.
'So, Majid. What will you do? Could you maybe speak with Imam Wassim and ask him to intervene on your behalf, between your father and you? I am very worried about the tension between you.' Omar knows that he is taking liberties by speaking to me in this way but I know his heart is in the right place. He has been like a father to me for so long I can't correct him now for caring.

'I know it has only been a short time since Shadia died but part of you died with her,' he continues. 'It is time to wake that part of you up once more and begin to live again. It is what Shadia would have wanted. Majid... I have never tried to hide how I feel about you. Since the day you were born you have been like a son in my heart, but that heart is heavy with your troubles right now. How can I leave for two months knowing what you are going through in my absence?'

We have reached home and Omar swings the car around to the front of the house before looking over at me, and I smile. I can feel the smile course through my veins, because I mean it, and I take his hand in mine.

'Your words are my lifeline, Omar. I'll be okay when you're in Pakistan. You've no need to worry.' I squeeze my fingers around his but before he has a chance to say another word I jump out of the car and run towards the house; my steps full of promise and hope; leaving a slightly baffled, but more at ease Omar in my wake.

*

Omar sat on the deck and watched as Dammam and Saudi Arabia got smaller and smaller while the boat sailed further and further away. With each mile he put between himself and the

40

tensions of the Al Faisal family, he felt his heart lighten and he
started to look forward to this special trip, with Karima at his
side.

In the distance the sound of the last call to prayer was vaguely
audible and Omar joined his fellow travellers in their washing
and preparations. In the absence of the Mullah, the boat's captain
led them in prayer. Further up the deck, Omar's attention was
drawn by a silhouette bowing and rising against the backdrop of
the setting sun. The movements of this person seemed so familiar.
Young, agile, completely immersed in his praise of Allah. Omar
found it harder and harder to concentrate on his words. He
bowed his head with the others but each time he raised his face
back up he squinted into the sun to get a better view of the other
passenger. By the time the prayer was finished, Omar was in no
doubt as to who his fellow traveller was. He folded his mat and
walked slowly towards the youth.

'You have been many things to me over the years, young man,
but I never before took you for a fool.'

I turn slowly and smile triumphantly at Omar.

'Asalam a lakum, Omar. It is good to see you.'

Omar stares hard and then sinks slowly to the deck and sits,
defeated.

'Your father will kill you, boy and then he will kill me. What
are you thinking, following us to Pakistan? Are you completely
crazy?'

'Certain people would say that I am. Yes.' I'm still smiling,
delighted to have got this far. 'But getting away from Riyadh was
the only solution and following you here was the most immediate
one. I took all my savings with me. I was surprised how much I
had, but I suppose I haven't been spending much this last while
with my lack of social life. I bought this kurta to wear, from one
of Aunty Ranya's servants and paid him handsomely in exchange
for his silence. I thought it would help me to fit in on the boat.' I
laugh at poor Omar's stricken face.

'Don't worry about a thing, Omar.' I try to put him at his ease.

'Relax and enjoy the journey. My father need never know how I came to be here.'

Omar takes a deep breath and blows out his frustration. We know that the boat's captain will never turn back now and there'll be no ports until we reach Gwadar. He has no choice but to allow me to continue my mad escape until we reach Pakistan.

'Leave telling Karima for as long as you can, Omar.' I have it all worked out. 'Sheltered with the other women she mightn't see me on board. Let her worry later.'

Sailing from Dammam, Omar tells me that I'm shedding the skin of the belligerent teenager a little more with every few miles of sea. 'The peace and solace of the boat trip are somehow transforming you,' he says. 'Or at least erasing some of the harshness. Replacing it with something… better. So I'll take my cue from you boy. I'll sit back and look forward to going home. What else can I do?'

I've never left Saudi before. The excitement of the experience drains the pressure of home and family as we round the coast of the United Arab Emirates and I begin to talk to some of the other passengers on the boat.

Somewhere out on the Arabian Sea, I meet Ali Al Aziz.

The twenty-five-year-old Pakistani is everything that I wish to be. His tall stature allows people to look up to him. His long beard and dishevelled hair give him a deeply religious air and I resolve to be like him. I watch in awe when he speaks about the West; at the way his eyes go from warm brown to dark and huge; glazed with the injustice of everything. As the boat glides through the sea, past the coast of Iran to our left and the coast of Oman to our right, I talk and Ali listens in respectful silence. I speak; my eyes filled with tears; of the Irish family who should never have been living in my country. I'm rewarded with Ali's understanding smile. Ali… the one person who agrees with me that it was that terrible friendship with the Irish girl that killed my beautiful Shadia.

Ali's ear is attentive, understanding, and as we draw within sight of the Pishukan coastline, he tells me in his calm, sweet voice, how Allah is good, how Allah shows us the way and how Ali feels that I have something special to offer to Allah. Ali talks and I listen. Oh, how I listen and oh, how Ali's words sink into my heart, my mind and my very soul. By the time we dock into the port of Gwadar; I catch myself as I say the words Ali and Allah with one breath.

Chapter ten

'SHONA.' Tommy stood in the doorway of the baby's room and tried to get her attention. Shona was sitting in the chair with her one-week-old daughter in her arms, rocking them both back and forth. Tommy noticed the way Shona was being comforted by the closeness of another body. She was staring ahead at nothing; her eyes glassy; sunk into her white face. It was almost 4am.

'Shona. Where were you?'

Still no response. Did she know he was there? The baby's room was filled with strange smells. Stale body. Dirty clothes. Vodka. Three days old.

'Shona. Give me the baby. I need to put Ruby back in her cot. She needs to sleep. It was so hard to get her asleep. She was screamin' for hours. She's exhausted. And so am I. Where were you, Shona? I was really worried. Your mam and dad were frantic. We called the Gardaí. Nobody knew where you were...'
Shona didn't take her eyes off the nothingness that was out there. The only response that Tommy got was the tears that fell and ran down her dirty face.

Tommy leaned forward and took the baby from her mother. Or what passed for a mother. Shona hadn't made much effort yet to show her maternal instinct. He had no idea how she felt about her baby or what she thought of *him*. He didn't want to think about the feelings he had or didn't have for *her*. He put the baby into the cot and covered her warmly. She was so beautiful. How could Shona have abandoned her for three days? She hadn't moved from the chair. She was still in no man's land. He went and sat on the floor beside her.

'What can I do, Shona? Is it because of what your mother said..?

About your adoption? Or is it a bit of postnatal depression..? I read about that in the book your mam gave you about havin' a baby. Come on, Shona. Answer me. I'm tryin', Shona. I really am.'

Still there came no response. Only silent tears.

Tommy leaned down once more and lifted Shona out of the chair, scrunching his nose at the smell. She was so slight. A slip of a woman. Woman? No. Still a girl. He carried her into their room and laid her on their bed. How strange it was to share a room and a bed with a person who was a total stranger to you. He began to gently peel off her filthy clothes. There was no resistance, but there was no help offered either. When he was finished, she curled up on the duvet taking part of the sheet in her grasp, pulling it over her face. Tommy looked down on her beautiful body. He seldom saw her naked, even though they'd shared a bed those few days after Ruby had been born. It was easier for the night feeds. She looked helpless; her floral tattoo out of place on her childlike neck. He left her and went to run the bath. When he lowered her into the hot water, Shona cried out; the shock bringing her to her senses. She looked up at Tommy and half-smiled.

'Thank you... I'm sorry.'

Tommy half-smiled back and handed her a cloth, then he left her to it.

Back in bed, Tommy lay awake listening for sounds of movement from the bathroom that told him that Shona was okay. He listened for sounds of movement from the back room that told him that Ruby was okay too. What about himself? Was he okay? Probably not. Nothing he could do about that for now though. There were too many other pressing matters on his mind. He was nearly dozing off at about 5am when Shona got into the bed beside him. She was wearing the t-shirt that he had discarded on the floor of the bathroom after his shower. Her long hair was wrapped in a towel to keep the wet from the pillow. She was clean. The smell of toothpaste had replaced the other smells. She lay on her back looking up at the ceiling. *Where had she been? Why?* He knew he should scream at her. How dare she disappear for three days? But instead Tommy reached over and held her hand. Shona squeezed his fingers in return.

'Are you okay, Shona?'

'Not really, Tommy. I'm sorry. It'll get better. Won't it?'

'Ah, yeah. I'm a bit spaced out myself, I have to tell you... But we'll sort somethin' out. I promise you. It *will* get better. We have a beautiful daughter, Shona. We're a family – you, me and Ruby. It's all a bit crazy at the moment, but, sure, we'll talk about it... In the mornin' though. I'm shattered. Come 'ere.' Tommy shifted awkwardly over to Shona's side of the bed and put his arms around her as she nestled into him.

Tommy wanted to comfort her. He didn't even know why he wanted to do that after everything she'd done to him lately, but he did. She remained on her back, one hand wrapped behind Tommy, the other limp at her side, staring up at the ceiling – feeling beyond tiredness. Tommy lay on his side, both arms around Shona, and took in the beauty of her vulnerability. Tired and all as he was, he too felt that he wouldn't sleep.

And still she lay oblivious to him, staring beyond the ceiling; thinking of something out there that she might never tell him. Would he and Shona ever be able to get it right together?

'Maybe you'd like to talk tonight, Shona? We can. If you need to.' Tommy wanted some sort of response from her. Talking was better than indifference.

Shona turned to him and smiled. A smile that curved the corners of her mouth slightly upwards and reached her eyes momentarily, taking away the haunted look for just a few seconds. Long enough for Tommy to believe that she was grateful for everything. That she wanted to be there with him at that time. That she needed him. As the smile began to recede; Tommy; in an attempt to keep it a little longer, leaned over and kissed it gently and was rewarded by another one. Maybe things would turn out okay.

Tommy definitely fancied Shona. But love? Well he was only eighteen and they had ages to work that one out yet. For now he gave her a hug and they talked. Well mostly Shona talked and

Tommy listened. She told him some things about her childhood. About never feeling that she fit in anywhere... the rows with her mother and the constant guilt she felt after.

'When I realised that I was never going to get it right, that I literally wasn't the child that Norah had ordered, I guess I kind of gave up. I didn't know then that Norah really had sort of ordered me. I could never quite figure out how I could be so different from everyone I was supposed to be related to. They're all tall on both sides of the family, and flat chested.' She smiled up at Tommy's grin. 'I was always so short in comparison to my cousins. I was so very different to them all. If they had told me why, I really think that I would have been more accepting. That I would have tried to conform a bit.'

'I don't think you're the conformin' type, Shona. But sure life would be dull without you.'

'You mean life would be good without me, Tommy. I'm useless to have around the house. I'm a pathetic mother. I'm unreliable. Even on a good day, I find myself in a total mess with Ruby. You'd both be better off without me. Sure you as good as told me that yourself.'

'We all say things in the heat of the moment that we don't mean, Shona. You've said a few choice things to me, over the past while, that I think I'd be better off forgettin' and I'm sure we'll have a few more things to say about each other in the years to come. But we can't dwell on everythin' that's been said. What's happened has happened. Thinkin' about it and keepin' it sittin' in your head forever is hopeless. It gets you nowhere.

'I know that your mam and dad not tellin' you the truth about yourself was wrong but it's done and we can't change it. They desperately want to make up for it. They love their grandchild and they love you, and they want to move on from here. There's only so many times they can say they're sorry. You have to give in a little. For Ruby's sake if not for theirs.'

'You know what you said earlier, Tommy about *in the years to come?* I wonder where we'll be. You and me and Ruby. Will we still be together? Or will I have wrecked everything by then?'

47

'Learn to be more acceptin', Shona and I'll try to do the same. Life's actually not so bad, is it? We've a lovely baby and a grand house. My weekend job's not too bad. I'll do the Leaving Cert this month and maybe even get to college. You can do it next year when life is quieter, easier. There's a lot much worse off than we are and they cope. We'll be fine. You and me and Ruby.'

They lay silently again for a while until Tommy broke in.

'Shona. Where did you go? When you disappeared.'

Shona pulled away slowly and turned over at the same moment that Ruby let out a wail and Tommy looked at his watch. 7am. Another sleepless night. Maybe life would get better. Things would look up. Whatever happened he wasn't getting an answer to his last question right now, but they'd made progress all the same.

'I'll go to her, Shona. You get a bit of sleep.' Shona's eyes were already drooping. Tommy sat up in the bed and kissed her forehead. 'It'll be alright, Shona. Okay?'

But she didn't answer and he guessed she was already asleep.

Chapter eleven

WALKING from the bus stop I feel like I've stepped out of a black and white movie and straight onto a technicolour set. Pakistan is like a collage of colour, shapes and sizes. Nothing matches, yet everything looks at home with everything else. Coming from Riyadh with its straight lines and its people clothed in black and white, I breathe in the scent of diversity that is Gwadar.

'We need to cross over here, Ali. We'll be taking a different way to you I think.' Omar reaches out to embrace our new friend and says goodbye.

'I hope you'll allow me to visit you while we're home, Omar? And you must bring Majid to visit my family. We would be honoured.'

The two men talk briefly, exchanging addresses; one outdoing the other in how welcome they would be made in each other's homes. I embrace my new hero with awkward shyness and we say our goodbyes for now. Then Ali is gone, leaving me standing with Omar and Karima. The reality of my time in Pakistan is ahead of me and I watch as the couple exchange a knowing look. Karima shakes her head. She hasn't spoken to me since she came up on deck and found me standing with Omar.

Omar puts one foot out on the busy road answering the question in my head about how we are going to get across. Boldly is the answer. Trucks painted every bright colour conceivable, boasting the most intricate detailed designs and teeming with bodies, are in competition with jeeps, motorbikes, battered cars and pedestrians. Nothing seems to have any real direction but no doubt everyone will eventually get to wherever it is they're headed. In the meantime their main job seems to be to raise enough dust to choke me as I reluctantly follow close to my minders. My adventure begins to take on a dangerous feel.

'Omar! Karima!' A man on the opposite side of the road is waving excitedly, obviously delighted to see old friends. When we eventually reach him the two men fall on each other with delight, clutching each other and smiling from ear to ear.

'I can't believe it's you, Omar. I heard you were coming home. It's wonderful to see you, and looking so well too. You look for sure the wealthiest man in Gwadar. And Karima! My wife looks forward to seeing you. So who's your young friend? A stranger to these parts... Did you kidnap him from the Saudis? Is that it? Ha, ha...'

Relieved, at first, at having made it to the other side of the road in one piece; I'm almost tempted to run back across to escape this toothless man wearing his filthy kurta. I'd have mistaken him for a beggar if he hadn't so obviously been a friend of Omar's. The man is holding on to my shoulder now with his other hand outstretched wanting me to actually put my hand in his in greeting. One look from Omar leaves no doubt as to what he'll have to say if I cause a scene, so I gingerly slide my hand into the wrinkled grime of dirty fingers and allow myself to be officially welcomed to Gwadar and Pakistan. I am speechless, so Omar speaks for me, introducing Naimul and a *nephew of my friend in Saudi* to each other. *Nephew of..?* I suppose he has to explain me away somehow. I am dressed in a kurta, but I speak no Pakistani dialect.

'You must come into my shop. Have some refreshment to break your journey.' Naimul has Omar and me by the hand, with Karima trailing behind, and is leading us down a laneway that seems to have come from nowhere. As we walk, he and Omar chat away to each other in Baluchi, breaking into English or Arabic for my benefit and then back into their native tongue again.

'Most people in Pakistan speak English well, as this is the official language of the country,' Omar tells me. 'Muslims also speak Arabic as this is the language of our religion.'

I nod and attempt a smile.

Halfway down on the left we fall upon a shop where two other men are sitting on their wares looking like they don't have a care in the world. The men don't rise to greet us but indicate that we sit somewhere. Karima is ushered into a back room, no doubt to meet with Naimul's wife.

I'm tired, hungry and thirsty but I don't want to sit on an upturned tin pot, and I certainly don't want to eat whatever it is that Naimul is now holding out to me expectantly. I do sit though, and I eat as the men speak to each other in Baluchi leaving me with no company but my Arabic thoughts. I look around at Naimul's shop in amazement. It's total chaos. He sells everything and anything, new or old. How does he know where or what anything is? To any visitor it merely looks like a lot of colourful objects scattered around with larger objects seeming to hold up the faded green crumbling paintwork of the walls of the shop.

One hour later, after endless food and drink and lots of promises of visits, we are on our way again, headed for Omar and Karima's home at last. My head wants a pillow. Another short bus journey and we are walking along a coastal path. I drag myself after Omar and Karima who are walking with a spring in their step on the way to see their family, giggling like children.

It's 7.30pm and the sun is setting when the pair suddenly break into a run; Omar's bag hopping along beside him. They point to the family home in the distance. Omar shouts at me to go faster but I've no push left in me. I turn my nose upwards and tut. Omar and Karima run on without me, leaving me to trudge along with the weight of my bag, filled with the ridiculous things that I thought I would need on my escape.

By the time I reach them, the power of the Pakistani welcome has reached fever pitch. How can they all be related to Omar and surely everyone doesn't live in this same tiny house? Is this a house? A second storey is being constructed on top of a tiny bungalow that looks like it's been sitting on this ground for all of time. A woman shuffles towards me, her bangle-adorned arms outstretched, life's map on her wrinkled face, her eyes shining with the return of her precious son. I don't understand a word the woman says to me as she wraps me in her arms but I know they're kind words and that I like this lovely lady. Her veil falls from her head revealing her long silver hair as she pushes me gently to arm's length; not letting go of me until she's taken my measure and told the waiting crowd what she thinks of Majid Al Faisal. It's most probably the effects of the sun setting behind her and the rich colours of her cerise salwar and kamees but I see a pink glow surrounding this beautiful old lady and I feel happy and peaceful. When she lets go I feel the loss.

Having introduced me to his parents, Malik and Razina, Omar then leads me from person to person saying my name over and over until I can't even recognise it as my own. I long for a bed but Razina calls out to her daughters and granddaughters and soon they are all rushing about spreading cloths on the ground and scattering cushions, of every conceivable colour and size, for everyone to sit. Then the food is brought and the party begins.

I wonder is Ali's homecoming like this? He told me that his parents are dead and that his older brothers brought him up. Perhaps he's having more rest than I am. I hope he visits soon.
I wonder now if you can die of tiredness.

I wake at 5.30am with the sunrise filling the room; a ray of light reaching in and touching each sleeping body. Omar's nephews continue to snore and I wonder how I've slept through the din. I barely remember lying down last night. When I hit my mat I passed out.

The muzzein call to prayer makes the other bodies stir and one by one they drowsily raise themselves up, ready for the first prayers of the day. I look forward to the visit to the mosque. Perhaps I will see Ali there too.

I feel like a child on his first day at school. Where should I go and what should I do? Who should I speak to; what's the custom? Omar's nephews regard me with their eyes full of Pakistani intensity. Are they being hostile or are they at as much of a loss at what to say as I am? One boy speaks to me.

'Our grandmother,' he stammers. 'She thought that you might need a fresh kurta after your travels.' He hands me a kurta that's crumpled, but clean, and walks away. I swap my dishevelled clothes and, head bent, I drag my feet out of the house and after the others. I pass Razina with her daughters and granddaughters, immersed in domesticity, and am rewarded by her mothering eyes on me as her look tells me it'll be alright.

When we arrive at the Mosque I realise that she is completely right. The Pakistani men are here for prayer, as I am. I'm amazed to see Chinese men there, also praying. Everything is different but everything is the same. The familiarities are woven in with the differences in a fabric, which I feel comfortably wrapped in. I wash and kneel, bow and pray and I'm a Muslim. I feel a part of a whole world where I can always take refuge and where I'm safe. Insha' Allah. With God's help.

When we walk out into the dawning of a Pakistani day, the sun has risen over the mosque and is shining down on Ali and Omar, greeting each other. As I get nearer to them I can hear Omar introducing Ali to his brothers and the invitation to join them for their morning meal is a balm. I follow on behind. I won't crowd Ali. If our talks on the trip from Saudi to Gwadar mean anything then he will seek me out.

Later that morning, when those who must work are gone from the crowded house, and only those who are resting are left, I'm proven right as Ali walks towards my shady tree and sits with me. At first he smiles and leans his head against the trunk, closing his eyes in silence, but once a peace has settled around us he breaks into my thoughts.

'The mosque was not so full this morning, my friend.'

'No? I thought a lot of people were there. The sound of prayer was loud and purposeful.'

'Those who were there were lifting their voices to Allah to make up for the loss. Ten years ago, Majid, this same mosque was teeming with bodies that spilled out into the open air. No man in Gwadar would ever miss his morning prayer. But now... they think that they do not have so much to pray for.'

53

'But I get the feeling that the people here are quite happy. There doesn't seem to be an air of gloom around Gwadar. Surely they would pray their thanks to Allah for their happiness? No?'

'Ah your innocence and trust, Majid. You see, the construction of the new port in the bay has brought huge economic development to Baluchistan. This port is to be the root of Central Asia. The Chinese – a great wealthy power – have sent their engineers to build this port. There is an enormous growth now in the fish catch and it is increasing all the time, enhancing seafood export.

'You see the happiness amongst Omar's family? They are mostly fishermen. Lack of money worries brings their happiness. Omar's brother, Jafar, tells me he has bought a new boat this week. Bigger and better. You see that Razina has won her battle over their house and a second story is at last being built to accommodate their growing family. In the village, shops are also building second and even third stories to sell their wares. People here in Gwadar, and our neighbours in Pishukan, are hopeful that other Pakistanis are going to come to our area and buy land and property here. There are roads being built now to the main highways to bring the Baluchi people closer to what they are calling civilisation.... Ha!'

'But, Ali. Isn't this all good news? Omar has told me often enough about the poverty of his family when he was growing up. Now they have wealth and they have hope and they are happy. How is this a bad thing and what has it got to do with the numbers being down in the mosque?'

'Everything, Majid. The villagers had nothing and they prayed to Allah for their very lives. Now they have what they need, they pray less and less. They are getting greedy and they know that greed is a sin, but they want to enjoy life and not be reminded of humility. They do not see that we must not only petition Allah; that we must thank him for what he provides as well. The more they have the less they feel a need for him. The less they feel a need to pray. They forget that nothing is anything without Allah. They are forgetting the words of the prophet Mohammed, peace be upon him.'

'Ali, in my country there is great wealth and the people are still very religious. What of that?'

'Ah, Majid but these are two very different nations with very different governments. My government is lenient on people about their religious beliefs. Your government is intolerant of any other religions and insists that its inhabitants obey and live by the Qur'an. Your country will not be tainted by wealth as ours would be. They say that Gwadar is turning into the next Dubai. As if this is a good thing. Look at the Western world and tell me that wealth governed without religion is a good thing... No, my friend it is not. Western greed and Godless lives are like a disease; and I, for one, will fight to keep them away. This disease has no place amongst the people of Baluchistan. We need to stay pure. We need to fight with our prayers... and with other things if necessary.'

Ali closes his eyes and leans his head against the tree once more in contemplative silence. I follow suit. Ali's my guide now. He'll lead me on Allah's straight path, but when I open my eyes he's gone and Razina's bending over me, wrapped in an orange shawl, holding out a bowl of water.

'Drink, boy. You can't sit in this heat without water.' I reach out to her and drink thirstily.

'These troubles that fill you with anger, Majid... Do you wish to talk about them?' She takes the empty bowl from my fingers and replaces it with her gnarled, gentle hands. 'You can't keep it inside you. You are a well that is overflowing with poisoned water. You need to empty it all out and be cleansed to begin again.' Razina looks into my face with her own healing eyes shining their encouragement.

So I tell her about Shadia and my family and how the West, especially the Irish, are to blame for everything and, slowly but surely, some of the poison drains from me.

Chapter twelve

'HAVE they her name down for the local national school, do you think?' Norah was standing doing the dishes; one rubber-gloved hand steeped in bubbles, the other spraying her husband as she wagged her fingers in his direction. Des looked up from his newspaper, his attention caught as the football tables were drowned with fairy liquid.

'She's six weeks old, Norah. She's hardly ready to learn her ABCs yet.'

'There'll be a waiting list if they don't get her name down soon. That's the way it is now with all the schools. They'd want to get a move on or they'll be left behind is all I'm saying.' Norah plunged her hands back into the grease and grime and Des thought it might be safe to turn back to the football results.

'Of course, they won't get her in if they don't get her baptised first.'

Des took his reading glasses from his face and put them down on his newspaper.

'So that's what this is all about. It has nothing to do with your granddaughter's education. I might have known. What has getting baptised got to do with going to school might I ask?'

'Do you ever read the news, Des, or do you only buy the paper for the sports section? Do you even listen to the radio? Sure everyone is talking about it. Most of the schools in Ireland are Catholic, so if you want your child to go to a Catholic school, they have to be baptised a Catholic. If they're not, they have to go to school somewhere else with all the Muslims and Buddhists and Protestants and that. The poor mite has her work cut out for her already fitting in anywhere with that ridiculous name her unreasonable mother has saddled her with. They'll have to baptise her, Des and you'll have to tell them because they'll never listen to me.'

The finger stopped wagging and dived back under with the pots. Des looked down at the soccer pages and realised the futility of trying to read the soggy print, and he'd have to clean the suds off his glasses anyway. Could a man not read the newspaper on a Saturday morning in peace? He wished he didn't have to listen to Norah either but...

'I'm going to tidy the garden.' Escape was always a good plan.

'Don't forget we said we'd go over to Shona's later...'

He was nearly out the door. One foot on the first step...

'Are you going to leave that paper for someone else to tidy up?'

*

'Father Brian, how are you?'

'Nice to see you, Thomas.'

'Eh, it's Tommy actually. I prefer Tommy. Sorry, Father.'

'Not at all, Tommy. Norah told me it was Thomas. So I... Now... Does Ruby have a second name? You know, like a saint's name?'

Tommy looked blankly at the priest.

'For her Christening, Tommy... Maybe she could take her Granny's name or something?'

'I'll be right back, Father.' Tommy went running over to Shona and filled her in on the dilemma.

'No way she's going to be called Norah,' insisted Shona.

'I'm not sure Norah's a saint's name anyway but what about your mum's middle name?' asked Margaret. Shona had asked her own Godmother to stand as Ruby's Godmother too.

'No!' said Shona.

'Okay, maybe not Mary. What about Maria then? It's different, but we can still tell your mum she's called after her. Go on, Shona. It'll mean the world to your mother and it might go some way to showing her that you forgive her for everything.' Shona glared at Margaret.

57

'Well, okay, not everything. But it will ease the pressure on you all, Shona. Go on.'

Tommy sent Shona to tell Father Brian and he went himself to tell Norah. He told her it was Shona's idea.

Ten minutes later Father Brian was saying, 'I baptise you Ruby Maria Farrell...'

Shona got a fit of the giggles, which stopped the priest in his tracks and left everyone else looking around uncomfortably. Walking down from the altar Tommy raised a questioning eyebrow at Shona who whispered, 'Ruby Maria Farrell. I hope she can pronounce her *r's* when she's older...' leaving Tommy holding his sides laughing all the way back to his seat too.

The rest of the Christening went smoothly and Norah was delighted to carry her namesake out of the church. Des followed behind with his arm around his daughter. Maybe she was coming back to them. Maybe these last few weeks could be erased and they could start again. The reception that Norah had organised back at the house could be a new beginning. Norah was smiling at Des. Shona was smiling at Tommy. Everyone was smiling at the baby. All was well.

'We'll see you back at the house, Father.' Des had a few bottles of champagne in the fridge to celebrate. His building contracts might not be doing so well at the moment but nothing was too good for his first grandchild.

Shona sat in the house that she'd shared with Des and Norah all her life. Well most of it. Apparently she'd been somewhere else until she was one. For the first time since she had found out about her adoption, it occurred to her that she had never asked where that was. She had thought about who her mother had been of course, but she was reeling too badly to do anything about it.

She stared into her champagne glass and swirled the last drop around before knocking it back. Reaching forward to the ice bucket she poured a refill letting the fizz settle and topping it up until there was no room left in the glass. This was the first time she'd been here since before Ruby was born. This was the first time Ruby had been in her grandparent's house. Ruby's grandparents? Shona tossed the words around in her head for a while. It all made sense now, all those feelings of not belonging. Shona looked around the sitting room. She had never had many relatives and only saw them for weddings, funerals and Christenings. She had never really questioned that she didn't resemble anyone in her immediate or extended family. She looked over at her mother's much younger sister, Margaret.

They had been quite close when Shona was a child. Margaret had played the Godmother role wonderfully back then. Shona remembered trips to the Savoy cinema and to see Santa at Switzers. Magical times. But the quiet, caring Margaret had been no match for the wild teenager that unravelled later in Shona. She sometimes felt bad when she thought of the horrible things that she'd said and done to Margaret over the years.

But hadn't Margaret lied to her as well? No use feeling apologetic to this lot about anything. They were liars, each and every one. Des and Norah couldn't have kept their secret all those years without being aided and abetted by this bunch.

The anger filled Shona's body as she knocked back her glass in one gulp, pouring it in on top of a skinful from earlier. Well somebody had to drink the stuff she supposed. Des had opened three bottles and people had only had a few sips to toast the baby. Shona had felt obliged to drink the rest. The last bottle was empty so Shona looked around for something else and filled a large glass with red wine. She then followed her Godmother into the dining room where Ruby had woken up and was whimpering.

Margaret looked over at the wild-eyed look on her Goddaughter's face and knew she needed to get her out of there fast. If she could just get her upstairs and lie her down… maybe she'd pass out quietly before she got herself into trouble.

'Ruby's filled her nappy, Shona, love. Would you like me to take her up to change her? Maybe we should take her out of all this white lace and put something more comfortable on her.'

Margaret was holding Ruby lovingly in her arms, a big smile beaming in Shona's direction. Shona stared through her aunt, a very unpleasant look on her face, which Margaret recognised immediately.

'C'mon and help me. Okay? We, eh, won't be long...' The baby's whimper became a cry.

'You lied to me, *Aunty* Margaret.' Shona had her face now right up against her aunt's, demanding a reaction.

Margaret wanted to tell her that it wasn't like that. That her mother had always meant to tell her about her adoption when the time was right, but it never was. Shona's life was one long crisis. She stood back a little from her niece and put the baby back down in her buggy. Ruby cried louder in disgust. Margaret didn't look back at Shona. She was scared of that face. Those drunken, crazy eyes that said something horrible was going to happen.

'Yes, Shona, I lied by saying nothing and I'm very sorry. I wanted to tell you. But I... We'll get together soon and talk about it. But not today, eh? Not here.' She finished covering the baby and walked towards the front of the buggy to push her out of the room.

Margaret didn't see the blow coming but it left her sprawled across the table, which was spread with food for the party. The shock left her incapable of calling out and the sight of the baby's Christening robe, splattered with her mother's red wine, made her move protectively towards the buggy. She had to get Shona upstairs and try to sober her up... but she soon realised it was too late. Shona had opened the door into the sitting room and was now shouting wildly at the visitors.

'You're a crowd of dirty bastard liars! You should all get the fuck home to your own houses 'cause there's not one of you related to that baby in there.'

Ruby screamed above the hush of the guests.

'I've had more than I can take of all this stupid, fucking pretence. I've had enough of all your lies.' Shona flung her half-filled wine glass at the far wall covering people and furniture, floors and ceiling with blood like colours and shattered pieces of glass.

'Go on! Get the fuck out of here!'

Norah walked calmly across to her daughter and slapped her full across the face.

'Don't any of you move,' she said with her voice full of steel. 'It's my daughter who is leaving.'

She then turned to a bewildered Tommy. 'Thomas, take this drunk out of here. Leave Ruby with us. You can bring her home tomorrow. If her mother has sobered up.'

Margaret, standing now, looked over at Father Brian. He looked as if he knew he should be doing something, but in all his years as a priest Margaret was sure he'd never seen such a display at a Christening. The baby screamed louder, her face purple with anger, her little arms and legs kicking out at the injustice of being ignored. Norah picked her up and cradled her close.

Shona pulled herself back up and looked at her mother, her face stunned and disbelieving.

'You sh- should have t- told me...' she stammered. She held her cheek, rubbing the tears into the sting.

'You all lied...' The people in the room who had stood accused of not being related to her baby, looked around nervously; at the floor, the walls, out the window; anywhere but at Shona.

'Dad, you shouldn't have hidden that from me...' Des looked at his daughter and his shoulders shuddered. A noise rose in his throat like the beginning of a keening, the years of struggling to bring up Shona taking its toll, and he turned and left the room.

'They should have, shouldn't they, Tommy?'

Tommy put down his can of Guinness and took Shona by the arm before leading her away from the house where the silent lies had ruined her.

'Somebody should have told me...'

Her Godmother watched her being led from the room and, in her heart she knew that Shona was right.

Chapter thirteen

ALI strides purposefully through Gwadar's busy market, not looking to his right or to his left; his blinkered vision carrying him swiftly on to his goal. I on the other hand am struggling to keep up. The sights and smells are there to be savoured, not ignored. It isn't completely different from a Saudi souk, but everything is more intense. It's louder for a start. The sellers shout over each other to get the best attention from their clientele. They sweep their arms over their wares to show the attractiveness of their beautifully displayed fruit, their kebabs, their popcorn and their juicers. The naan are stacked high having been tossed and hung, the smell of them sweet in my nostrils, salivating my taste buds.

Ali turns and glares at me to hurry myself.

'But I'm starving, Ali,' I beg. 'Could we not buy something small? Very quickly...' I wear my most pleading face.

'If you were out of bed on time this morning, you lazy good for nothing little runt! If you hadn't missed your morning prayers! If you hadn't been so sluggish about your dressing! Then you would have had time to eat... So, no! Now move it!'

I shrug my shoulders and push my hungry body forward to catch up with him. Marching beside Ali, my temper is scrunched between clenched fists. But then he relents, stops beside a stall and asks the seller to hurriedly pass him some karaye, which I hoover up from the cardboard plate. A small smile returns to my face and all is better with the world for now.

'Laziness and greed... a bad start to your day and a waste of good rupees. We were supposed to meet Sameer ten minutes ago. He's a busy man Majid. Do you think he has nothing better to do with his morning than sit around waiting for the likes of you?

Come. Get a move on.'

With my temper quelled by food, I wonder what this Sameer has to do that's so important he couldn't hang on for a few minutes more. Ali's been bringing me on visits to Imams, teachers and philosophers for days now and I haven't seen any of them doing anything other than sit around and talk. If talking could solve the world's problems then this lot would have the globe well and truly cleaned up by now.

Having said that, their talk is amazing. I've had so much food for thought recently it's a wonder I'm ever hungry.

'I know what has you so tired and so hungry, young man and its nothing to be proud of I can tell you.' Ali speaks in a way that leaves no doubt as to how disgusted he is with me, and my skin burns from my shoulders upwards as I wonder how he can possibly know what I'm so ashamed of. I look sideways at him to try to get a clue of what he knows and how he found out.

'Do you think that nobody noticed how you were staring at Intizar last night? Do you think that nobody realised why you were suddenly unable to eat the wonderful food that Razina had prepared for you? Omar's nieces are not there for your entertainment, Majid. Did you know that she was slapped, hard, by her father for not wearing her veil last night? Your dirt-filled looks got the poor girl into trouble. There was a big row after you left to go to your room early too. The brothers were saying that you must leave their house. Go and stay somewhere else. Their daughters cannot even relax in their own home. So eat the food you're given in future and keep your thoughts on girls to yourself.'

Ali's words bounce off me. Poor Intizar. Now this makes me feel doubly ashamed. I hadn't realised that anyone had actually noticed. I'd left and gone to my room early because I was embarrassed at the things that I'd been thinking about Omar's niece while she was serving me my evening meal. If Ali knew what had actually happened when I returned to my sleeping mat, what would he be saying about me then? Had someone actually seen? Was I followed up? No... I'm sure I wasn't. My skin warms again as I remember the feelings, lying under the sheet, in the place I normally share with so many others. When I first realised what had happened I didn't mean to start touching myself. But once my hand started to reach down and the pictures of Intizar got clearer in my head; well, there was nothing I could do. I felt the guilt, of course I did, but even thoughts of Allah and attempts at prayer couldn't stop it happening.

I called out. I'm sure of that. Did I call her name? I don't think so, but… What if someone saw and heard? Ali speaks about laziness and greed. He shows how disgusted he is about my so-called thoughts about Intizar. He knows nothing of what happened later – the thing that stopped me from going to the mosque this morning.

I slept restlessly but when I woke early this morning and heard the muzzein call to prayer I threw the sheet over my head and buried myself in shame.

'Should we wake him?' Sharif had asked his older cousin.

'Leave the bag of dirt where it lies. He's not worthy of prayer,' was the response.

And now Ali's bringing me to another Imam and I can't bear being in the presence of someone so perfect, knowing myself to be so imperfect. How can such sins be cleansed? But the worst thing of all is I'm not that sure I want those thoughts to be cleansed. The devil has taken over, well and truly, because the pleasures that I felt under the sheet last night were absolutely wonderful and I know that I'd want to repeat them again. So, what's to be done? Well for now I'll patter along after Ali and think later.

I wonder what Intizar's doing now and the image of her face and bare hands come to me so clearly that I fall behind Ali's step once more for fear he'd notice and chastise me again. I think that this sin; the one where I want a woman; is probably going to be the one sin that I'll find hardest to overcome.

Then she's there in my head again. Shadia. The day I kissed her at Maeve's house. Of course it was Shadia who initiated it. I was shocked and delighted at the time and I never want to forget it.

My only kiss so far would be Shadia's only ever kiss.

Sometimes it's hard to be sorry for your sins. I could never be sorry for that.

Imam Sameer holds my hands and looks so deep into my eyes that I'm sure he can read every bad thing I've ever thought or done. These Pakistanis and their intense staring. I can't take my eyes from Sameer's either. They are so dark they're almost black, and, through them, I feel a hold grip me and lock me in a place I feel I want to be. I know that Sameer's taking my measure, as Razina had done on the first night of my visit. I see the knowledge in his gaze and feel the forgiveness sweep through his hands and reach into me. This man is surely sent from Allah. I leave the tears that wet my eyelids unchecked and don't feel any less the man for my emotions. We stay like this for only a moment in time, but it is a moment, I know, will stay with and strengthen me.

When Sameer let's go of my hands I feel a link remain between us. A thread so long and so strong that it could stretch to the end of the world and never be broken.

Sameer gently gestures his graceful old hands towards two rich, red cushions and we sit, legs crossed, backs straight, quiet and humbled.

'Forget all of your struggles from before, young man. Allah is with you from here on. I think sometimes it's hard for you to always follow his straight path? I know how hard it is. I was young once myself, you know.'

We smile at Sameer, trusting, soaking his words and allowing them space.

'I know, I know, I must seem like a hundred years old to you two, but I feel my youth inside me still. Though it was a good place to be, I know that there were some very dark times but I made room for Allah. Then the world was a brighter place and my heart was lighter.' He closes his eyes and we close ours.

I think of the times that I have Allah in my life and the times when I don't and I know that the difference between those times is the difference between complete darkness and intense sunlight. One fills the mind with fear and incompetence and the latter fills my heart with joy and a feeling of utter power in all I chose to do. Sameer's asking me a question and the answer is so incredibly easy that I wonder why I have ever had doubts.

'The way to happiness is through Allah,' I answer, 'and the way to Allah is through prayer and keeping to the straight path.'

'Words are easy, Majid,' Sameer says, 'but you must answer these questions with actions. Allah will lead and you will follow.'

I hear a scraping of feet and I open my eyes to see that Sameer's getting up.

'Has there been any news, Ali... of Khaled?' Sameer's face is filled with concern.

'No... Nothing,' Ali's eyes pain and he looks away.

Sameer smiles and embraces Ali. 'It will come good, Ali. Allah will see that he is rewarded. Khaled knows this and it gives him strength. Let it give you the strength to fight on too.' Ali tries to smile and the older man holds him once more.

Letting go, Sameer turns and gives me his hands as well as a long hard look. One that says *you know what to do and you can do whatever you want to. For Allah.* I hear the unspoken words. For me there's no smile, I haven't earned it yet, only a nod of encouragement and Sameer walks away.

Ali draws near and places his hands on my shoulders.

'You see now, Majid. Don't you? It will all be good, but it's up to us. I believe that Allah speaks through Sameer. This amazing Imam is telling us to forsake all the badness in the world and to embrace all the good. He has challenged us to fight Allah's cause and we will do this, Majid. Do you see?'

I see. I push my shoulders back and nod my head. I'm ready to take on the world in Allah's name.

'Ali? Who is Khaled?' I'm upset that the mention of someone's name can cause my friend such distress.

'Khaled is my brother, Majid. He is a guest of the American government in Guantanamo Bay. He is an intelligent, religious man, who has been wasting away for years, for the pleasure of a

Western government. But Majid, let's talk of him another time.'

We walk away from the meeting room with a peace I had not felt when we arrived. Ali does not take his hand from my shoulder and I feel his solidarity all the way back through the market, and back towards the house. When we get to the pathway that leads to Omar's family home, Ali stops and turns. He takes a deep breath and sighs, shaking his head from side to side as if the world is on his twenty-five-year-old shoulders and he has to shake it free.

'Majid. Sit down.' I look around and although there's nothing but dust and dirt at my feet, I sit. Ali sits too and there's silence for a few moments as we collect our thoughts before he speaks – his voice almost a whisper.

'Majid. You're in disgrace in the house where you're supposed to be the guest. Every man and woman has turned on you. I'm afraid that you'll no longer be welcome there. So listen to me carefully and I'll tell you what we must do, and if you're as clever as I think you are you'll agree. It's not completely honest but it's for the best and leaves everyone feeling good about you; which is important. The alternative is for you to go back to Saudi and I've a suspicion that you're actually enjoying your time here. Am I right?'

I nod my answer. I'm finding a peace in Gwadar that I haven't known for months.

'So go along with whatever I say back at the house. Yes?'

'Yes, Ali. You lead and I'll follow.' I know by Ali's smile that this is the answer he's hoping for.

*

The men of Omar's family sit on the sand and look out at the waves, sighing their disappointment in unison. I was shocked at how quickly they had all been summoned to this meeting. It amazes me how everyone in Gwadar has a mobile phone. I even see beggars on the street pull their mobiles from under their rags to call their friends. So here we are and it feels more like a court hearing than a meeting.

At first they murmur quietly in Baluchi and I can only guess what they are saying to each other from their tone of voice, or from the heated exchange and the looks they then give me. These begin as seething, but eventually become tolerant and finish with sympathetic nods in my direction. Then Ali makes a joke and Omar laughs. The others follow suit and before long they're all clapping me on the back, and the meeting-come-court-case seems to be over. Have I been let off the hook? It certainly seems like it.

I stand and smile contritely as the uncles and nephews, as well as the grandfather, all smile back at me and everything looks like it might be alright. They all begin to walk away from me, leaving me, I think, with only Ali for company.

'They fell for it, Ali. Whatever it was you told them, they believed you. I owe you. Thank you...'

'Yes, Majid.' A very familiar voice from behind me cuts in. 'They believed you. But I have known the little boy when he was saying he was sorry and I notice that the almost adult man is as insincere as the boy often was.'

I turn and Omar is standing there.

'Omar! I didn't know that you were there. I...'

'No. You didn't!' Omar spits his words.

Ali comes to my rescue. 'Omar, that's not what Majid meant. He told me earlier that he never thought that they would forgive him. He said that he didn't deserve their forgiveness. I can't tell you how ashamed he was of what he did. You know how young people talk, Omar. How they rarely say what they mean. It's normal for him to feel relief at what happened this evening. Especially after the things that I've said to him today.'

'He's right, Omar. I'm truly sorry.' I look at the man I've known all my life and I know that I need his forgiveness above everyone else's. I want to tell Omar the reason behind my attraction to Intizar. I want to explain that she reminds me of Shadia, but I know I can't say these things.

As I get older I realise that some of the most important things in life, the things that really need to be spoken, often have to be left unsaid – especially between those who love each other most. But maybe Omar understands. He puts his hands on my shoulders and hugs me, kisses me three times and walks away; nodding his head slowly up and down as if he has just realised something, and reluctantly agrees.

We two friends are left on the beach and we sit once more in silence. At 7.30pm the sun sets quickly and the bay is lit purple; the light stretching to the houses and along the cliffs that tower over them.

A fisherman finishes loading his cart with the day's catch and leads the donkey away from the shore. I smile at the blue hat that has been lovingly made for the animal, to keep the sun's rays off his head, holes cut for his ears. I follow the ornate carvings along the side of the cart and realise, not for the first time, that actually nothing in Pakistan is ordinary. Everything is colour and life. Nothing's as simple as it first seems.

Ali gets up and follows the donkey and cart and I catch up and fall in step.

'You're to stay with me tonight, Majid. It has been agreed with Omar's family. Tomorrow we will go to his house to pack some of your things, you won't need much, and you haven't, as yet, apologised to Razina. I promise you that these men will seem like a party compared to her wrath. You wouldn't believe the things that she's been saying about you.'

I shiver when I think of the wonderful, motherly, Razina and how I've betrayed her trust and care.

Ali's words break through my thoughts. 'I have two weeks left in Pakistan before I have to return to Riyadh to spend my days hosing down the grass for my Minister's garden. Such important work, eh?'

I smile in embarrassment. I've never given much thought to the men who hose the city's reluctant grass. I can't put this wise young man with these servants, but I'm beginning to see the equality of people. Muslims are the same the world over. Islam is a common bond, a strong link stretching across the globe. Our faith in Allah's the only thing that matters.

'I've many friends in Baluchistan that I want to see before I leave and I feel that you'll benefit from these visits,' Ali continues. You'll be made very welcome wherever we go. Your faith shines from you and my hope is that my Baluchi friends will keep that light alive and help to spread it further. While we are gone, Omar will call your father and put him out of his misery. That way Omar will be able to truthfully say that you are in Pakistan but that he has no idea where you are.'

And so we go; leaving the purple beach behind and, with it, my shame. As the cliffs soften to pink I can feel, from afar, Razina's forgiveness and a calm washes over me, because I now know that, somehow, everything will be alright.

Chapter fourteen

TOMMY was beginning to realise that he was, essentially, a single parent. He had put Ruby back to sleep, again, and looked over to the empty pillow on Shona's side of the bed. It was 5.20am. This was the third morning in a row he'd woken up alone and, he had to admit, it wasn't an unpleasant feeling, as he settled back down for another few hours shuteye. Between Ruby, working in the bar and doing his exams he was feeling exhausted.

Remembering the date, however, brought him conscious again all too quickly and he sat up in panic. It was Des and Norah's twenty-fifth wedding anniversary and they were coming for tea at four. Did Shona even know? Was there anything registering with her as she wandered in and out of the house oblivious to all of them? It was because of Shona that they weren't having a big party. Too soon after the chaos of the Christening to involve any extended members of the family. It was her fault her parents were coming to them as well. Shona hadn't apologised to them since their nuclear fallout and her parents were hoping she might make amends today. But why was Tommy feeling so worried about it all? They weren't his parents. Still, he'd asked his dad to come for moral support, or as referee or something. Imagine being married for twenty-five years. Tommy had a brief thought about what it might be like to be married to Shona and knew, instinctively, that they wouldn't get through year one.

He couldn't go back to sleep. It wasn't because he was worried about Shona. He was well beyond that now. The pattern of their lives over the past weeks was set. He looked around their room, his and Shona's, and wondered why they still shared. They shared nothing else. Especially looking after Ruby.

Tommy thought back to those last few weeks of Shona's pregnancy. She had been so excited. She had changed from wild party animal to Mother Earth overnight. He had come to like her most of the time, and sometimes he had thought she liked him. They were friends with a common cause. He even thought that they might come to something after all. When Tommy saw Shona feeding his baby girl in the hospital, after giving birth, he had been filled with so much love and emotion. That had lasted up until Shona's constant disappearing acts took over his life.

Since Norah's revelations about what Shona referred to as the lie, Shona had erased all signs of Mother Earth and had become a wilder than ever party animal – certainly the drunkest. That was the essence of it all. Ruby's mother had become a drunk. Blottoville was where she wanted to be and for all Tommy now cared she could stay there. He was fed up trying to pull her out of the mire.

Both he and Shona were only united in their efforts to keep the parents unaware of the extent of the problem. They needed them to pay the rent. Because of this, Shona had agreed to make some pretence at forgiving her parents for lying to her. Tommy pretended to his father because he was too proud to admit that he had made the biggest mistake of his life in moving in with Shona. He wondered how much longer he could keep them in the dark though. He snuggled back under the duvet. Ruby would be up at 7am, on the dot, so he needed to sleep.

*

'Shona! Shona! Wake up. Come on Shona. Wake up.'

Shona woke up, sat up and threw up, barely missing Tommy as he recognised the signs in time and jumped out of the way.

'Ah, for fuck's sake, you silly bitch!'

'Aaagh, sorry.'

Shona knew there was more to come and lurched in the direction of the toilet.

'You can fuckin' clean that up *yourself*.'

'I will. I'm sorry.'

Tommy flew downstairs in a rage and collected the necessary cleaning materials before storming back up to the bedroom and flinging them in the door at Shona.

'In case you hadn't realised, it's your parents' weddin' anniversary today and they're arrivin' here for tea and cake in less than an hour.'

'Okay. I know. I'll be down soon. I'll jump in the shower first.'

'Yeah. Please do. We don't want everyone passin' out with the...'

'I said I will. For fuck's sake, will you shut up?'

'Why pisshead? Am I too loud for your fragile head?'

Tommy slammed the door closed behind him, waking Ruby from her nap with a wail.

He had hoped to get another half hour out of her so he could finish cleaning up downstairs, but now they'd have to take him as they found him and if one of them so much as looked crooked at the pile of laundry in the corner he'd fist them one. After he'd floored Shona that is.

She had fallen out of a taxi soon after 6am this morning. The driver rang the doorbell and asked Tommy did he recognise the girl in his backseat. She had given him the address before passing out and he wasn't sure if he had understood her slurred speech. He didn't normally pick up drunks, he said, but he had felt sorry for the pretty little thing who'd obviously found herself in the wrong crowd where things had got out of hand. Tommy was tempted to say no, he'd never seen her in his life, but instead he ended up paying him with the money he was going to use to get Norah and Des a posh cake. The driver helped to bring her in, giving him some wise words on how to look after her. As if Tommy wasn't already an expert. Ignoring the advice, he had dumped her into bed and left her.

But now she needed to be up. Now they needed to show a united front against those who always thought they knew better. They needed to smile and be the perfect parents. Shona knew this too. Tommy knew that she would be down shortly and the play could begin. Mammy, daddy and baby make three.

Stephen had called earlier to say that he would bring a cake and a couple of bottles of bubbly over to celebrate the day, and after a few feeble arguments Tommy was delighted to give in. There would be a nice cake after all. He had prepared a few sandwiches himself too and even found time to make a quick print, in paint, of Ruby's tiny hands, which he framed for Norah and Des, who would love their present. For all her faults, Tommy recognised Norah's adoration of her granddaughter. They could all smile at the camera and put the photo up on the mantelpiece after. All friends together. As he picked his daughter up from the cot he practised his smile. Ruby smiled right back and, as usual, he melted into a soft gushy grin. Ruby would make everything alright.

*

'Bye Des. Thanks for comin' over.'

'See you, Mum. Thanks for everything. Happy Anniversary!' Shona had been the model daughter and mother. She had apologised to her parents for her behaviour at the Christening and assured them that it was all behind them. There was nothing like a binge to bring out the guilt in her.

Norah and Des had turned up at four o'clock that afternoon with Shona's giant old rocking horse in tow. They had unearthed it from the attic and cleaned him up. Now Buttons sat in the hallway, taking up half the house, and Shona was trying to thank her mum and keep a straight face at the same time. She would have managed and all if Tommy hadn't looked over at her at that particular moment causing the two of them to break into fits of laughter.

'Bye, son.' Tommy's dad shook his head and ushered Norah out the door before she realised that the laugh was on her and her addition to the household.

Tommy was still smiling when he closed the door and turned around to find Shona mounting the horse, rocking him back and forth as fast as she could.

'Fancy a ride, Tom?'

'Yee, haw!' Tommy climbed on behind and they yahooed over and back howling with laughter, letting loose the stress of the afternoon. One rock too many though and Shona flew over the horse's head landing on the floor with Tommy on top of her.

Tommy was laughing so much that he couldn't manage to move himself off her.

'Jesus, Tommy.' Shona laughed. 'When I asked did you fancy a ride I didn't know you'd take me literally, but seeing as you're here and everything and Ruby's asleep...?'

Tommy rolled off Shona and got up, then she stood and took his hand. Before he knew it he felt himself being led towards the stairs; the few glasses of champagne he'd had in the course of the afternoon fuelling a desire for Shona he hadn't known existed. They kissed halfway up and Shona slipped out of her stilettos. At the top they heard Ruby moan in her sleep and they froze while they waited for her to go silent again.

'Don't worry Tommy. She's a deep sleeper. Now where were we? Oh yeah.' Shona lifted her top over her head giving Tommy a perfect view of her very ample cleavage. Any doubts he'd had up to now, that this was a good idea, were expelled as they fell giggling into their bedroom to have passionate sex in the bed that they had never shared anything but sleep in.

*

Three days later Tommy decided that Shona was now officially missing. He had woken up on the night of the anniversary to find himself alone in the bed again. Presuming she was downstairs, he had turned over and gone straight back to sleep. When Ruby woke him at 7am Shona was out. Tommy fell over her shoes on the stairs and cursed her to hell for her habit of always leaving them there. How dare she have sex with him so casually like that and then feck off out for the night when she'd had her fill? How bloody dare she?!

But she had bloody dared and she'd kept going. She wasn't

answering his calls and her phone was going straight to voicemail. Now Tommy was in a quandary. He was beginning to think that perhaps something bad had happened to her. He knew he should contact her parents but that would mean telling them about Shona's problem. He really should call the Gardaí, but they would contact Shona's parents anyway and it would all come out. Maybe it was for the best, but Tommy didn't think he could cope much more on his own.

*

Shona tried to open her eyes but they were glued together. She lifted her hand up and prised them open gently with her fingers. The light blinded her and she shut them again immediately. Where was she? In that split second when her eyes were open she had recognised her surroundings but she still wasn't sure where exactly that was. The bed felt lovely and soft. The pillows cradled her head but she knew if she moved it would hurt. She opened one eye again and chanced a look to the side. She knew those curtains and that carpet. This room had been the same all her life. Shona had spent many nights here as a small child. This was her special room. Little Shona had been let choose all the decoration and obviously it had been kept that way ever since. She was regretting, now, the bright yellow walls and the curtains splattered with orange and purple butterflies. When she opened her other eye she could see the lilac bedspread, faded with age, but still there. How could she possibly have ended up here in this bed? In Aunty Margaret's house.

She could hear Margaret downstairs on the phone to someone. She hoped it wasn't her parents. The thought of that made her sit up in bed with a start and fling her feet over the side. The fast movement made her stomach lurch so she tried to sit still and take some deep breaths. Had she somehow made her way to her Godmother's house after two days... or was it three days drinking? She looked around the room but couldn't see her bag or her clothes. She was wearing a long, old nightdress and

Margaret had left her own battered dressing gown on the end of the bed for her. Her Godmother still didn't believe in shopping for anything new if the old one was still usable.

Reaching for the gown, she wrapped it around herself and tied the belt securely. She could smell soap and shampoo from her body and realised that she must be freshly washed, but she had no memory of having a shower the night before. Had Margaret washed her? The only way to answer these questions was to go downstairs and face her aunt. Her stomach turned again. The last time she had seen Margaret was at Ruby's Christening and Shona didn't want any reminders of what had happened that day. She used the headboard for support to haul herself up and out of bed, then dragged her feet towards the door before heading downstairs.

'Sit down, Shona. I've made some lunch.' Margaret's mouth was turned down in a scowl and her voice was frosty.

Shona pulled the heavy chair out and her neck and shoulders seized with the strain of the noise. There was a glass of water by her knife and fork with two antacid tablets sitting at its side. She wished Margaret would get up and leave the table for a moment so she could prepare the drink in peace without being glared at, but she knew she would have to go through it all. There was silence but for the drink fizzing between them. The post mortems of where she had been, where Margaret had found her and what state she had been in, were all looming. The only way to get to the end of them, and out of the house was to face all head on, then apologise and leave.

'Will we get it all out of the way, Margaret? What do you think? Shovel all the shit my way and get it off your chest.'

Margaret picked up her fork and began to slowly eat her pasta.

'This would be lovely with a nice, crisp glass of Chardonnay.' That was the last thing that she had expected Margaret to say. Shona picked up her glass and drained it of the drug that would hopefully make her feel a little better – or at the least well enough to take whatever it was that Margaret had to say to her.

'Except when you have alcoholics over for lunch, then you have to forgo things like that and leave only the water jug.'

That was way below the belt. Shona made to get up from the table.

'Stay right where you are, Shona Moran, don't you dare move. You're going nowhere until we've thrashed this out and made some plans for the future. Now sit down and eat every morsel of your pasta.'

Margaret had spoken quietly but there was enough authority in her voice for Shona to know that she meant what she said. She sat back down and force-fed herself as much of the soft cheesy dish as she could stomach. Through the whole meal Shona never looked up at her aunt once and neither woman said a word. Then when they had both put their knives and forks together Margaret got up from the table and put the kettle on.

'Your clothes are in the dryer. I had to put them through the wash twice to get the stains out so they won't be ready for a while yet and you'd look ridiculous in anything belonging to me so you're stuck here for a while.' Margaret finished making tea and carried it into the sitting room.

Shona sat at the kitchen table willing herself to get up and follow, but her legs seemed rooted to the worn lino. Margaret was holding no prisoners with the comments so far and she hadn't even started into the lecture yet. Shona caught sight of the raincoat and boots in a heap by the back door and thought about simply walking out, but it was a long walk home and she had no money for the bus. Eventually she managed to push herself up into a standing position and follow her Godmother into the sitting room.

She sat and let Margaret serve her the tea and they both began to drink with only the noise of the mugs being lifted and settled down again for company. Was Margaret going to let this go on for long or was she waiting for Shona to say something first? If so, she'd be left waiting. Shona had nothing to say. She didn't know where she had been for the last few days. She didn't know how she had gotten to be in Margaret's house. Maybe if she started by apologising for whatever it was she was supposed to have done.

It often worked with her parents.

'I'm sorry, Margaret, I don't know exactly what for, but you're obviously very angry with me so I'm sorry. And for what happened at the Christening. I'm really sorry for that too. You of all people didn't deserve it.'

'No I didn't, Shona but at the time you thought that I did and in some ways I can understand why you were so angry.'

Shona was once more floored by what Margaret was saying. She wasn't used to someone taking her side. She had resolved to be strong, take it all on the chin and then leave, but she could already feel the wetness in her eyes.

'I never agreed with your mother that you should be left in the dark about your adoption,' Margaret continued 'but I'm not your mother. She had her reasons.'

'What reasons could anyone possibly have for not telling me something as mind-bogglingly important as the fact that she was not my real mother? That there's some other woman out there who couldn't be bothered with her daughter so she dumped her in a home and walked away?'

Margaret took another sip of her tea and curled her feet up under her on her chair. 'There are reasons but there are no justifications for it. You may have noticed that your mother and I have a somewhat strained relationship, Shona. I fell out with her over her decision not to tell you about your past when you were about six. We were very close before that. But she was going through a very difficult period in her life. Realising that she wouldn't be able to manage another adoption after having you was taking its toll. It shook her relationship with your dad and that never went back to its original state. I was sorry afterwards that I wasn't much support to her, but we drifted apart and the rift never truly healed. So, as I said, she had her reasons.'

'What reasons?'

'You.'

'Oh, don't pull any punches will you Margaret? It's all my fault? Yeah, heap the blame on me. Go on, why don't you? It's what everyone else does. So you go right ahead too. I've been taking the blame for everything for as long as I can remember. At school. At home. For getting pregnant with Ruby. The works. So let's throw this one on me as well. No worries. I'm fine with that. It's my fault that my parents and both their families are liars.' Shona had spoken quietly but her words were thick with fury. She wanted to kick out at something. Somebody.

'Shona, your problems in life did not start the day you heard that you were adopted. Your problems have actually nothing to do with your adoption. You weren't treated any differently than if you had been Norah's own child but you had a temper, Shona. Sorry, you have a temper, and from the very beginning if you didn't get your way with absolutely everything you would lose it big time. Screams from your cot or your high chair are the earliest memories I have of coming into your house shortly after Norah and Des adopted you. By the time you were walking and talking, when it would have been a good time to begin to introduce you to the idea that you had another mother other than Norah; we were all so busy trying to stave off the next tantrum that your mother decided it was best to let it lie for a while. Norah and Des had hoped to adopt another baby around about then too but everyone agreed it was best to wait a while. So the terrible twos became the troublesome threes and the unforgettable fours and so on. Then you started school and you were never out of trouble from day one.'

'God, I hated school. I hated my parents for sending me to that snobby kip of a place and I hated the teachers and...'

'So you hate the system, Shona. I think we've sussed that one out. Is it because you hate everyone that you drink so much?'

'I don't hate everyone and I don't have a temper and I don't drink too much!' Shona took a deep breath after her outburst. 'I don't, Margaret. I don't hate everyone. I certainly don't hate Ruby. I love her more than anything.'

'Brilliant. Let's start from there then. Let's start from Ruby. When did you see her last?'

'Yesterday. No, the day before. We had a party for mum and dad's anniversary.'

'Right. Well it's three days since your mum and dad's anniversary, so at least we can verify how long it is that you've been on this particular binge.'

Shona went quiet. Had it really been three days? Her head and her body certainly felt like it could have been. She brought her knees up under her chin and hugged them close. Shit. She was crying. She had hoped to avoid that but Margaret had always been great at wording things in such a matter-of-fact way that she laid you open for emotion. Her aunt was over by her side immediately.

'Shove up in the seat there.' Shona moved over to the edge of the sofa and Margaret put her arms around her. She held her through waves of sobbing and said nothing. Just kept Shona grounded while she felt that she was being swept out to sea in a gale. Margaret didn't speak again until the storm was beginning to clear. Then she loosened her grip and sat back in her own chair.

'Shona, look at me.' Shona reluctantly pulled her face up to find Margaret. 'Are you going to do something about this mess? You need help, sweetheart. Help to manage your anger and to curb your addiction to drink and I'm all yours as much as I can be. I've always been there for you whenever you wanted. I'm here now, but there's only so much I can do.'

'I'll try.' Shona was nodding but she knew she wasn't convincing either herself or Margaret.

'In what way?'

'I don't know, Margaret. Today is a difficult time to talk about it. I've been drinking solidly for three days and I agree that that's excessive. I will do something, but not today. I feel like death and my head's a mess.'

'Fine. I'll bring you home and I'll call into you tomorrow after I'm finished at work. Spend the next twenty-four hours thinking up a plan of action, Shona.'

'Will you come in with me when I get back? I don't know if I can face up to all of Tommy's bloody accusations right now.'

'Tommy will be fine with you. He always is. One of the things that you might think about tomorrow is changing your attitude towards him. He's a brick, Shona. I can't understand why he hasn't done a runner so far, but he's still here and you can thank your lucky stars for that.'

Shona wasn't sure if she could cope with the St Thomas bit today. She tried to pull herself into standing to announce her departure but stumbled over the long nightdress. In a heap on the floor, she took a deep breath and used the coffee table as leverage to haul herself up once more. Her humiliation was complete now so she thought that she might as well ask Margaret where she had been when she found her.

'My neighbour called me at work to tell me there was a disgusting, filthy-looking, female curled up in my doorway who kept yelling obscenities at her each time she tried to approach. She wanted to know should she call the guards or leave it 'till I came home and you know what, Shona? I wasn't a bit shocked or worried about it because I knew immediately it was you. I left work a bit early and came home to find you still lying in the porch and not making a blind bit of sense.'

Shona didn't want to hear any more so she turned around and walked towards the clothes dryer in the kitchen. She needed to get out of here, but Margaret was hot on her heels and wasn't letting go. She caught her by the shoulder and turned her around.

'Look at me, Shona. You were out of your mind on booze for three days and you still somehow made your way to here. You swear that you hate the family but when the going got really tough you crawled on your hands and knees towards the people that love you most in the world. You love your family more than you let on.' Shona tried to pull away. 'No! Stay put. Hear me out.' Shona looked back at her aunt, blinking to try to hold the tears in. 'Your parents and their whole family completely let you down. We lied. You're right. In trying to protect you and keep you safe from a truth that we felt would mess you up; we managed to do exactly that without ever intending to.

'Shona you have to find it in yourself to forgive your parents. They have worshipped the ground that you've walked on since the day they met you. They've done their best.'

'Well they fucked up.' Shona was letting the tears fall now.

'Yes. We all did. You included. So now that's done. Now we have a chance to say, where do we go to from here?'

'So where do I go to from here, Oh Wise One?'

Margaret drew a deep breath. 'You know the one thing your mother did wrong was insisting that she would never smack you, because if ever a kid could've done with a good arse walloping, it was you. Is you.'

'I'm not a kid.'

'Then stop acting like you're ten. You're nearly eighteen and you have a child. Go home. Sober up. Look after my great niece. Look after yourself.'

Chapter fifteen

A KICK in the backside wakes me on my sixth morning away from Gwadar. I sit up, furious, and lunge at the man who's cackling a toothless laugh over me. I still haven't a clue where we are and I haven't seen Ali for days. We arrived in the Chagai Hills last week and I've no idea how we got to this particular spot. I know that I'll never find my way back to the nearest village alone, that's for sure.

The ground is bare granite and it took me a long time to fall asleep, the first few nights, on the roll of matting Ali gave me, surrounded by snoring men who smell as bad as I probably do myself. I yearned for a shower at first but I'm used to it now. The only women I've seen here come regularly to the edge of the nearest hill and leave water and food. Then, like exotic birds in the distance, they seem to fly away and disappear from sight.

The kick in my nether regions is to let me know that it's time for prayer. I love the familiarity of this, always, as everywhere, five times a day. All of us kneeling and praying and bowing in the same direction. It isn't long before I feel at ease in my rocky home. With every prayer time, comes a speech from the heart, from older, wiser men; leaving no man wondering what exactly it is that Allah wants us to achieve.

Many of the men are about my age and I chat with a Saudi boy called Nawab. At night, sitting by the fire, I'm sedated with delicious meat, cooked on a spit and shared with everyone. Although we have long discussions about all things Islamic or philosophical; Nawab won't fill me in on his background, where he's from in Saudi or why he's here. He carries a gun, as does every man I've met since I arrived.

'In this region guns are carried as a sign of manhood, nothing more,' Nawab explains.

'They're freely available, being as close as we are to the Afghani and Iranian border. Trafficking is rife,' he laughs, 'and the smugglers are constantly able to find new places to hide their booty without getting caught.'

The terrain is rough and the men in their filthy kurtas seem a tough bunch, but the atmosphere in the camp is generally one of prayerful peace. Nawab has been with these men a while and speaks enough Brahui to get by, and to translate a little for me. I was getting used to a little Baluchi in Omar's hometown and find it amazing that yet another language is spoken in Chagai. But it seems this camp is home to many languages and that's why Arabic's used so much to bind them together. It's the language of Islam after all. I breathe in the air of the place and let it fill me with excitement and peace in equal measure.

I'm with the men for almost a week when Ali, who's hardly come near me in all that time, comes to speak to me. Another man, who doesn't introduce himself, sits on the ground opposite and stares at me until I feel I have to look away. Ali's taken on a particularly grave expression.

'Ali, it's good to see you.' I smile at my friend. 'Where've you been?'

Ali sits beside me on the rock, retreats into his usual silence for a while and then speaks.

'Majid. The time has come to test your allegiance to Allah. Some senior men here seem to think that you don't have what it takes.' He glances over at the stranger.

'I don't understand. Do you mean they doubt my sincerity to Islam? Are they mad?'

'Okay, my friend, don't be so jumpy. Today a man called Ahmed Al Alfi wants to talk to you. Be careful what you say to him. If you want to be taken seriously then you will have to show him that you would literally do anything for Allah.' Ali's eyes burn into mine.

'To do the work of Mohammed the Prophet, peace be upon

him, we have to first get to the root of Islam's problem, Majid. Tell Zarrar here what you think that is. What do we need to fight against if we are to have a better world run in the Islamic way?'

In my mind I know that the greatest rot in the world, the part that's filling the rest with a terrible disease, is undoubtedly the people who've caused Shadia's death. I've no problems with the answer.

'The West!' I spit out the word.

Ali sits quietly, his eyes closed as if in silent prayer.

'Ali...' My voice shakes a little and I clear my throat. 'Ali, what is it, this work that we have to do?'

Ali turns away and his eyes shine angry in the morning sunlight. The two men stare at each other and I try to read Ali's thoughts. He shakes his head slowly.

The stranger spits on the ground and speaks for the first time. 'I was right, Ali. You have brought us a boy who has no idea how to follow Allah. No focus. *The West?* You couldn't be a little more specific, rich kid. Eh?'

'Give him a chance, Zarrar. We all have to start somewhere.' Ali tries to placate the man.

'Majid, you must learn to put your life in Allah's hands if you truly want to follow him. Don't question what Allah wants you to do; but follow his lead. There are wise men here, who recognise the injustices that are committed against innocent men in this world. Men like my brother Khaled. I have been talking with Ahmed this week about a way in which you could help my brother. He wants to meet you and assess your suitability. *Don't* let me down.'

Then he stands and gestures for me to follow him and Zarrar and soon we are in a tent with an older man that I haven't met since I arrived here. A nervous, thin young man crouches in the corner. The older man closes his eyes and begins to chant verses from the Qur'an and the others follow his lead. We invite Allah into our thoughts and beg him to help us in making the right decisions. The men then open their eyes and my interview begins, half in Brahui, half in Arabic, with Ali translating when the need arises.

Who are you? Where are you from? Who is the one and only God? Who are your true friends in the world? Who are your enemies?

The questions are simple to begin with.

As Muslims, how do we believe that we should deal with those who are misguided? What does jihad mean to you? When is it right to rise against an enemy in a jihad?

I have to really think now, make sure I get it right.

Why are you here? Where do you see your future, servant of Allah? What do you want from life? To what extreme would you be willing to give of yourself to the work of the jihad?

The words fire out like bullets and I begin to get breathless.

What do you think Allah wants of Majid Al Faisal?

This continues for an hour. Some questions I have the answers to, other questions confuse me. The old man becomes angry when the answer doesn't please him and his face becomes mellow and friendly when the words are what he wants to hear. I go from fear to pride to happiness, back to fear and finish full of revenge for those who slight Allah. I am ready to do whatever is necessary to win this jihad.

When they're finished, the older man introduces himself as Ahmed Al Alfi and gets straight to the point.

'Majid, sit.' He points to the ground in front of him where I'll be looking up to him. 'We can see that you have a calling to help your fellow Muslims.'

Ahmed picks up two blown up photos and places them in front of me. One's of an airplane displaying an American flag with military personnel standing nearby, the other is of a man, probably Pakistani, who I think has something familiar about him.

'Islam has already shown its strength in America and in those countries that have come to their aid, but one government has been consistent in helping them to hurt our Muslim friends. The American armies have been allowed to land their planes there and refuel.' Ahmed leans forward and prods the offending photo with his finger. 'Planes that we know are full of innocent

Muslim men. Good people who are being brought to prisons to be tortured and humiliated.'

Ahmed pauses to let this information sink further, giving me time to think about what he's saying. Will I be asked to go there? My mind is swirling while I try to keep up.

Ahmed continues. 'The small island of Ireland has been a neutral state for many years. It still calls itself one but this is no longer true. They are not a country against war. The Irish have always been in cahoots with the Americans but *this*…' Ahmed picks up the photo of the aircraft and puts it into my hands.

'This is a picture taken by Amnesty International. It's an American plane, claiming to be refuelling in Ireland on its way to its final destination. Amnesty insists that the journey's end is to locations where they are dropping detainees to be questioned. Places known as black sites. The American government has recently made a big gesture of stopping this from happening, but we know that it's continuing and growing. The filth bag CIA makes its own laws and the American authorities stand back and let this shit carry on.' Ahmed speaks quietly, the fire in his eyes giving volume to the words that come out in a whispered spit. The old man bends closer, making sure he has full eye contact.

'The Irish are not listening to Amnesty and continue to allow this brutality to happen.' He takes a deep breath and exhales loudly. 'We will make them listen.'

I stare at Ahmed, my eyes wide with understanding. I knew it. The Irish are as bad as all the others. Worse even. I've been right in everything I said. They're to blame for Shadia's death. As if they had planted the bomb themselves…

'Majid.' Ali stands and takes the second photo and turns it towards me. 'This photo is of my brother Khaled, before he was imprisoned. You can see how he was. He is as tall as I am, but a stronger man. Khaled was taken from his home for questioning because he was a friend of this man.' Ali points to the man in the corner whose hands shake involuntarily.

The man stands and walks unsteadily towards me and speaks.

'I was with Khaled on his journey from here to a black site in

Europe. I never found out where it was, as I didn't last long there before I was let go. I never found out why, but the important thing is that when I lived in Abu Dhabi some years ago I worked for an Irish family.' His voice trembles as he speaks. Ahmed nods at him to continue.

'On my journey with Khaled we stopped at an airport for some hours. A door was open to the outside whilst the plane was refuelled and I heard workers speaking. I recognised the accent, it was similar to my former employers, and unmistakably Irish.'

'Majid', Ahmed interrupts. 'I understand from Ali that you have recently lost someone very dear to you and Ali is right in what he says. If that Irish family were not there corrupting Shadia then she would still be with us. They most likely did not mean her any harm but the error of their ways rubbed off on your Shadia, as the errors of the Irish rubs off on all of Islam.'

My eyes brim with tears as the reality of Ahmed's words begins to sit in my chest. My breath is heavy and I cough to hide my fear.

The young man, who's shaking more now, continues to speak. 'When I returned to Gwadar I knew that I had to do something about this. I went looking for Khaled's family and found Ali. He brought me here and together we know that we have to act against the ignorance of these people. The last time I saw Khaled he did not look like this man in the photo. He had lost an incredible amount of weight. His body showed signs of...' he looks over at Ali and drops his head... 'torture; being force fed. His eyes were sunken in his face and he carried himself like a man defeated by life.'

Ahmed looks deep into my eyes as if he is searching for the faults that might show me to be the wrong candidate for the job. I swallow and take a deep breath. I strengthen my face to his and hang on the words that spill out and around him.

'We have nobody in Ireland who would be as able and willing as you are to make them see the error of their actions. Tomorrow you will return to Gwadar with Ali. He will inform you of your cover story for your time here, travelling and visiting in the Chagai Hills. From there you will go to the airport saying that

89

you are heading home to Riyadh.'

I look up sharply at the old man.

'No! Please! Not yet…'

'It's alright. I understand your reluctance to travel back to your family. From what Ali tells me they have been completely lacking in understanding of what you have had to endure.' Ahmed reaches out and puts an old, wrinkled hand on my shoulder. 'From Riyadh you will actually be travelling on to Ireland. We've spent the past week getting you a visa and all the arrangements have been made.'

He hands me two passports. One is my old one, and though the other holds a photo of me without my glasses from when I was younger, it has a different name and it looks worn. My own hasn't had much use. I look back at Ahmed, puzzled.

'So, you will travel to Riyadh as Majid Al Faisal but then you will get lost. You will swap your baggage with Zarrar in Riyadh. He will hand you luggage much more suited for your stay in Ireland and you will travel on to Dublin as Jameel Al Manhal of Riyadh in Saudi Arabia. When you get there you can invent your own family, friends, school etc. Be whoever you want to be but be consistent. You will stay near a mosque in Dublin. Ali will travel a day before you and will settle you in when you get there. You will attend an English language college as this is what your visa allows. When asked, you will say that you are perfecting your English for university in the fall. Then you will wait to hear from Ali as to what is expected of you.' Ahmed drops his hand and indicates for me to get up.

'There will be no link to us. From now on you are a boy setting out to go to college in Ireland for the summer; before heading back to Riyadh to attend university in the fall. You are nothing else. You have never been here and you will not speak of your time here. You will do nothing unless you are told to by Ali or Zarrar. When we need you, you will know, but always be ready. Go, Jameel Al Manhal, with Allah. Follow the Lord.'

Zarrar stares intensely at me as I walk away, daring me to fail, so I stand tall and with shoulders held back I turn and follow Ali from the tent. Darkness has fallen while we were changing the world and I stop and look up to the sky. The constellation of the *Summer Triangle* is there. *Vega, Deneb, and Altair* telling me now to follow the straight path to Allah.

Chapter sixteen

STEPHEN hoped that Tommy wasn't going to stay much longer. He loved seeing his son and granddaughter but they had a habit of overstaying their welcome. He knew it was a real expedition for Tommy to get a baby ready and drag her from the southside to the northside, on two buses, halfway across Dublin to see her grandfather. He appreciated it and he knew that it was the journey home that Tommy was probably dreading so he had offered to give him a lift.

'Not at all, Da. Sure Ruby loves the bus.'

Stephen had suggested that Ruby stay with him overnight and he would bring her home in the morning, to give Tommy and Shona a bit of a break for a while. He had wanted to give Tommy a few bob to take Shona out for a bite to eat but his son had looked at him like he had suggested a dive into the sea on Christmas morning.

'Eh... You're grand, Da. I wouldn't dream of takin' your money for trivialities like that. I think Shona's goin' over to her Aunty Margaret's tonight, but you're very good to offer.'

So Tommy had got up to make another cup of tea ...a sandwich ...a slice of cake ...then he needed to change Ruby's nappy ...then she fell asleep ... it was a shame to wake her ...sure he'd give her half an hour ...then they'd go ...but there wasn't another bus for twenty minutes and they'd only be waiting at the bus stop...

Would they never go home, for God's sake? Stephen caught sight of his wife's photo. Sometimes her eyes seemed to follow him around the house when he was doing or saying the wrong thing. Admonishing him. Mona Lisa, only much more beautiful, and still his conscience after all these years. Tommy was his only son and he clearly didn't want to go home. Stephen knew that he should ask him why, but he also knew that Tommy would probably tell him. This would open a dam so powerful that there would be no going back and Stephen would have to take charge. He would have to tell his son that things were going to work out fine, but anyone standing within three hundred feet of Shona and Tommy could see that things were going to be far from fine.

Stephen picked up the paper to give him time to get his thoughts together. What should he say? What could you say without letting it all fall apart? Shit, sometimes he hated being a father. Heading for forty in a few months, Stephen had never had a serious relationship with another woman since Sinéad had died. At first he was too busy looking after seven-year-old Tommy, while stricken with grief, but lately he had been lonely enough to venture out and dip his toe in the water. The temperature had never been quite right up to now. He had kind of given up but he was still a young man and the next forty years were looking a little bit bleak. There still might be someone out there for him but most women his age came with a whole load of baggage and he had enough baggage of his own to contend with. Who was he to talk to his son about relationships? He shook out the middle pages of his paper and spread them out in front of him, hiding his face from his responsibility.

'Do you want to talk about it then, son?'

A silence. Tommy sat back into his chair.

'What, Da?'

'The time bomb, Tommy, that's tickin' away in your house; waitin' to explode at any given moment.' Stephen lowered the paper and showed his son the concern on his face.

'*Shona,* Tommy. Do you want to talk about Shona?'

'Here it comes,' thought Stephen and his fists tightened around the pages as if a piece of paper could protect him from the approaching flood.

'I can't bear to live with her anymore, Da. I hate havin' her in the house with me. I want to throw her out and I can't because she's being all Mother Earth-like since she came back from Margaret's.

We were about to split up. The nightmare was about to finish. I think she would've gone. I think she'd had enough too and she knew she'd have to give up Ruby. She's not fit to be a mother. At least she wasn't before Margaret made her see reason.'

Tommy was up now and pacing the room, flaying his arms around for emphasis.

'I seem to bring out the worst in her as well. It's a two-sided thing this feelin' of not wantin' the other around. I don't want her, but I do want Ruby. Sometimes though, I even find myself feeling angry with my own baby because she's the reason that Shona and I have to stay together. I feel completely trapped and I need out. I want to run but I won't. I can't because of Ruby.'

Tommy picked up his daughter as she woke from her nap and he held her tight.

'I hate your mother, Ruby. I absolutely fuckin' hate her.'

Ruby let out a wail and Tommy realised he had been holding her too tight. He passed her to his father and sat back down on the still warm chair. Stephen thought he looked better already. A trouble shared.

'Maybe I should get out... Maybe I should take Ruby and cut my losses before I end up in the looney bin. What do you think?.. Da?'

Stephen was feeling the other side of a trouble shared. He felt the energy sap out of him and was filled with a sense of dread. He was holding his beautiful granddaughter, the spit of her grandmother, and listening to their son telling him that he intended to abandon the mother. The Morans would have a field day in court. No way. Ruby would end up in the hands of the completely screwed up Shona Moran?

'Tommy. I've no intention of allowin' you to walk away and leave Shona to drag Ruby up in any way she deems fit. She's hardly been the model mother since she gave birth to her. Has she? She's left you with full responsibility for her daughter since she was born. So she's on the dry right now. That doesn't mean she's suddenly Mother o' the Year. No way, son, I'm afraid walkin' out is not an option at the moment.' Stephen watched his son's face screw up in pain once more but he had to tell it the way it was.

'Listen, son, Shona's not the girl for you. We both know that but she's the mother of your child and walkin' out on her right now, when she's doin' the best she can would be madness. You'd lose any right you had to Ruby. The law's still old-fashioned enough to overlook Shona's past and give her custody of her daughter. You can't do that to her or to yourself. Or to me for that matter.'

Stephen gently rubbed the back of his fingers down the side of Ruby's soft cheek and she rewarded him with one of her heart-stopping smiles. The like that filled her face and gladdened the heart of anyone privileged enough to be on the receiving end. Losing her was something that Stephen would never risk.

Shit. Now Tommy was crying. He'd have to come up with something better than that. He looked over to Sinéad's photo again. Come on Sinéad; help out here. I'm out of my depth.

'It doesn't have to be forever, Tommy. Bide your time. You've lasted a few months together so far. It won't be long before Shona'll go back to bein' her wild self again. That'll be a good time to leave. You can come back here if you like. We'll manage the baby between us.' Jesus. What was he saying? Stephen mentally kissed goodbye any chance he might ever have of a woman in his life now.

Would you like to come back to my place? This is my son Tommy and this is his baby. We all live here.

Mmm. Change tack a little maybe.

'Or I'll help you to get another place of your own. Whatever you want, but hang on in there for a while. Put up with her for now, Tommy. See what happens.

'Now come on and take a lift home with me. We'll stop off for a take-away and if Shona's there she can eat it with us. If she's not well we'll manage it all by ourselves. It'll be easier for you if someone else is there. Don't be makin' any life changin' decisions yet, Tommy. The only decision you have to make tonight is whether to have Chinese or Indian.'

'Fish n' chips.'
'God, you were born awkward!'

Chapter seventeen

IT'S my eighteenth birthday and I awake on a bus headed back to Gwadar; a man; I have arrived. In all my years of dreaming of being an adult I never thought it would happen like this. It's only been three weeks since I left Saudi.

Three weeks from boy to man.

I look over at Ali as he sleeps. My friend can sleep through anything, anywhere. The bus journey from Chagai District to Gwadar has been long and bumpy. When I first came to Pakistan I was astonished at these buses, or trucks as they're known. Such works of art. The driver is the owner, the artist and the conductor. A one-man show. The competition between the drivers to have their truck designs better than anyone else's is strong too and it feels fitting to wake up on my eighteenth birthday inside such a masterpiece.

We're coming into Gwadar now. I can see the small, rough houses as they reach out into the waters of the bay; the cliffs rising up around them, protective but authoritative. I shake Ali gently so he can be fully awake when the truck comes to a stop near the market place. I take a peek as we pass by the part of the market reserved only for women and Ali cuffs me on the head, but laughs.

'The ladies will be the undoing of you, my friend. When you get to Omar's house this morning, remember to keep that weakness of yours in check and don't even think of looking in Intizar's direction. You've apologised to Razina and her family but that's only words. Until you leave, you'll show them the greatest respect to prove to them that you're sorry. I've told Omar that you will leave for Riyadh in two days' time and he has passed this news to your father.'

I soak up this information with dread. Ali notices the look on my face and speaks in a whispered voice.

'Majid, when we leave this bus you'll walk to Omar's house alone. When I called Omar from Chagai yesterday, he told me that you are to fly home to Saudi, first class. Your father insists that you return immediately. There's some trouble between Omar and your father. He blames Omar for your absence, but I'll allow him to explain.' I feel anger flaring inside me and Ali reaches out a calming hand.

'Remember what Ahmed has said to you. Don't let him down... *Jameel*. I will call you this from now on. It will be easier on both of us. I told Omar of the change in you. I remarked to him that you had met a good many holy people on your travels and that they had made a great impression on you. I told him that you were ready to return home; that you had reached manhood in a way that he would hardly recognise as the same young boy that left him two weeks ago.

'I'll fly to Ireland tomorrow and prepare the way for you. At Riyadh you will be met by Zarrar with your suitcase. Only transfer what you really need from your own luggage and hand it to him. When you land in Dublin Airport take a taxi to the mosque in a place called... eh, must be some Irish name. You know they have their own language there, but they choose to speak English instead. Crazy. Here's the address. I'll be waiting for you.'

The truck splutters to a stop on the opposite side of the market. Ali grabs his bag and walks swiftly towards the door, leaving me staring disbelievingly after him. I pull myself together, put my bag on my back and hurry after the man who has become, to me, as vital as the air that I breathe.

'Ali!'

Ali turns and smiles, his eyes speaking volumes, as always.

'I wasn't going without saying goodbye. I'll walk with you a little bit of the way. Whatever happens, Jameel, you must remember what has been said and copy our words with your actions. Let's walk.'

I float beside him and wonder, not for the first time, how such a smart person can end up watering grass in Saudi. I suppose the answer lies in his upbringing. Ali didn't go to school beyond the age of ten and his brothers sent him to Saudi to make money to support the family.

But Allah has work for Ali and this is what his life is really about. We stop beside a group of boys playing cricket and Ali spits in disgust in their direction.

'Why do you do that, Ali, every time we pass a cricket game? I thought that all Pakistanis loved cricket. It seems to me it's like a national obsession here.'

'A dirty Western game, like that terrible soccer that you're so fond of.'

I resolve to hate both games intensely from now on.

We leave each other on the same side of the road where we parted when we first came to Gwadar together. There are no long drawn-out goodbyes. Ali will be in Dublin when I get there. He smacks my shoulder hard and pushes me towards the road.

'Go. Go on. Do it.'

I find my way across the crazy road and when I turn to look back Ali has disappeared into the crowd and the mayhem. I feel my boyhood threatening to return. Ali's gone. I'm on my own. Nobody knows where I've been or what's in store for me. I hardly know myself, but I think of Ali and how he trusts me to get it right so I throw my shoulders back and march off to face Omar. When the house comes into view, however, my marching comes to a stop.

It's Razina who comes to greet me as I stumble uncertainly along the track. Omar remains in the doorway of the house. There's no sign, on Razina's smiling face or in her shining eyes, of her anger from before but it might be harder to get around Omar. In everything I say or do until I leave, Omar will be my biggest test. I walk towards him and catch his shoulder before feeling his strong hands on my arms. He looks me up and down for the changes that Ali has spoken about and in his look I see clemency and warning in equal measure. I want to drop my eyes but I know I have to be strong and I hold Omar's look with one of my own that says *I'm sorry. It won't happen again. I'm stronger now. A man. You'll see.*

I want to apologise again to Razina but she's obviously putting it behind her so I will too. I will do what Ali said and show her how sorry I am by my actions. Razina puts me at my ease immediately, babbling away in her Arabic English.

'Majid. You are very welcome back to our house. Your short time away has changed your face, my boy. I see a beard is trying to push through your soft skin. It won't be long now. Eh?'

I smile awkwardly at my reception and finger the fluff around my chin. I look nervously towards the house and Razina, guessing the cause of my apprehension, turns and beckons me to follow, talking as she goes.

'You will have to excuse our hospitality for your last days here, Majid. My daughters and granddaughters have left to prepare a cousin for her wedding. They won't be back before you leave but they send you their best on your journey home. Come. I have prepared a cold breakfast for you.'

I follow, relief and hunger pushing me on.

'The men are working and Omar here has to go out. They won't be back until this evening. I myself am going to visit my sister, so I will be gone most of the day. I am sorry to leave you alone Majid, but perhaps you could use the rest after your travels?' Her words drain the anxiety from my face. She places a hand on my shoulder, which feels like an injection of assurance. 'Help yourself to food throughout the day and do rest.' I have missed her and I smile.

She turns her attention to her son. 'Omar, you mentioned something about going somewhere tonight? A celebration or something?' Omar raises his eyebrows at his mother and throws his hands in the air, the surprise aspect gone from his plans for my birthday, but Razina takes the blame from herself immediately and scolds her son. 'Eesh! How am I supposed to know it was a surprise if you didn't tell me?' She launches into a torrent of abuse at her son in Baluchi and I watch in amusement as the grown Omar is threatened with a cooking utensil and chased out the door like a naughty child. Razina slams the door in his wake, then turns her toothless smile to me. We laugh together at the scene. She hugs me once more and she lifts her hands to wrap her bright green dupatta around her head and shoulders. Then she is gone, taking all her colour with her.

I feel the bareness of the room without her. What is it that I feel with this woman? Is it the motherly way she has about her? So different to my own mother, and I wonder now what my grandmothers were like. I try to imagine them back in my early years but it's too long ago since they both died. They were not like this woman, I'm sure. I sit back on my cushion and relax for the first time in weeks. No months. Actually I can't remember the last time I felt like this. I'll have a whole day alone. I'll sleep for a while and walk for a while and not worry about the face I must wear for others. I'll use today to brace myself for the many things that Omar will want to talk to me about.

Where is it he's taking me this evening I wonder? Something special for my birthday, a celebration. Omar will never know quite how much an event it really is. So much to celebrate, but for now I can be myself and breathe easy for a few hours. Then the long unspoken lie will begin.

*

For my birthday, Omar has brought me to the bay at Pishukan where he's organised to meet with some of his childhood friends and their sons.

'This was my playground when I was growing up, Majid. Surfing was my passion. These men here? They were the competition. This is the best place for surfing in the world. Look at those waves! Summer is, of course, the best time. The conditions for surfing are at their finest when the offshore winds blow from the North and North West. At high tide, there is nothing that can beat the thrill of this. We had no money, but what we had we

101

spent on making the best boards. This was life. When I look at this scene, Majid, I am reminded of my youth again. What do you think?'

'Are we going surfing, Omar?' I look at the man who's well into his forties and presume he's gone mad.

'Allah, No! We are going to sit and watch. Remember and enjoy our memories. Today you are eighteen years old and we are going to celebrate your youth and recall our own.'

'What about the other young men, Omar, they're getting ready to go surfing? It looks like so much fun. I'd love to try it. And anyway, why are there so few people here in the sea? If it's as you say it is, the best place and the best time, then where are all the surfers?'

Omar smiles at me. 'There is the small problem of taking your life in your hands, Majid. You might meet a few friends you didn't want to bump into. You must be more than a good surfer to play here. You need the skill of dodging the sharks and the sea snakes.' I reward him with a look of terror on my face and he laughs heartily. 'Come on young man. Let's have a party.'

There's a fire crackling and some chickens are roasting over a makeshift spit. The smell of the food is killing me. I'm starving. Becoming a man hasn't diminished my teenage appetite at all and when someone who looks too old to be Omar's childhood friend hands me my food, I'm positively salivating. The great outdoors is definitely the place to eat and for a moment I wonder how I'll ever get used to eating at home in such formality again. Then I remember that I mightn't be going home for some time. I'm about to experience another culture, another language. Life has become so exciting in just a few short weeks.

I smile and nod my thanks at the man who is all eyes and no teeth.

'Omar, all your family are fishermen, right? But we seem to eat an awful lot of chicken. Why's that?'

'We used to be big fish eaters in these parts, but the business sense has taken over now. You can buy two chickens for the price you can get for exporting one fish! So fish has become almost a

102

delicacy. Do you see?'

I nod, but it sounds ludicrous. I watch the surfers and the more I see the more I want to have a go. As the evening becomes night, the surfers begin to give up and abandon their boards in exchange for the delicious smells of food. There are a few adventurers still left, balancing their feet, and watching for sea snakes if Omar's right, in a world of their own. I wander down to the water's edge. The sun renders everything purple as it dips lower and lower on the horizon. Such a majestic colour and fitting for a place so full of majesty. As I drag my feet in the sand a boy of about sixteen is coming in, his day as king of the waves over.

'Can I have a look at your board?' I ask instinctively. 'Could I borrow it, for a few minutes?' I know I won't use it. The snakes and sharks won't feast on me this night but I want to stand on it, to imagine what it might be like. The boy generously hands it to me and I place the board on the sand before climbing on top. With the sound of the crashing waves in my ears, I close my eyes and picture what it might be like to do something so crazy and dangerous that you are literally putting your life in jeopardy. I like what I feel. I might not be stupid enough to tackle the hazards of the Bay of Pishukan but when Allah calls, I know I can take on all the perils of the world.

*

Walking back along the beach towards Omar's home, I'm not ready for the bombshell that he has in store for me.

'I don't understand, Omar. Why are you not going back to Saudi? You and Karima have always lived there.' I'm angry. Omar and his wife have been the decor of home life for as long as I can remember. It's all I know. Going back to Saudi, whenever that may be for me, without Omar there is wrong.

'I'm sorry, Majid. It has already been decided. Karima and I have been away too long from our families and our country. We always thought we would stay in Saudi until we had children. Then we would return to bring them up with family and friends.

This never happened. Allah had reasons to keep us in Saudi. Alone. And we were alone. We have friends in Saudi, certainly, but not long-term friends. Our Pakistani people went to Saudi to earn money and then returned home. It is time for us to do the same. Job opportunities in   Gwadar are better than they have ever been with all the new development.'

All of a sudden I am a child again, the one that Omar has known since birth, vulnerable, needy, discontented. Majid Al Faisal... Always reaching out for something else.

'When will you come back to visit, Omar?' I'm pleading; my high spirits from the birthday party erased with this news. Omar stops walking and stares out to sea.

I sink down onto the sand. How can I say goodbye to Omar and never see Karima again? It isn't possible. We sit in silence for a while, deep in our own thoughts about the separation. Despite the soft breeze from the sea, I'm sweating in my kurta. In two days, I'll wear my disha dasha and face another new beginning. Will I ever want to go back to Riyadh again? With no Shadia and no Omar I will be alone to face my parents. Omar can't bring himself to look at me when he speaks.

'It is not so easy for us to visit Saudi without a visa, Majid and there is also the expense. But I will write and I will email you in Saudi and when you are settled in your new university I will keep in touch with you there.'

Omar turns at last to face me and helps me to stand up. He takes both my hands and looks deep into my eyes.

'We may not see you again, Majid, but Karima and I will never forget you. You have our love and good wishes for a long and great life. You will live in our heads and our hearts every day.'

I'm trying to keep the tears back. 'This time in Pakistan, Omar, has been such an exciting time. I'll cherish the memories as I'll cherish my memories of growing up with you, always caring, always there.'

'You know you shouldn't thank me for the goodness that Pakistan has given you,' he says. 'Use what you have learned to lead the best life that you can. Eh? Trust in Allah. Pray to him for guidance and follow where he leads. Okay?'

When it's time to let go, we embrace and I feel the grief of loss begin.

Chapter eighteen

BE careful what you wish for.

Tommy shook his head at the old saying his granddad used on him as a kid. He put the phone down after speaking to Norah and lifted the roaring baby from the crib.

'Come on then guzzler. I'm sure even your mother hasn't had this many bottles today… wherever your mother is. Wouldn't it be great altogether if she got so sozzled that she forgot where she lived for a few weeks?'

Shona had been all promises to her Aunty Margaret when she stayed over there but she just couldn't keep it up. Within days she had started going out drinking and somehow managing to come home again in a terrible state. He wanted to throw her out, and he would. Soon.

She had been gone two days now. Tommy should have become anaesthetised by her behaviour at this stage but he still found himself wondering where she was and whether or not she was okay. With the Leaving Cert exams behind him, Tommy had taken up Mick's offer of a full-time job in the bar and was using his salary to pay a lovely childminder who lived just across the road from them. Norah didn't know as yet. She thought her lovely reformed daughter was doing all the mothering, and he hadn't managed to tell her the truth.

Ruby's routine had become his routine and he walked around in a haze of bottles, nappies and work at the bar, in between catching an hour's sleep here and there. Thinking of the childminder made Tommy wish Ruby was with her now so he could go back to work for a rest. To think he used to say that pulling a few pints was hard work. And where was her mother through all this chaos?

Out. Out of her head. Somewhere else. |

Be careful what you wish for.

Norah had been on the phone again this evening asking for Shona. Thank God he had managed to divert the conversation. Shona hadn't come home the night before. Tommy had been dressing Ruby for the childminder that morning when Norah rang and he told her that Shona was asleep upstairs. How long would she continue believing everything she was told though?

So many lies. Shona's lies to him. Shona's lies to her parents. His lies to his father. His lies to family and friends. Life was one big cover-up.

Tommy got the smell of the nappy he had changed ten minutes ago and sighed. He put Ruby back down on the changing table, still kicking and screaming for her bottle, and opened the drawer to get another nappy. None. He looked at his daughter and willed her to stay still while he ran across the room to get her changing bag.

There was no nappy inside either so he had to open another new pack.

'Shite,' he swore, as he fumbled with the packaging, but by the time he got his hands on one it was too late.

His daughter's screams filled the room with a sound Tommy never wanted to hear again. As he ran towards her limp body on the floor he took in the drop from the changing table to the ground and could barely contain his own screams.

One fed the other as Tommy's horror fuelled his baby's fright and both sat for a moment, the baby girl in her daddy's arms, before he realised he'd better get her to the hospital.

He had walked away and left her on the table. Something he'd been told never to do. Tommy felt sick but he pulled himself together.

'Right. Tallaght Hospital or Crumlin? Tallaght. Too much traffic from here to Crumlin.'

He called a taxi and with Ruby's wails in the background the company didn't have to be told that this was an emergency. They said they'd have someone around in a few minutes.

The taxi swept through the evening's traffic thanks to the bus lanes. As Tommy rushed through adult casualty to get to the children's area, he tried not to let the uproar in the corridors feed his panic. He raced past two Gardaí handcuffing a drunk to a trolley and edged around a man sitting on a chair, bleeding all over the floor. Walking past elderly people groaning in pain and others neglected on trolleys, he wondered was this Ireland or a scene from the Second World War? When they reached the children's area Tommy's face fell. The place was heaving. He was sure the triage nurse would take one look at Ruby and realise that she had to be admitted. They wouldn't have to wait long…

Three hours later as the doctor was examining Ruby, and Tommy had hung drawn and quartered the minister for health, in his mind, a hundred times, Ruby was proclaimed a case for admission.

'The x-rays show that there's no fracture.' Tommy felt himself breathe properly for the first time in hours. 'But she's badly bruised and in view of her fall and her age, we'd like to keep her in for observation overnight. You'll be able to stay with her of course. The nurses will be in and out for obs and such.' Then he was gone, leaving Tommy near to tears with the relief of Ruby's wellbeing and the knowledge of how close they had come to something much worse..

'Are you all right Mr Farrell? Is Ruby's mummy here?'

There was that question again. From the nurse this time. How many different ways were there of asking why the child's mother wasn't there? Tommy didn't know how to answer any of them. Shona might not show up or she might stumble in the door at any minute. He hoped it was not the latter. An invisible Shona was way better than a drunk one trying to act sober. He wished now that he hadn't left her a message. At least they had stopped asking him the question about how Ruby had sustained her injuries. Waiting for him to get it wrong – let it slip that he had meant to harm her.

Ruby started to cry again. The poor little mite was beside

herself with tiredness. Every time she tried to fall asleep, someone needed to have another look at something.

On the walk up to the ward Tommy held his baby girl like he was never going to see her again. He thought he might be about to cry once more and he didn't know how to stop himself. Grown men don't cry. Tommy had cried when the Dublin footballers had lost the All-Ireland when he was a kid. That was allowed. That was football and his dad and granddad had been close to tears too, but now he was weepy all the time.

Come to think of it when was the last time he had stood on Hill 16 and watched the Dubs play in Croke Park? That life was a million years ago now but he didn't care. Ruby was all that mattered. At that minute he'd give anything to take her place. The doctors and nurses had said that she had been very lucky not to hurt herself badly. She could have though and Tommy knew it was his fault. He also knew he had no intention of telling any of her grandparents where she was spending the night or why.

Somebody's mobile began singing a song. Tommy thought how irresponsible that was at this time of night with sick children everywhere, sleeping – then he realised that everyone was glaring at him. Before he pressed the off switch, he saw Shona's mobile number flash up on the screen.

'Nearly there now,' the nurse behind him touched his elbow. 'She'll be fine you know. We'll settle her down and then you can go and get yourself a nice cup of tea.' Soft words. Kind eyes. Tommy stared at her as if she were mad. Did she really think he would leave his baby for one minute? What if she woke up and no one was there? Tommy was going nowhere.

Walking down the corridor, he felt more alone than he ever had. He needed someone right now and wished that he had a brother or sister, or even a best friend. Someone he could ring and say, 'Hey, I'm in a bit o' trouble here. Can you lend a hand?' But his school friends had all let go, slowly but surely, over the last few months. There was only Barry, and he was working in London for the summer. Like all the others, Barry was living the life of an eighteen-year-old. The world was his oyster. They were all as far removed from living with a drunk and bringing up a baby as was possible.

For the first time in years, he imagined what life would be like if his mother had lived. That ache that had sat in him for years after she had died came back… when his father was stunned and heartbroken and Tommy felt like the only person in the world.

He should ring his dad. He would lecture him no doubt, but at least he would support him. Tommy looked at his watch. No wonder he was exhausted. He stared down at Ruby and heard himself praying.

'Please, God, make her alright.' Apart from the Christening, Tommy hadn't been to mass since he made his Confirmation. A bit late coming back now? Suddenly his prayers were interrupted by a commotion behind them in the corridor. A man was shouting.

'I don't care who you say's in here, you're not goin' any further in that state. Now get back outside and stay there!'

There was a crash, something falling, and then it went quiet for a moment, but Tommy turned around just in time to see Shona thundering towards them.

'Where'sh my baby? I want to shee her now!'

Tommy gently handed Ruby to the nurse.

'I'll be back in a minute. Sorry.'

A security guard was right behind Shona.

'This your girlfriend?' he asked.

You must be joking! Thought Tommy. 'I'm afraid so,' he said.

'She'll have to leave the hospital immediately. She's caused absolute mayhem for the last ten minutes. Will you be able to handle her?'

Tommy looked at Shona. She didn't look like anyone's mother or anyone's daughter. What a mess. She was disgusting.

He answered his question of earlier. He didn't care about her anymore. This was the last of it, but he cared about Ruby. He had to get Shona out of here quickly, for her sake.

'Ruby's fine, Shona. She's… eh… back at your mother's. I came back to pick up her coat and stuff. Come on. I'll put you in a taxi and you can go and see her but I need the loo first. Sit down there and wait for me.' Shona swerved around and fell down on the nearest chair.

Tommy begged the security guard to stay with her for a minute, then ran into the loo and called Shona's mother.

'For goodness sake Thomas, it's nearly midnight. What is it?'

Tommy went on to explain that Ruby was in hospital, that Shona had turned up very drunk, he was getting into trouble with the staff, and that he was going to put her into a taxi and send her to her house and…

'Stop, Thomas. You're not making sense… Is she alright..? Ruby I mean… What hospital..? Tallaght? Okay. We'll come up in the car now. Meet us outside the main entrance in about twenty minutes. My God, what a mess your lives are all the time.'

Gone.

She was something else that woman.

Tommy would do what she told him. He would go outside and wait for Norah and Des. It meant that he wouldn't be there to settle his baby when she got to the ward but he had to get rid of Shona.

He went back to the corridor where he had left her. The security guard was gone and she was lying across the seats, out cold, saliva dripping from the side of her open mouth. Tommy shuddered before heaving her off the seats towards the hospital entrance.

Chapter nineteen

I DIRECT my motorbike into a parking spot near the beach. Taking off my helmet I lock it to the bike and turn towards the sea. The early morning fog obscures the horizon and I have to squint to get my bearings. Once more I haven't been able to sleep, but the wonderful thing about going walking at this time of the morning is the stillness of everything before the Dubliners wake up and disturb the peace. The fairground rides that I saw advertised earlier in the week have now been set up all along the promenade. I take a step towards the beach and stop short as I hear a noise. Someone is singing.

Turning back towards the ghost train, I peer in to get a closer look. The horrible scenes along the outside seem to move with the fog and make me shiver. The song's coming from behind me and I turn around to face the carousel.

A girl dressed in black, with long, dark, curls is lying across a white horse, with her arms around the horse's neck, singing a song.

'Hush little baby, don't say a word.
Daddy's gonna find you a mocking bird.
If that mocking bird won't sing,
Daddy's gonna buy you a diamond ring.
If that Diamond turns to brass,
Daddy's gonna buy you a looking glass.
If that looking glass gets broke...

'Well that'll be mummy's fault because everything always bloody well is.'

I stare at the girl amid the swirling fog and step a little closer, calling out her name.

'Shadia...'

No. Not Shadia. It can't possibly be her, but the resemblance of the girl on the carousel is striking. It's the surreal image created by the smoke-like foggy weather that has transported me back to earlier this year and Shadia on the white horse of another carousel. The girl sits up and pulls one leg over the horse's head to sit side saddle. I can see her more clearly now. Her heavily made up face is eerily zombie-like and I find myself looking back at the images on the ghost train.

'Shadia? Is that a name? It's pretty.'

I say nothing in reply but shift back around towards the girl and the carousel.

She's talking to me? I want to run off towards the beach, but instead I continue to take in the horses and the golden princess carriage... like the one that Shadia and Maeve were riding in before...

'Nice motorbike. You're out early. Do you work around here?'

My feet are moving slowly now. I feel myself walk towards the ghost-like figure expecting her to fade into thin air as I get closer.

'Are you foreign? Do you not speak English? Here I am talking to myself again.'

I climb the steps to the carousel slowly and stop in front of the brown-eyed girl. The fog no longer covers her and she looks uneasy at my sudden nearness. Her eyes dart around as if she's looking for an escape route.

'I'm sorry. I didn't mean to frighten you. You... you look like someone else that I know. I'll go. I'm sorry.'

'No worries, it's okay,' she answers. 'It's all a bit creepy around here this morning but the fog is beginning to lift. The sun'll be shining soon and we can all enjoy the sea and the hills in all their splendour, without feeling that Hallowe'en has come early. Are you okay? You look a bit shocked or something.'

'I'm fine. As I said I only came over because...'

'You thought I was this Shadia girl...'

'Yes... but I can see now that... you're not.'

'Don't look so disappointed. I'm Shona. I guess that's near

enough. Is she your girlfriend? Shadia.'

I know the best thing to do is to turn and run away from this crazy-looking girl, who close up doesn't look anything like Shadia, but she's asking me about Shadia and I'm so hungry to talk about her.

'Yes. We were to be married.' I sit on the top step still facing the girl.

'Were? Did she leave you then?'

Did she leave me? No. She's still with me every minute of every day. Pushing me forward. Leading me on. But she left me the day that she climbed on board that carousel and…

'Yes. She's gone. Shadia's gone.'

'I'm sorry to hear that,' she said.

I close my eyes and I take some deep breaths. When I open them again and look back up at the horse where the girl was sitting, it's empty. I didn't hear her go. Where's she gone?

I'll go for my walk. It's what I came to do. I stand and walk through the fog towards the fall and rise of the sound of the waves.

She's ahead of me, walking slowly along the shore. She looks over her shoulder and waves but keeps on walking. I'll have to walk slower if I want to lose her. I stop and pick up some pebbles from the sand and begin to throw them into the water as far as I can. Each one disappears into the fog and announces its decent into the water with a small splash that breaks the quiet of the early morning. I look over to see if she's moved further on but I can still make out her blurry figure through the fog. I'm tempted to backtrack and go home but why shouldn't I have my walk?

Eventually she stops to sit on the sand. I'll have to speak to her now. How embarrassing.

'Hello. Again.' She stays sitting, looking out at the sea as if she can make out anything through the swirling fog.

'I like it better later in the day when all the people arrive. Especially in the summer when they put out the rides and the atmosphere is buzzing. I think I was here last night, actually and…' She stops and makes to stand up and I find myself holding out my hand to help her. She takes it, smiling and she holds it as we walk together.

Her hand feels strange in mine but I'm reluctant to let go. I still feel the shock of thinking that she was Shadia. Though I'm walking with the girl on the beach, even with her hand holding mine, I still feel as if I've left something on the carousel. Looking back now, the fog is beginning to lift from the rides and they look normal.

Shona. Is that what she said her name was? She's smiling up at me and biting her lower lip.

'So, what's your name then?' she asks.

'Maj… I mean, Jameel. Jameel Al Manhal,' I splutter.

'Well, Jameel Al Manhal. It's nice to meet you but… Well… It's kind of nice holding hands and walking along the beach with you like this but… it's sort of weird too. Don't get me wrong. It's just that… well maybe we could walk without holding hands for now?'

I pull my hand from her and step back.

'I'm so sorry. I don't know why I did that. I didn't mean any offence…'

Shona laughs. 'Oh, none taken,' she says. 'It was nice actually but… another time maybe. Ah, come on. Let's go for that walk and you can tell me all about Shadia and how she broke your heart.'

My smile fades and I feel the loss of Shona's touch. We walk on along the sand in silence at first. The fog has completely lifted now and the sun's trying to make an appearance over the hill. At least it isn't raining again today. Summer in Ireland is something my Saudi bones will never get used to. I shiver.

'So. What did she do that was so bad? You sound upset.' Shona doesn't look up at me as she speaks. 'You should talk about it. Talking's good.'

I stop and after a moment Shona stops and turns around.

'She died. Four months ago,' I say.

'I'm sorry,' she says. 'That's terrible. Was it sudden?'

I think about the split second between Shadia being full of life and happiness and then suddenly dead, and I look up at Shona.

'Yes. It was sudden.'

'Was she here in Dublin?'

'No. She was in Riyadh in Saudi Arabia, where I'm from. I only came to Dublin last week. I'm perfecting my English before I start university.' I think about why I'm here in Ireland and realise that I should cut away from this girl. Ali'll go crazy on all counts. I'm getting to know someone I don't need to know. And chatting with a girl I've never met before. Never been introduced to.

'But your English sounds better than mine,' she smiles. 'You have a bit of an American accent too. Did you live there for a while?'

'No. And I have no wish to go there either. My teacher at school spent most of his life in New York. He's left me pronouncing my words in an unfortunate manner.'

'I don't know. It's kind of sexy.'

Her teasing face is too much.

'I need to go now. It was nice to meet you, Shona.'

I don't like the feeling that her fallen face gives me so I reach out my hand to shake hers and she takes it again and holds it as she had earlier.

'Walk a bit more with me.'

Shona's hair falls across her face like Shadia's used to... when she was little... before her hijab hid her away from me. I should smile and thank this girl for her company and walk away, but her hand feels so right in mine.

'Okay. A few more minutes.'

We walk some more towards the hills and I tell Shona all about my years with Shadia and our plans together.

'Her father's my father's cousin. We grew up together and we always knew we were promised to each other.'

'An arranged marriage?'

'Yes, but one which we were both delighted to be a part of. Not many men in Saudi go into marriage knowing that they are marrying someone as intelligent and caring as Shadia is... was. She was like a gift. My parents never knew each other before they got married and they never seem to like each other very much. Shadia and I would've been so different.'

Shona slips her hand out from mine and continues walking. 'She sounds perfect.'

'She was. We had our arguments of course. Shadia was not a nice girl if she was crossed. What a temper!' I smile, remembering Shadia's ability to lose it at a moment's notice if things didn't go her way. 'But mostly she was, as you say, perfect.'

We've reached a cluster of rocks at the end of the beach. Shona sits down on the edge of one. 'I'm sorry that she died, Jameel but it sounds like you had it all for a while. Hang onto that. Some people never have that kind of love in their whole lifetime.'

'Well. Unfortunately I lost her before we had a chance to truly appreciate each other.' Allah forbid that I'll start to cry in front of this girl but talking about Shadia after all this time is so soothing, yet at the same time makes everything raw again. I take out my mobile and pretend to look at the time before starting along the beach again.

'I really must go. It's been a pleasure to meet you, em, Shona but I'll be late for my English class if I don't hurry.'

'No worries.' Shona stands up to walk back with me. 'Where are you studying?' She falls in line with me as I hurry back along the beach.

'In Dundrum. I'm staying in an apartment there too.'

'I live near there. Perhaps we'll bump into each other around and about.'

'What do you mean?' I'm not sure I like her tone.

'Just joking, Jameel. I don't suppose you could give me a lift back to Dundrum on your way? I've lost my bag and my phone and I've no other way of getting back to my mum and dad.'

'I've no spare helmet. Isn't that against the law here?'

Shona links her arm through mine and steers me towards my motorbike. 'I'm sure you're not as conservative as you pretend to be, Jameel. I bet there's a rebel in there waiting to get out. We'll take our chances you and me. Okay?'

I don't feel this is such a good idea. Though it's been so good to

117

talk about Shadia again, it's best to walk away now in the politest way that I can. I unlink my arm from Shona's and pat her hand. I reach into my pocket and pull out a wad of notes.

'I really am late I'm afraid but I won't see you stranded. Here, take this,' I say and hand her a fifty Euro note.

'No. I can't take that much money. I won't know where to find you to give it back.'

'Please. Take it. It's alright.'

But Shona hangs her head, folds her arms and walks slowly away from me. I unlock my motorbike swallowing guilty feelings. I get on and rev up the engine before riding out onto the road. Looking back I see her climb back up on the carousel. I rev the engine again but I can't make myself drive off. I turn and call out to her.

'Shona! Come on! I'll take you home.'

I'm rewarded with a smile. She jumps down from her horse once more and runs towards me.

'Thanks,' she says. 'I appreciate it.'

'You'll have to give me directions and we have to hurry. I'm late as it is.'

As she nears the motorbike I start to feel a bit nervous. Shona'll have to sit behind me on my bike and she'll be in very close proximity to me. I feel her climb on and immediately remember feelings in Pakistan when I was lured by the beautiful Intizar. I hadn't touched her, but that never stopped me getting into a whole heap of trouble.

I take a deep breath and turn the ignition on my bike once more. I'll drop this girl home and from now on I'll stay well away from girls resembling Shadia. No girl in the world will ever really come close.

'Hold onto the bar at the back of the bike,' I call out. That'll help to keep some distance between us. I wobble a little and then race away from the beach.

*

Shona had never been on a motorbike before. She clung on to the back of her seat at first, but as Jameel sped along the roads she shifted her hands to his waist and ended up wrapped around him and the warmth of his leather jacket. At each traffic light she eased her hold, only to find herself gravitating towards him as he put his foot to the accelerator again. She knew that she should only be thinking of getting back to Ruby. And she was... But the way that Jameel was making her feel, she wanted this journey to go on forever.

Shona directed him to her mother's house. She couldn't face Tommy if he was at home and obviously she hadn't mentioned Tommy or Ruby to Jameel.

Her father's car wasn't in the driveway. Maybe they were with Ruby. Shona felt herself sobering up more as she eased herself from the seat and away from Jameel. She thanked him. They said their goodbyes, but as Shona reached up to kiss his cheek he covered her lips with the tips of his fingers and shook his head. His touch on her lips was enough to send shivers through her. She walked away reluctantly towards the back of the house where she knew the spare key was kept and turned it in the lock of the back door. She didn't see, but she heard Jameel rev his engine and take off back to wherever it was he lived. She didn't know. She didn't have his number. It was best. He had said so. But what if she was to go back to the beach some time... early one morning... and happened to bump into him again...

Shona heard a noise and looked around to see Mrs O'Connor looking over the back wall at her. No doubt she had witnessed her mode of transport home. Normally, Shona ignored her nosy neighbour, but hey, she was grown up now and maybe she should act that way.

'Good morning Mrs O'Connor.' Shona smiled and waved. 'Lovely morning isn't it?' Mrs O'Connor continued glaring at her. So much so that Shona forgot she was grown up now and sticking her thumb under her nose, she wiggled her fingers in her neighbour's direction and stuck out her tongue as far as it would go. God that felt good! Then she went inside to sort out her returning hangover and to work out how to get to the hospital to see her baby girl. Passing the clock on the kitchen windowsill, Shona noticed that it read the seventh of July. She had missed two days. Her stomach lurched. Where had she been? Shona sat down at the kitchen table and put her head in her hands, the euphoria of meeting Jameel receding for now.

'Oh, Ruby...' She sobbed her daughter's name out loud. She had really let them down this time. She was so lost in her crying that she didn't hear her parents come in behind her until her mother spoke.

'Shona! Where were you, you selfish cow?' Shona could feel the disgust spat out through every word and jumped up running past her mother's anger and her father's bewilderment to the downstairs toilet, barely making it there before she threw up.

Chapter twenty

I STEP out of the shower and reach for the large, white bath towel before wrapping it around myself and pulling it tightly. I've stayed under the water for an endless amount of time trying to free my body of the sea salt and the feel of the girl on my skin. I shiver. I've been cold since I got back to my apartment. Cold and shaking. How crazy to go out walking on a foggy morning – and the Irish call this the summer?

The reality of the morning's hitting me hard. The girl's mad. She's everything that I despise about Western girls. So outgoing with a boy she doesn't even know, teasing my masculinity mercilessly. But I know that there's something else too. I don't doubt that I'm attracted to her and for this reason I feel guilt.

Shadia. I called this girl Shadia. How could I possibly confuse her with my beautiful fiancé? My lifetime friend. The girl I was to spend the rest of my life with until.... Four months ago Shadia was my world... But now...

I grab some clothes and dress hurriedly. I need to go out again. I have to run. I'm always running, from the hurt and from the rage. I'm the angriest eighteen-year-old in the world. I'll get revenge on those who made me this way though. I run from the apartment once more and get on my bike. I forget my helmet. No matter. Nothing matters. I want Shadia back but she's never coming back.

I called this Shona the wrong name. She was obscured by the fog and dressed in black with her dark curly hair. On a carousel as Shadia had been.

I rev the engine and speed away towards the motorway. The picture of Shadia won't go away. Those beautiful laughing eyes seconds before it all ended. I travel on and on. One motorway becomes another and still I see her. Her last day rolls through my mind and won't be moved no matter how fast I speed. One hundred kilometres, one hundred and twenty, one hundred and forty and my head's still full.

Tears blind me as I remember my beautiful fiancé's face laughing in the lights of the fairground, followed by the image that haunts me, of the ball of flames crawling towards me.

The driver of the car in the middle lane beeps his horn loudly as I manage to bring myself out of my reverie in time to realise I've swerved out of the outside lane into the path of a black Passat. I straighten my bike and indicate to move into the inside lane but other cars join in with their horns until I feel deafened. I slow the bike to a stop in the hard shoulder. I breathe in deeply, allowing the sound of the car horns to block out the sound of the bomb that killed my beautiful girl.

Running to Pakistan hasn't lessened the pain and the hurt, no more than running to Ireland will. But I breathe in once more, filling myself with resolve. I'm in Ireland for a reason and I'll never allow anything to get in the way of what I'm here to do.

Shona let me talk about my Shadia. She understood and told me to rejoice in the short-lived love that we shared. I climb back on the bike and make my way out onto the motorway again.

The girl I met today with the floral tattoo creeping up from her chest is not Shadia –Shadia's dead.

Chapter twenty one

TOMMY and his pals fell in the door laughing like a bunch of schoolgirls. They'd left the pub at closing time and decided to continue the party back at Tommy's house. Tommy had decided he needed some time with his old friends and had got in touch to see who was available for a night out. He'd had a blast. Felt like a real person again.

'Is Ruby asleep, Tom?' whispered Peter, the most responsible of the four.

'Fast asleep', giggled Tommy. 'In my Da's house. We've agreed that he'll have her one night a week to give me a night out. Isn't that great? His only condition is that I don't let that *silly bitch of a woman*' back into our lives. His words not mine. But I have to say; life's been nice and quiet over the last few weeks without her. I could get used to this, so I could.' They followed the other two towards the sitting room.

'Eh, Tommy...' As they carried their six packs with intent, Niall pointed to the couch. 'You have a visitor.'

'Yeah. It's the silly bitch of a woman,' slurred Dave. Five pints of Guinness and Dave was fit for nothing. Especially diplomacy.

Tommy on the other hand sobered up on eye contact.

'Hello, Tommy.' Shona stood to face him. 'Sorry to spoil the party.'

Tommy drew in his breath in anger at the sound of Shona's voice.

'Spoilin' things is one of your strong points. I'm well used to it.'

The lads shuffled on their feet. Peter looked towards the others and gestured his eyes towards the door.

'C'mon guys. Tommy, will we leave you to it? Yeah?'

'Yeah…Okay…Sorry guys…some other time maybe. I'll give a ring durin' the week.'

'Will you be needin' your six-pack or will we take that with us? Probably besht not to leave that hangin' around here.' Dave's delicate touch again, complete with exaggerated eye gestures towards Shona.

'Jaysus, Dave. Will you come on?' Peter pulled at his arm, but not before Dave helped himself to Tommy's Guinness.

Tommy listened to the sounds of his old school friends filing through the hall and out the door. It had taken a lot of nerve to ring them up and presume they'd let him slip back into the old crowd after not being in touch for so long. They wouldn't be back. Shona sat down on the couch.

'Don't even think of makin' yourself comfortable there. You can turn around and walk straight out of here you drunken little cow.'

'Said the pot to the kettle.'

Tommy was disgusted. Of all the times that Shona could have walked in, it had to be when he was a bit worse for wear himself. On any other night over the past couple of weeks, she would have found him busy with Ruby or housework or something. It enraged him more.

'What are you *doin'* here? What do you *want*? I thought I'd made it perfectly clear that you were finished with us. There's no place for you in this family. So get the hell out of here.'

'It's not that simple Tommy. You didn't answer any of my calls. You wouldn't come over to talk to me. So I *had* to come here.'

'Talk about what? There's nothin' to say. Are you completely mad? Get out! Get the hell out!'

'Tommy, stop shouting. Let's sit down and discuss this like two grown-ups. We're not kids. Shit… The last thing I thought, coming over here tonight, was that I'd find *Saint Thomas* drunk… Maybe we should sleep on it and try to work things out in the morning… You're not making sense right now.'

'Really? So when did Shona Moran become so sanctimonious and clean livin'? I might have had a few drinks but compared to your binges, this is nothin'. But you're right. I'm in no mood to talk to you right now. I'm goin' upstairs to bed. My bed. You can fall asleep on the couch. Second nature to you, I'd say. And in the mornin' you can scuttle out of here back to the stone you crawled out from under.'

Tommy stormed out the door and thundered up the stairs, slamming his bedroom door into its frame.

*

'Tommy, I've brought you a cure.'

Tommy heard Shona's voice but he couldn't open his eyes. And someone was hammering on his head. A cure? She'd probably made him a *Bloody Mary*. That would be Shona's idea of a cure alright. He turned his back to her. God his whole body hurt. He wasn't used to drinking any more.

'Fuck off back home, Shona.' His voice came out as a hoarse whisper. 'And you can shove your *Bloody Mary*, or whatever it is, where the sun doesn't shine.'

The room went very quiet. After a few minutes, Tommy presumed she must have left so he turned around slowly and lifted himself awkwardly into a semi-sitting position. Shona was sitting in a chair by the window, holding a photo of Ruby. Silent tears ran down her face.

Tommy wasn't going to be caught out by her attempts to get him to sympathise with her. He looked away and his eyes caught the tray.

'What's all this stuff?'

Shona quickly wiped her eyes and put the photo back on the windowsill.

'Honestly. It'll make you feel a lot better, Tom. A pint of water to rehydrate you, two antacid tablets to clear your head and your stomach, a glass of orange juice to replenish your vitamin C and a slice of toast to give you a little bit of energy. I'll make you a proper breakfast when you're feeling a little better.' Shona smiled down at Tommy's shocked face. 'A *Bloody Mary* would only make you feel better for a short while.'

'You don't say?' Tommy rubbed his eyes and shook his head.

'This cure is what you might call a more permanent solution.'

Tommy busied himself with the contents of the tray. He didn't want to look at Shona. What was she up to? What did she want to say to him? He was feeling very vulnerable in this position. It was no place to be having a serious discussion.

'Why don't you get through that Tommy and have a shower? Come down when you're feeling a little better.'

And then she was gone; before he could protest or shout her out of the house or even say okay. She really timed it well to come back.

Come back? There was no way she was coming back. Tommy's anger was rising again and he flung his plate of toast against the wall. He sat further up in the bed and took some deep breaths.

'No way is Shona Moran comin' back here.' He spat the words out of his mouth, lay back down and turned over again. This was all proving too much for him this morning. He'd go back to sleep and when he woke up again Shona would have got the message and left. He closed his eyes and waited for sleep to take hold of him. He waited, and waited.

It was no use. He was wide awake. Maybe he should get Shona over and done with after all. He sat up again slowly and eased his legs over the side of the bed. Oh God, all this movement. His mouth felt like the Sahara Desert so he reached for the pint of water. Down in one. His stomach started doing somersaults. Maybe he *should* have the antacid tablets. After he took his medicine, making faces as he tried to swallow the foul stuff, he lurched like prehistoric man towards the shower. He allowed the water to beat down on him and after about ten minutes emerged feeling almost at the caveman stage. As he dried himself the toast leaning against the skirting board caught his eye. He was starving and so, against his better judgement he sat on the bed and hoovered up the food, washing it down with the glass of orange juice. Shona was right. He was already feeling a lot better and was getting nearer to modern-day man all the time. She was a master at curing hangovers, he'd give her that.

Now to face up to the mess that was his life. Time to put the last few months behind him and to move on. Shona was getting her final marching orders.

Walking down the stairs and through the hall, Tommy felt there was something wrong. There was a wonderful smell of bacon wafting from the kitchen and something else. The kitchen was gleaming. In fact the whole house looked as if a professional team had swept through it. So... Shona had thought that a little bit of housework would butter him up. Well, she could think again. Nothing was going to change his mind this time. She was out of here. He would eat the bacon butty she was holding towards him and then the eviction could begin.

It took the same amount of time to eat his sandwich as it did for Shona to fill him in on the details of her last two weeks. He wanted to interrupt her but he was too hungry, so he let her continue. It was a mistake.

'Tommy. I know I'm an alcoholic.'

Tommy nearly choked on a piece of bacon rind.

'I thought because I didn't need a drink every morning when I woke up, that it meant I didn't have a problem. I realise now that the binges are just a different sort of addiction, but I haven't touched a drop since the night of Ruby's accident. I've been to visit the centre at St. John of God's, Tommy. Mum came with me. You wouldn't believe how wonderful she's been.'

'No. I wouldn't,' thought Tommy between mouthfuls.

'It was the thought of Ruby being in hospital that did it. It made me realise how much I love her. Sometimes I think that giving birth to her was the only good thing I've ever done. I'm sure you think that was the only thing I ever did for her. You're probably right. I don't know where to start with her to make amends but the one thing I do know is that I need your help to get better. You've come to know me better than anyone Tommy. Will you help me..? Please Tom?'

Shona's eyes were filling up again but she was doing her best to hold back the tears. Her face looked so sad. Her eyes were so

127

imploring.

Look away, Tommy thought to himself. Don't let her get to you. We've been here before. Well maybe not this very place, but near enough… though she's never actually admitted to being an alcoholic before. They say that admitting it is the first step to overcoming it. Maybe… Oh God, I can't make this decision. Not this morning.

'No!' Tommy surprised himself at the vehemence of his reaction. He took a few deep breaths as he realised the mistake of eating his sandwich so quickly.

'It's too soon. I'm happy that you're beginnin' to get yourself sorted out. I really am, Shona. You even look so much better already, but I can't accept that it could all be that easy. Maybe sometime in the future we can talk about it again but not yet.'

Tommy walked towards the window, his back to Shona once more, his fists clenched in resistance. He had to hold out on this one.

'You're right Tommy, about it being early days. It's going to be a long time before I can cope with every day like other people can. I know that alcoholism is something that's going to be part of me all my life. I want to overcome it though.'

This sounded nothing like Shona. Was she up to something?

'The centre told me I needed the help of my family and friends. Particularly those that I'd treated the worst throughout. That's you Tom. You and my parents. They're already willing to help, but that's easy. I'm their daughter. They love me unconditionally. Look at me Tommy. I'm shaking. I need a drink. I'm so *far* from being sorted it's scary.'

Tommy turned to face her. Another mistake. He took in her slight frame. Her need. Her vulnerability.

'Tommy. You and I don't share a love that couples should share. My mother dragged you into this but what we do share is one of the most wonderful human beings that ever lived. I trust you so much, Tommy. You're the only real friend I've ever had. Please let me stay with you. With Ruby... For now... I know you can help

128

me.' The tears were coming heavy and fast now.

'What about us Shona? Me and Ruby. Who's goin' to help us?' Tommy's voice began to catch.

'We'll get through it together, Tommy. We need each other.' She reached out and took his hand. 'I don't mean that we should be boyfriend and girlfriend. We don't... well, we're not, you know... But you'll see Tommy. We'll get there with Ruby. You'll see.'

Tommy thought of the last four months and then thought of the next four months and suddenly it was all too much for him. He broke down. He tried to swallow the sobs that were bursting through his throat but they came anyway. Great big gulps that shook his body. Shona put her arms around him and they sank to the floor together crying and shaking. They seemed to stay like that for a long time and were only interrupted by the sound of a text message coming through on Tommy's phone from his dad.

I'll be over with Ruby in an hour!

Tommy read the message and pulled himself together. He knew he had to get rid of Shona before his dad got there. He'd probably be furious at the way Tommy's night had ended up.

*

Shona looked over at Tommy reading his text. She reached up and took a tissue and passed another to him. She tried to work out what he was thinking. It was hard to lie to him. She had spent all of their time together lying but in her sober state it didn't come so easy. Shona had no intention of staying with Tommy but she needed him on her side. She loved Ruby and she wanted to be a part of her life. Tommy was her key into that world. Slowly she would put all of the mess behind her; pick up the pieces and put them back together. That meant splitting with Tommy for good, but for now she needed them to be friends.

Now that she was free from the crutch of drinking she could take on the world. And her plans for the wonderful man that she had been seeing almost every day since she had met him on the carousel, had given her a forceful purpose. An energy she had never had before. Jameel was her way forward. Shona knew that she could take their friendship further. She'd make him realise that they shouldn't deny how they really felt about each other. It was out there... almost ready to reach...

Chapter twenty two

THE couple in the coffee shop shivered in their damp clothes enjoying the cosiness of the heat and the inviting smells, after the in-your-face summer downpour on Grafton Street. They wrapped their fingers around the steaming mugs and laughed again at the antics of the waitress who'd served them. Shona started to mimic her again.

'*Would-you-like-milk-with-your-coffee-sir?*'

Jameel joined in.

'Yes. *Have-you-a-brain-behind-all-that-brown-skin? Can-you-understand-me*? You'd think I was stupid instead of dark-skinned and accented.'

Jameel smiled and then came to the waitress' defence. 'You know, I think she was only trying to be nice, in her own way. To her I'm different and she was worried for me in case I didn't understand. Believe me, I've come across worse cases of racism since I came here.'

'Do you really get that much though, Jameel?' Shona asked. 'I think the Irish are pretty good at accepting those who aren't like them. To many people here, you're sort of a new kind of black man.'

'What do you mean?' Jameel asked.

'Well not so long ago in this country some people were referred to as black men because of their religion. I remember my grandfather talking about a family of blacks who had moved in next door to him in Dublin. They obviously weren't dark-skinned and when I asked my grandmother what he meant, she said it was because they were Protestants.'

'I suppose it's similar with my religion. I am Sunni Muslim. If I brought a Shi'ite Muslim back to my parents they would disown me. I must say though I never really thought of Christians as being anything but Christians before.

'But I'm glad then that I'm the right kind of black man in Ireland,' Jameel smiled. The smile encouraged Shona to edge right in beside him in a very proprietorial manner.

But to her disappointment Jameel pulled slowly away from her, frowned and raised his eyes in question.

'Why must you persevere, Shona? These things aren't possible.' His face was angry but where Jameel was concerned, Shona was determined.

It was three weeks now since she'd met this man on the beach. She had returned two days later and her wish had been answered as soon as she saw the familiar motorbike parked in the same place as before. They'd met there many times since but this was their first time in the city centre. Shona took it as a sign that Jameel wanted to move things along. In the short time since she'd woken up on the carousel and seen Jameel looking like he'd found the woman of his dreams, Shona had known that she'd met the most wonderful man in the world.

She hadn't had a drink for three weeks. Norah had been gobsmacked when Shona agreed to go to Alcoholics Anonymous with her. After two excruciating sessions, she'd persuaded her mother that she could go alone and promptly never went back again. As far as her parents were concerned, she'd been going for long healthy walks in the morning and her AA meetings once a week. She'd actually replaced her cravings for alcohol with daydreams and longing for this gorgeous man. She'd started to go to bed on time too so that she could be up and gone to the beach early in the morning.

At first Jameel had been very hesitant, but she'd cultivated their friendship. Shona had decided that this man was the love of her life and she wasn't going to let it go. Now she reached over and took his hand.

'Because Jameel Al Manhal, I love you. Quite simple really.'

I look into her eyes and take in her look of complete and utter trust. The tilt of her face is the same as Shadia's was. I think of Shadia now, surrounded by the flashing carousel lights before she died. Her beautiful loving face. Now Shona's beautiful loving face prompts me to squeeze her hand before I pull gently away. I push my chair back.

'Don't go yet, Jameel. Please. I'm meeting my Aunty Margaret here, in a few minutes. I want to introduce you to her.' Shona's face pleading as always. 'Margaret has always been so good to me, Jameel. She always seems to see another side of me, one that others can't. Have you ever known someone like that? Someone you can trust with anything?'

I stare at my empty coffee mug and think about the friend that I made when I ran to Pakistan and without meaning to, I speak Ali's name out loud.

'Ali Al Aziz? That's a lovely name. Sounds friendly alright. Are you very close? Maybe I can meet him sometime?'

'He's like my brother...I'd trust him with my life...' I shake my head to bring me back to reality and stare at Shona, shocked that I've let Ali's name slip so easily.

'I have to go, Shona. I'll call you.' I walk away as a woman comes through the doors and heads straight for Shona giving her a kiss by way of greeting. She looks at me suspiciously as I leave and I know that it's time to let go of Shona. What am I thinking of being around this girl? I'm lonely. Where is Ali? Why is he not in touch?

*

Margaret sat and ordered two more coffees while Shona poured out all her news. With a dizzy smile she told her aunt of the man she was completely in love with. The man who had given her back her reason for living. This wonderful person who she knew would turn her world around. Of course he had misgivings at the moment but she was making him see reason.

She and Tommy would be better off without each other. Tommy was a lovely man and a wonderful father, but they had no future together. Except for bringing up Ruby. She would never give her up of course. But Jameel was such a good and kind man and everything would turn out wonderfully. She was sure of it.

Margaret tried not to look aghast at Shona. She hid her worries behind a smile but the boy she'd seen leaving this table and walking out of the café, with a pained expression on his face, didn't look at all ready to settle down with Shona's plans for them both.

'That's lovely, Shona,' she said, 'but take things slowly for a while eh? Things are never as easy as they seem.'

Chapter twenty three

ANOTHER horrible day in Dublin but there's no queue for taxis on Stephen's Green, so I'm able to jump into the first car. I reach into my rucksack and pull out a hat and scarf. Almost a month of living in Dublin hasn't hardened me to the damp weather. It's supposedly the middle of the summer but nobody's explained this to the low-hanging sky and the harsh winds. I'm not sure that all my shivering is to do with the cold but if I concentrate on the temperature, then I don't have to face what's really on my mind. I'm frightened and I whisper his name over and over. Omar.

I direct the driver to my apartment in Dundrum and pull the scarf higher up over my chin.

'Have ye come from somewhere hot?'

I sigh. Another chatty Irish taxi driver. At home in Saudi, they never dare to speak. But here? They talk and I don't want to talk. I want to close my eyes and think about my meeting with Ali and let the significance of it all sink in.

'No. I've been here for a while,' I answer, 'but I can't get used to the cold.' I look out the window to end the conversation.

'And are ye here on holidays then? I'm John by the way.'

'No. I'm attending English college for the summer.'

'Right. Grand. And will ye be visitin' anywhere else?'

Allah, where's a good Polish or Lithuanian taxi driver, with no English, when you want one? I'm stuck with wonderful Dublin hospitality all the way back to Dundrum. It felt too cold to take the motorbike earlier, but it would have been better than this.

'No. Only Dublin. To perfect my English.' I smile. I can be patient.

'That's brilliant. How long more will ye be here then?'

'Em, another few weeks, I think.'

'That's just amazin', so it is. And what else are ye goin' to do between now and September then?'

I'm silent. I take a deep breath. Ali has told me now what I'm going to do. The taxi driver's question leaves a big lump sitting in the back of my throat. I can't answer. A few days ago I was getting used to being in Ireland. But now..? I close my eyes and exhale as the whole, crazy meeting with Ali explodes my thoughts. Twenty-four hours. How can a life change so dramatically in such a short time? It was only yesterday when the text message from Ali burst in on me.

Meet me in Stephen's Green Park beside the main entrance at 5pm tomorrow.

I hadn't heard from him since I came to Ireland at the beginning of July. The fires that were lit in my heart by Ali and the Pakistani men that I met in June had almost gone out. Without any word from him in all these weeks, I was beginning to think they didn't need me to help after all. I felt rejected. I missed my friend.

When I first arrived in Ireland, Ali settled me in quickly and returned to Saudi. His lack of communication afterwards hit me hard. The time in Dublin at the beginning was lonely and full of emptiness, but on Ali's insistence I made no close friends. Apart from Shona, I got to know no one in Dublin. I barely spoke to the people in my English class, arriving just on time each day and leaving immediately after. As the time moved on I felt the loss of contact with Ali less. I still harboured the same ideals as the men who I met in Pakistan. I still felt the same about wanting to make a change but as the weeks progressed with no word, I worried that Ali's leader, Ahmed Al Alfi, didn't need me after all. I thought that maybe I should finish the English course, see a bit of Ireland and return home to Riyadh to face Baba's rage. I had made up my mind to do exactly that when Ali sent me the text.

We met in the city centre and he seemed delighted to see me, talking non-stop to me through the park. He had lots of news from Pakistan. He told me Ahmed Al Alfi had been asking for me and that he, at last, had some work for me to help them with. Some work... but then Ali changed the subject.

It was like losing a loved one, spending time getting over it, deciding it was over and moving on; then meeting up and finding it rekindled and feeling it grow until the flame burned brightly once more. It didn't take Ali long to hook me and reel me in again. I'd do anything for that man.

'So, Ali. This work that I'm needed for...' I eventually said.

Ali looked uncertain. 'There's time enough to talk about that, Jameel. Let's spend some time catching up first. Okay?' I nodded but nothing could have prepared me for what he told me next.

'Jameel, you've not mentioned it so I presume you've not heard. I'm sorry to be the bearer of such sad news from Pakistan. I know you were very fond of him.'

My heart was thumping in my chest, I could not imagine what he might say but implored with my eyes to continue.

'Omar passed away last week, Jameel. He had a heart attack. He died quickly and his wife, Karima, said he asked after you before he died.' Ali reached out and put his hand on my shoulder.

'I really am sorry.'

At first I stared at him in disbelief but when his words began to take meaning I raised my hand and hit him a blow across the head.

'No!' I shouted at him. 'It's not true!' Ali fought off my hands and dragged me to the nearest bench to sit. I dropped my head in my hands and wept for Omar. How could this be? I wanted to go home to Saudi. I needed to erase this new life. Nothing mattered now. How could Omar be dead? I had promised to email him regularly but I wasn't able to tell him that I was in Ireland. My true father. Omar. My real Baba. Gone. I cried and ignored the stares of people passing by.

'Why? Ali. How could this have happened?' I asked.

Ali turned my face towards his and told me what had brought about Omar's fate. 'Omar and Karima weren't able to return to Saudi because your father threatened to have them arrested, Jameel. For kidnapping you. When you didn't return Nazir said he was sending people to Pakistan to find you. I suppose the stress of it all was too much for Omar.'

I'm shocked and quiet. After twenty years of caring for my family, Omar and Karima still meant nothing to them. They were merely servants. My anger with my family momentarily takes over my grief for Omar.

'Tell me the rest,' I say, rubbing at the tears.

'Omar had to make a bargain with your father. Nazir had booked you on a first class flight back to Saudi Arabia. If Omar was successful in sending you back to Riyadh, Nazir would agree not to press charges against him for kidnapping you. Nazir was adamant that Omar and Karima would never set foot in Saudi again and never have anything to do with you or any of your family. Omar could not tell any of this to you at the time as he knew it would make you angry and you might not return so easily. Pretending it was Omar's and Karima's decision to leave Saudi was the only option, but there was a piece of Omar's heart that broke away from him with every lie he told you. Before he died, Omar told me that you were the nearest he had ever got to having a son.'

Ali was kind and concerned.

'It's okay, Jameel. Omar knew that you cared for him and he loved you too. He knew that you were meant for great things.'

'How could that man do those things, Ali? To Omar...'

'Let Nazir go, Jameel.'

'But my mother...'

'She could have persuaded your father to do the right thing by Omar and Karima... She did nothing. Come on, Jameel. Let's go.'

Later, we sat in a restaurant; just another two guys eating our meal. Inconspicuous. Our voices low. Ali spent the time keeping the tone of the conversation easy at first to take my mind off my grief, as if that was possible. We discussed chapters of the Qur'an that Ali said have been occupying his mind. We talked about Pakistan and then about Omar. We talked further about my family and their treatment of Omar. I eventually brought the conversation around to the work again but Ali stalled.

'Later, Jameel,' he said. 'Come now. It's Isha. Time to pray. There's a place close by.'

Ali took me to a small prayer hall in Stephen's Green where he seemed to be on very close terms with many people. He had obviously been here before. Many times.

The Imam stood to speak after the prayer and his words had the followers of Allah breathing in his language deeply. I noticed that a lot of the men there were about my age. After the Imam had been talking for a few minutes I was as enthralled as the others and soaked up his words like magic. I felt that the words were for me alone – that Allah was speaking directly to me through this man. I sensed Omar speaking to me through his words too.

'There are times when we move away from the real reasons for our being here.' His words reached out and caressed my pain. 'We forget what it is that Allah has designed for us. We don't remember to give him enough space in our lives. We don't allow him into our minds and into our hearts. We recite the verses as we always have but we don't speak them with meaning.

'Mohammed, peace be upon him, told us exactly how to live our lives. There is no room for compromise. There is no room for half measures.'

I listened and my heart filled. The messages that I had heard loud and clear in Pakistan, I had put to the back of my mind. Filed under 'later'. Well, now it was time. Ali was here and he was asking for my help. Back in Pakistan, Allah had called. Now was the time to answer. The Imam continued to speak the words that I needed to hear. They quenched the thirst of months where I wasn't able to find a reason to live.

'Only in answering the call of Allah can we truly find ourselves. He always has a message for us. It is for us to listen and to do our duty. For some these duties might be quite light and they might feel that they aren't doing enough for Allah. But for these people, it is up to them to pray fervently for the lost, for those that need help.

'For others it may feel that their task is too difficult for them to perform. That it is almost unbearable. But you my sons of

Mohammed... You will find the best reward. For you the straight path might be filled with unimaginable obstructions but you must push through and you will find the only thing worth having in the end. The love of Allah.'

'Allah Akbur! Allah Akbur!' I took up the cry with the other young men in the prayer hall. God is Almighty. There is only one true God. That is Allah. Each time I said the name of my beloved God, my hunger was satiated more. I felt alive and as I chanted the prayers with the other men, I realised that the Imam was speaking to us all. That we were there for each other. I wasn't alone. I was part of this wonderful Islamic world and we each had a part to play to keep it alive in the hearts of all Muslims, everywhere.

Well this new Jameel Al Manhal would listen to the call of Allah. I would play my part. I would take on the job that Ali had planned for me and I would be a cog in this wondrous wheel. When I left the prayer hall I was filled with a purpose that I hadn't known for some time. Losing Omar had taken away my heart but strengthened my purpose. I walked with Ali outside, ready to do whatever was asked of me and at the top of Grafton Street, he pointed in the direction of the park. Inside we sat on the same bench as before and Ali gave me my job.

Back in the taxi I open my eyes to reality again. The driver's waiting for me to answer a question. Many people will be asking me questions where I'll have to lie to them in the coming weeks. Shona. I'll definitely have to let her go. I take a deep breath and try to answer.

'I'll be staying in Dublin for the rest of the summer. There are some things I need to sort out here before ... I go.'

Whether it's the troubled way that I speak or the look of dread on my face; something makes the driver go quiet until we get to Dundrum. After I pay him and leave, I look back and see him staring after me. I'm going to have to put myself back together again after Ali's revelations, but first I go into my flat and curl up on the couch where I cry again for Omar, and for Shadia. For everything that is lost.

Chapter twenty four

SHONA sat on the sand and watched the familiar figure park his motorbike before climbing off. He locked the helmet to the bike and began to walk in her direction. He was dragging his heels slowly. She felt a pang of hurt at the idea that he didn't look as eager to see her as she was to see him. She had bounced off the bus and leaped over the railings in her hurry to feast her eyes on the man who had spent the last four weeks turning her world around.

When Jameel was with her she felt that her life was filling with… well all those things that she'd always been looking for. She felt strong and worthy. The words that he spoke to her filled her with resolution and hope.

When he had given her a lift after their first meeting, she had hoped they would meet each other again. Even if she had orchestrated it... coming to this beach in the early morning... he didn't have to come back there if he didn't want to meet her again. Texting each other back and forth when they were not together, she was inseparable from her mobile, obsessed with his words, healing her. With Jameel, Shona had been able to reinvent herself.

She knew she should tell him about Tommy and Ruby, but she was afraid he would do a runner. When they knew each other a little better she would introduce him to her daughter. One look at her gorgeous face would be more than enough to make him realise how wonderful she was anyway.

For Jameel and Shona, the beach had become their place to be together. He was behind her pushing her on. He was in front of her leading her. He was beside her holding her hand. They had only known each other such a short time but their relationship meant so much to Shona. She was wrapped up in Jameel.

Her face was bursting with admiration and wonder as Jameel eventually arrived beside her, but she took one look at his face and she knew that he was going to leave her. She would stop him. She had to. This was Jameel.

'What? What is it?' Already she wished she hadn't asked.

'I came here today to tell you... I won't see you again, Shona. We're not... right for each other. I'm not what you think you see... I'm...'

'...perfect Jameel. You're perfect. Forget what you said. Look what you've done for me in the weeks since I met you. For the first time in my life I feel good about everything. I've always blamed myself for anything that was wrong. I've never looked around me and questioned other people's faults. I've never felt that other people could have made me what I am, what I believed I was until I met you. That gap I've always been trying to satisfy... It's been filled... with you.'

Shona reached her hand up to touch Jameel's cheek. He stepped back.

'No, Shona.' He gripped her hand. 'You know that there can never be anything more than friendship between us. Never. How many times...?'

'Okay. Okay. I hear you...'

Shona, as always, felt the punctured loss. When would she learn? To hold on to Jameel, to his friendship, she had to play by his rules. Usually he held her hand. That time, when she had cried, he held her to him, in friendship but never a touch that was meant to arouse. Never a caress, or a careless touching of mouth on bare skin. Even so, it was the best that she'd ever had and she never wanted it to end.

They had reached their rock. That part of the strand that was always a place of silence and calm. In their many visits there, they had sorted out the world's problems; international and personal. Always in this place, there had only been peace. She had learned about Jameel and his beliefs. His feelings about

143

Eastern and Western society. Women were to be revered. Shona was to respect herself in order to have others respect her. She stood lonely on her pedestal.

Shona laughed now, releasing the tension of the moment.

'You're something else. You know that Jameel Al Manhal? How can you stay so true to your beliefs? I know how you feel about me.'

'You know nothing about me!'

'I know when two people should be together!'

'You only know what your body tells you.'

'And my heart.'

'Well…luckily one of us uses our head…eh?'

Jameel kicked off his shoes and waded into the sea to his ankles. Shona watched helplessly as the cold water strengthened his look of resolve.

The cloud had thickened and chilled the sands. She felt as if all her senses were racing through her veins. What was he staring at out there? What was he searching for? The rain that had been threatening the sky began to touch her face. First as a caress, then a welcome release.

Shona's fingers touched the grainy surface of the rock and trailed its rough and smooth areas. The soft, welcoming, polish fighting for space amidst the hard, jutting, cutting edges. She could never fathom Jameel. He intrigued her. He was wonderful and he always left her wanting more of him, elated, full of promise.

'I'm leaving for Saudi tomorrow, Shona.' He didn't turn around to face her.

Panic built in her stomach and her eyes welled.

'What! Since when? You said you were going to stay and study English until the end of August. Is it for a while? Are you coming back? Look at me, Jameel. Answer me!'

He turned slowly and waded back in towards her, still unable to look straight at her. 'I've changed my mind. It was a wrong decision to come here. I want to go back to Saudi. I'll be finishing my studies at home. There'll be another girl in Saudi, Shona.

My parents will choose her. What you and I have... it's wrong. I can't...'

The horizon was slowly disappearing through the rain. The soft breeze that had spiralled at her feet began to lift higher. Faster, louder, round and round. Upwards, reaching her ears with a dizzying force and then the rain tumbled down. Flapping sheets. Surrounding them. She slithered down the rock and knelt, looking out; far out there... The straight line of the horizon had disappeared. Sky and sea were fighting together.

Jameel knelt down beside her, taking her hand.

'Shona, I'm saying goodbye to you today.'

Sinking, soaking; the saturating storm all around her, pulling at her, tugging. Her free hand clung to the rock; her eyes were searching that place where only minutes ago, the sky and the sea held their silver hands, at peace with each other... out there... Would she ever reach that place?

She turned and his face was beside her, his eyes exploring hers.

'Jameel...'

Shona only realised she had been kissed because of the overwhelming sensations that filled her body, her head and her heart. Passion consumed her and not realising the destruction his kiss would cause, he reached for her again, his mouth drinking in her senses, emptying her life and creating anew.

'Shona. Remember me. Be strong. I am with you in here.' His hand touched the curve of her breast, pointing to her heart. As he brushed along her Fuchsia tattoo he nodded his resolution before turning and walking away.

Shona wanted to run, pull him back, but the weight of the water held her there. Seawater, rainwater, tears.

145

Chapter twenty five

FOR the first two days, Shona lay in her bed in her parents' house. She wanted to drink but despite her parents' pleas, then demands to move herself, she hadn't the energy to go out. Somehow though, on the third day she woke up and realised what she had to do. Shona had to make plans for the long-term. It was as if Jameel was somehow still there helping her along. Although he had been the one to cause her all the pain by leaving, the memory of his last words was enough to give her strength now.

She knew that Tommy would never give up Ruby but they'd come to some arrangement about equal access. They'd be friends, her and Tommy. It was the best they could offer their daughter. It would work out. And maybe... sometime in the future, she'd meet someone who made her feel like Jameel had done.

Having persuaded Tommy to let her live back with Ruby to try things out for a while, they were now trying to clear a space in the spare room for Shona to move into.

'Come on Tommy. Get up and help. Get your head out of all that old stuff.' Shona teased.

'That old stuff, as you call it, is very valuable to me. You know... I can't believe I haven't been to Parnell Park or Croker to see the Dubs play in all these months. Would you look at this, Shona? That's Jason Sherlock's signature on this shirt. Jayo himself. And look. Dessie Farrell signed this hat when I was a kid. These are amazin'. To think I stuck them up in the spare room when we moved in and never touched them again.'

'Did the writing not come out in the wash? Seems like a stupid place to put a signature if you ask me.'

'You don't wash it, Shona. You keep it. As a souvenir.'

'Yeuk. You mean you never washed it when you took it off all those years ago and it's been stinking out our spare room all this time? They'll have to go. I'll never be able to sleep in here with them. I knew there was something smelly in the wardrobe.'

'I'll put them into my room with all my other things and you can bring all your things in here once we've done a thorough clean of the place.'

'I can't imagine how I'll be sleeping in here, Tommy. Are you sure there's a bedroom under all this stuff?'

Tommy wanted desperately to say that he was sure she'd slept in worse places but they were doing their tiptoeing on eggshells impression today and he didn't want to scramble the balance. Shona was going to move back into the spare room while she continued to put her life back together. They should try to be friends at least, Shona had said, if they were going to raise a child together. She was making a huge effort to stay off the gargle, he had to admit, so for his part Tommy had to watch his p's and q's and say the right thing.

Shona pulled him up off the box he was sitting on and gave him a friendly hug. Tommy pulled back and smiled awkwardly down at her. There was a time when Tommy might have been persuaded that hugging and kissing Shona was worth the odd hiccup in his life but he knew that, right now, living together would not help Tommy and Shona feel anything for each other but embarrassment.

'Come on Shona. Let's get the job done. Your mam'll be back with the baby before we've even made a start. I'll just put these things in our… in my room; get them out of the way.'

Tommy walked away, holding his Dublin shirt and hat lovingly in his arms, promising himself that they would feature once more in his life. Sure Ruby would love Croke Park. She'd look so cute in her little Dublin shirt too.

Shona turned her back on Tommy, embarrassed by her failed attempt at intimacy. She wondered how long she would have to stay living with him to show how committed she was to her daughter now. Being a caring mother was no problem. She had developed a bond for Ruby that she never thought she'd possess and Ruby was responding to her with all the love of a baby for her mother. She was sure being nice to Tommy couldn't be that difficult for a few months. She did care about him but she wasn't in love with him. She knew he didn't love her either. She'd never loved him and never would. Not in a passionate way.

Certainly not the way she had loved Jameel. She had no doubts about her feelings there. They had only been together for a short time and she hadn't even made love to Jameel but she knew instinctively that if she had, it would have been fantastic; like nothing she had ever felt before.

As Shona kept busy with the folding and throwing things out, she tortured herself with thoughts of how her life might have been if Jameel hadn't gone away. He wasn't coming back but it didn't stop her fantasising. She swallowed the emptiness.

Reliving that kiss, Shona felt that Jameel must have had strong feelings for her. So he'd had great difficulty with the fact that it was so soon after losing Shadia, but if he'd stayed for longer she would have made him realise she was the best thing that ever happened to him. Shona sensed that now she'd met Jameel Al Manhal, there'd never be anyone else who could measure up to him.

Jameel was gone back to Saudi, to a future arranged marriage, that was probably as doomed as her own relationship with Tommy. Life wasn't fair. Two people who loved each other should be allowed to be together. Shona balled up the hoodie in her hand and flung it into a drawer.

She had to sort out her life; to concentrate on what she valued most, create her life around Ruby. She'd carry the strength that Jameel had cultivated in her and use it to work at being a real mother. Jameel had given her this.

It would take time to build up Tommy and her family's trust in her. She was beginning a new phase in their relationship. It would be hard to live with Tommy but she needed to be here until she'd convinced them all, that she was more than capable of sharing in the care of her baby. There was no way she could leave without access to Ruby and to have that she had to be Tommy's best friend. It wasn't so hard anyway. Sure he was a great guy when you thought about it. She could have chosen a lot worse to have a baby with. They could live together for a while. Then they would sit down sensibly and discuss why it wouldn't work for them long-term. Tommy was going to college in September. They'd make plans for Ruby's future, but that was all.

She continued sorting her clothes with a sad little smile. She had to put Jameel away. All that emotion, she would use towards building a new life with Ruby. Shona had lived five weeks without taking a drink. She could do this. Jameel had told her she could and she would.

For the rest of the day, memories of her love for Jameel whirled around her, wrapping her like a cloak. She felt the ache sit inside her. She coiled her long hair around her finger and stared down at her black curls remembering Jameel's words the second time she'd met him.

'It was your long, black, curly hair; so like Shadia's; that drew me to you.'

Had Jameel only been interested in her because of her resemblance to his fiancé? Was it Shadia he'd been thinking of the day he kissed her? Shona loved her hair but she flicked it behind her shoulders now, out of sight. People always remarked on her thick, shiny hair but if it was going to remind her of Jameel all the time then maybe she should get it cut.

*

'… and you're mummy's little beauty… what a gorgeous baby you are. I could eat you up. All smelling nice after your splashy little bath…'

Tommy stood in the doorway watching the scene with amazement. Shona was curled up with Ruby on her lap content with her world. The baby was bathed and in her pyjamas. The room was tidy, and there was a smell of something cooking in the kitchen.

The Dubs had won the match... Another bit closer to the All-Ireland Final. Tommy had loved being back on Hill 16 again, swaying and shouting and swearing and saluting his heroes. Come... on... you... boys in blue...

This was the first time he'd left Shona on her own with Ruby and he'd been so worried he'd turned down the offer of a pint with his dad after the game. But Shona was fine. Better than fine, she was great.

Tommy felt happy. He really did, but there was something else tugging at him too. One day with her mother, and his baby was sharing out her affection in equal measures.

'Hi, Shona. Everythin' okay?'

Shona was smiling like she'd won the lottery.

'Wonderful, Tom. We've had a fabulous day. She's just had a bath and she's ready for bed. Say goodnight to Daddy now, Ruby.'

Tommy watched them walk upstairs without him; Ruby snuggled fast asleep in the crook of her mother's arm, instead of her daddy's, and he felt the happiness of his day deflate. When Shona came back downstairs would they sit together watching telly for the evening like a normal couple? What was going on? He hated what went before, but he wasn't too enamoured with this new development either. Jesus, was he never satisfied?

Five minutes later, Shona came bouncing down the stairs like a child and insisted Tommy sat down at the table she'd set so beautifully, while she served him his favourite dinner. Tommy stopped himself from saying *okay, let's play mammies and daddies.* He wasn't sure he liked this game but he felt he had to go along with it for now.

Maybe he'd spent too long being angry with Shona to be able to forgive and forget so easily. Maybe he should be trying a little bit harder, as Shona was, and maybe in time...

No. He didn't love her. He never would.

Chapter twenty six

'WELL now, isn't that lovely dear? A picnic. In Stephen's Green? What a lovely way to spend your birthday. You're going in on the Luas? A nice treat for you all…'

Shona could hear the disappointment in her mother's voice down the phone, but she wasn't going to relent. She was determined to go through with this family day out. She had the food all prepared. Unfortunately, the chicken drumsticks were blackened and binned; the smell of smoke still sitting in the kitchen. But the sandwiches would be fine. It was the idea of the picnic that was nicer than anything.

A family picnic for three, not five.

'We've kept today free for you as we always do on your birthday, love, but I'm sure we'll find something to amuse ourselves. I've a cake for you, Shona. I could drop it round before you leave if you like…'

'No, Mum! That's lovely of you. It really is but we'd like to leave soon. Get the most out of the day, you know, and we want to pick up that gorgeous new buggy while we're in there. You're so good to give us that money. Five hundred Euro is such a lot.' God but her mother was never done with making her feel guilty.

'Sure she needs it, Shona. The size of her now. She's growing out of her little pram already.'

'I suppose when we're back later, maybe 6pm or so, we could have the cake then, Mum. Is that okay?' Tommy'd kill her.

'That'd be lovely, Shona. We'll be there at six and if you're not home yet, sure we'll wait for you. Ruby will still be awake then too, I'm sure. We'll see you later, so. Have a lovely day, Shona.'

There. That did it. Shona felt oddly happy that she'd given in a little. Her mother sounded so pleased. It didn't take much after all to make her happy. Did it? And it would be nice for them to see Ruby at the end of the day.

'Tommy, I hope you don't mind. I…'

'I heard you. Are you mad, Shona? I thought you were goin' to stand firm on this one. The house is a bit of a mess. Your mother'll be tuttin' and turnin' up her nose, as she does, and Ruby'll be tired at that time of the evenin'. We've to go to get the new buggy too. One day to ourselves Shona. How hard can it be for God's sake? This new you can be a bit hard to cope with sometimes. All this tryin' to be nice to everyone, it's wearin' me down. Come on. Let's get her into the sling and get out of here. Before we end up bringin' your parents with us.'

Shona wished she'd asked them now after all. His dad too. A big family get together. It was her birthday after all. Tommy was becoming increasingly grumpy lately. Living with him again was proving to be harder than she thought. Well it wouldn't be for too much longer. She was confident of that. In the meantime, she had to stay on good terms with everyone so that when the time came for her to suggest a break they'd know that she had tried hard too. She took some deep breaths and followed him out of the house.

'Tommy, I'm sorry. Don't worry. It'll be fine. We'll have a lovely day today. Wait and see.' Shona put her hand into Tommy's hand and felt him wince. She pulled away. He wouldn't miss her when she went. She'd stay on good terms with him in the meantime, but it was killing her. She fingered the silver locket he'd given her for her birthday. Inside were photographs of Ruby. It was a beautiful, thoughtful gift and Shona knew she was a little bitch to be thinking badly of the man who was trying so hard to do the right things. They walked towards the tram stop through the tension, which thinned out in places thanks to Ruby's endless baby noises.

As the day wore on Tommy found himself smiling more and more at Shona's antics with Ruby in Stephen's Green. Her squeals of laughter were infectious and he even began to join in. They could pretend to the world right now that they were a normal, happy family on a day out. It was lovely to see them this way but just as he got to the stage where he completely forgot that this was Shona; then he would remember and he would check his laughter.

Shona had been booze-free for over five weeks now. This was what Tommy had wanted for months. She looked beautiful. Radiant. Her new haircut was dead sexy and any other man would be delighted to be in Tommy Farrell's place right now.

But not Tommy himself. Tommy wanted to be very far away from this place. He did not want to play happy families with this woman for the rest of his life. He was scared at the prospect.

Since Ruby was born, Tommy had been the knight. Now that Shona looked set to join him he was shaking in his armour and he knew he wasn't so shiny anymore. Squeaky-clean Tommy could dump his dipso girlfriend and nobody would ever blame him, but this new improved model was not quite so disposable. If he abandoned this radiant beauty he'd be letting go of Ruby as well. No way. Never. As long as Shona was living with him, his daughter was his full responsibility. So Shona was staying. Tough luck Tommy. He'd just have to try much harder with the give and take that other couples took for granted.

Shona smiled at Tommy and he winked. He could play this game too, but right now he could do with some time on his own with his baby.

'Shona, we've to go to pick up the buggy. I'm knackered. I don't suppose you'd like to do it yourself?'

Shona took the bait. 'Sure, Tommy. Will you be alright here with Ruby for a while?'

'No bother. We'll go feed the ducks with the crusts from the sambos and then we'll go for another walk. Ring me when you're ready and I'll tell you where we are. You have the money your mam gave us. Stick it deep down into your bag.'

Shona nodded enthusiastically.

'Don't be too long. Remember you told your mother you'd see her at six.' Tommy rolled his eyes and Shona smiled her most charming *I'm so sorry* smile.

'No worries, Tom. Be good Ruby. Back soon.' Shona kissed her daughter's head and Tommy watched her walk in the direction of Grafton Street with a bounce in her step and a thrilled smile on her face. Why could he not come to like, never mind love this woman?

'Come on then Ruby and we'll feed the quack quacks.' Tommy was delighted to have his baby to himself for a while and he allowed himself a rare smile.

Chapter twenty seven

SHONA traced the rim of the glass with her finger. Round and round. She stared at the ice cubes melting in the clear liquid. She wouldn't pour the tonic in. No point in diluting the desired effect. She threw it down her throat in one swallow. The burn was painful and delicious at the same time. Just like Jameel's kiss. She could still see the back of his head and the beautiful shape of his body, disappearing into the crowd on Grafton Street.

How dare he tell her that he was leaving to go back to Saudi and then stay here in Dublin? He'd kissed her on the beach and made her believe that he loved her; then dumped her when he was good and finished with her. Shona had been used by someone once again. Join the list of users, Jameel.

'Another vodka, please. No. No tonic, thanks.'

On her way to buy the buggy she'd seen him walking out of a building on Stephen's Green. She'd called out his name; all memory of why she was in town forgotten in that instant. Jameel had looked across at her for a moment. His face was shocked and he ran as fast as he could up the busy street, getting lost amongst the bodies in seconds. Shona had stood staring at the space where she'd seen him – the reality of the situation hitting her hard. Jameel had not left to go back to Saudi. He'd lied to her. The only thing that Jameel had left behind was Shona.

So she had wandered to the nearest pub. She raised her glass to her lips now and drained it.

'Happy birthday, Shona Moran.'

'Another vodka, please. No ice.'

'A double vodka... please.'

'nother double vodka.'

*

Tommy sat on the park bench and thought of Des and Norah sitting in their car in the driveway waiting for them to come home; the birthday cake balanced on Norah's lap. Hopefully they'd have given up by now and left. Tommy couldn't bring himself to return the countless messages they'd left on his mobile. He might make an excuse for Shona tomorrow. Then again, he might not. He'd called her countless times but she was ignoring him. Ruby was asleep in the sling. She'd been getting cranky. The heat of the evening was getting to her. Tommy stood up and walked towards the Luas stop outside Stephen's Green.

'Shona!' This was the last place he would have looked for her but there she was sitting on a steel bench leaning against the shelter, singing a song. She was slurring her words, those she could remember, and looked in the general direction of her approaching family with wasted eyes. Tears came. She mumbled something to Ruby and Tommy looked away, embarrassed. Shona may have made her own way back to the tram stop but how would he manage to get her into a carriage in this state? He wanted to walk away to the next stop and leave her there, but she was calling something out to him and he couldn't turn around and go.

Shona leaned her head against a pole and closed her eyes. Drunken words tumbled chaotically out of her mouth. She began to smile. A mad, crazy kind of smile. Then she began to laugh. Louder and louder. Ruby woke up and started to cry again. Tommy had no bottles left for her. The crowd shuffled forward craning their necks to see if the Luas was coming yet. The elephant in their company was rendered invisible.

Tommy's hatred for Shona consumed him but then so did relief. She was disposable once more.

Chapter twenty eight

I DON'T stop running until I reach the top of the street. I slip my heavy bag from my shoulders and crouch down, then take some deep breaths. I wish I'd stopped and spoken to her. I owe her an explanation of some sort. Lies, yes but better than what she's thinking. Her poor face when I turned towards her. The short haircut threw me at first, but there's no mistaking that tattoo. I could ring her. Maybe speak to her on the phone and tell her my departure's been delayed but I'm still leaving. It's not that far from the truth. Or maybe I should leave things. Maybe speaking to her would use up all my energy and I need every drop of strength to face what's in front of me today.

Walking back down Grafton Street, I'm uncertain whether to keep an eye out for Shona or to keep my head low and steer well clear of her. I decide to go to Bewleys for a coffee. Something to pass the time, and if Shona goes there too then it will be okay, we can talk. I have to stay around people, stay on track. Seeing Shona isn't a problem. In fact it's given me strength. I can do this thing. It's the only thing to do. My phone rings.

'Hi, Ali. Everything okay?' I'm almost hoping there's a last minute change of plan.

'Just checking where you are right now. Are you with anyone?'

'No. Like who?' Ali's silent for a moment on the other end of the phone.

'Tell me again exactly what you have to do tonight, Jameel.'

'Ali. I haven't forgotten. I've to be on the Luas leaving Stephen's Green for 8pm. You'll meet me at the Balally stop and drive me to Limerick. Zarrar will meet us at Bunratty Castle and swap cars with us. He'll drive me from there to Shannon Airport.'

'Exactly, Jameel. No changes with flights. The U.S. Air force is due in at midnight. The soldiers will be coming through the café shortly afterwards. That's when it will happen. You have everything?'

'Yes.' I look down and pick up the bag that I've been dragging around with me for hours now. 'I didn't expect it to be so heavy, Ali.'

'It's powerful, Jameel. Be careful. The remote? Is it still in its box?'

'Yes, Ali.'

'All good then, Jameel. See you at about 8.25pm.'

No goodbyes. The line's dead.

Sitting at a table at the back of the coffee shop, I think about what's ahead of me. I pray that I'll be able for it. I put my encounter with Shona to the back of my mind and think about Shadia. It's Shadia I love. The friendship with Shona is madness. I should have run away from her at the start, but I was lured in and it's almost cost me dearly.

It was the loss of Shadia that sent me running from Saudi all the way to Pakistan. Running alongside Omar to meet with Ali. Today I'll make Ali proud.

I breathe his name into my heart now, with Omar's and Shadia's, then I drain the last of my coffee and stand up to go. I'm ready. I pick up the heavy bag and walk back up Grafton Street towards Stephen's Green. I look around expecting to see Shona at every glance then I shake my head to banish her face.

Chapter twenty nine

STANDING waiting for the Luas, Tommy felt his disgust for Shona eating away at him. Thoughts of loathing echoed through his head. Over and over. Louder and louder. But it couldn't block out the sound of her and the burning in his eyes couldn't hide the sight of her.

'I hate her.' Tommy's thoughts scorched his mind while he smiled at the man beside him.

Not an unusual sight, Tommy thought, if it was a Saturday night and they were waiting for the last tram home. Maybe then she wouldn't have looked so out of place but at 7.50pm on a baking hot evening, with a baby in tow, they were attracting attention.

Tommy felt worn down with the weight of little Ruby in his arms. He struggled to make conversation with the man in the queue who had offered to hold the baby bag while he tried to sit Shona up.

'I hate her. I – hate – her. *I hate her!*' Tommy could feel something filling him like a sickness. Tears threatening. The mantra continued in his head as he nodded his agreement to the man in the suit.

'Yeah, it's hot.'

'Better than yesterday though. There's a bit of a breeze in it today.'

'Yeah, but you wouldn't mind a drop of rain for once.'

The doors of the Luas tram opened and Tommy pulled Shona into a standing position. Not for the first time he wished he could leave her where she was. She would have found her own way home eventually anyway. She always did.

The sweaty Dublin throng pushed them forward as he moved

swiftly to grab a place where the three of them could sit together. A seat where a drunken girl might look less conspicuous. When he reached to drop Shona down on the seat, she fell over into the aisle.

'Shite... Get up, Shona, for God's sake.' He pulled her off the floor and she flopped onto the seat.

'Jaysus! Watch where you're goin'!' Tommy snapped at the crazed-looking guy who pushed past them with his oversized rucksack.

'Bloody weirdo!'

*

I'm sick with fear and longing. I sit back in my seat on the tram and try to allow the nerve endings in my body to tell me that this is right. I will it to be over. Two days ago I arrived back at my apartment to find everything I'd need for the operation sewn cleverly into my mattress. A few uncomfortable nights of sleeping on the floor and I'd never have need of the bed again. Was it Ali who left everything ready for me? I wish he'd let me work alongside him. It's a lonely mission. I could do with some camaraderie.

Now the time's arrived. On the eighth day of the eighth month. A date to remember. I'm ready.

Ali's words sail in and out of my head... *'Retribution...My brother in Guantanamo... Shadia... For Shadia, Jameel. Do this for Shadia...'*

'Insha' Allah!'

'This task is your life.'

'Insha' Allah! I will not fail Allah. I will not fail Ali. Or Omar or Shadia. I'm not afraid.' I swallow the bile in my throat.

'Ali...' Ali's given me full training, in mind and body, in what I'm about to do. I only need to sit and think of his words and it'll be okay.

'You are chosen Jameel. You are pure of heart. You have Allah's blessing. You have the blessing of all Muslims worldwide. You will

160

be revered, with love and with thanks for delivering us from the darkness of Western societies. Ma'a salama Jameel. Go with Allah.'

I think of the beautiful woman I met this summer; of the feelings she's awakened in me. If Ali knew of Shona, he wouldn't have said those things. Shona... No. I mustn't think of her... I know that seeing her this afternoon has almost robbed me of my direction.

I wouldn't have changed what happened this summer for anything. In fact, I'm convinced that it's all been part of Allah's map. Being with her has helped to psyche me up. All that nervous energy inside me I've poured into my friendship with Shona. In a way I have loved her. I've loved being around her. She's very beautiful and she loves me so much, I know, but in my head I've been calling out Shadia's name.

I've been honest with Shona that our friendship can't last. I haven't told *her* of my plans. I can't expect her to ever understand. On the beach I told her goodbye. For good this time and when I walked away I didn't dare to look back at her.

'The Qur'an tells us to travel the straight path Jameel. The path to Allah.' Ali's words are in my head once more and I'm on track. I think of the constellation that Omar told me about, minutes before Shadia died. The sky's clear this evening. Later tonight before I go into the airport I'll look up at the sky and find the Summer Triangle and I'll follow. 'It is made up of Vega, Deneb and Altair.' That's what Omar said. 'Good Islamic names for stars that guide us on the right path.'

*

It was 7.55pm by the time Tommy sat on the tram, with Ruby asleep in his arms facing the object of his disgust. Shona's head lolled forward making her snore softly. He looked across the aisle and he smiled and shook his head. The weirdo was sitting now caressing the rucksack on his lap, his eyes closed and his lips moving in silent speech. A mad man. Great company for Shona.

Tommy tracked the flight of a painted lady butterfly, flapping its way in through the dull crowd, still squeezing in past the open doors, to keep his mind off Shona. He watched as the lovely creature fluttered its black and orange wings around windows and light. Trapped, it flew about the carriage, circling, finally coming to rest, wings closed, on a stain on Shona's jeans. It settled a moment. Tommy followed as it rose again, zig-zagging its way up before circling Shona's head. Making its way back down again, it brushed against her cheek. She shook her head and reached out a swipe at the beautiful insect. The colours stained her face orange and the butterfly fell to the floor writhing. You could always rely on Shona to ruin a good thing. Tommy stared for a moment and then moved his foot to put the butterfly out of its misery.

*

With just minutes before the tram pulls out I sit with the rucksack on my lap and the small box in my pocket. Within hours it will be done. I can feel Omar and Shadia with me, helping.

I close my eyes and think of her and of the man who detonated the *bomb* that took her. Was he frightened or simply angry enough with the West to kill? I think about Shadia's friend Maeve who was killed with her. At sixteen they were still children.

But as Ali says, Maeve lured Shadia to be her friend. Money lured Maeve's family to Saudi. Westerners are at their worst, their most un-Godly, when money's involved. The man was right to do what he did. In its aftermath less and less Westerners are coming to work in Saudi and more have left. The message is being read correctly.

For a while I thought that maybe the way to change humanity was through talk and reasoning, but I was wrong. My little voice crying to be heard over the evils of the West would be nothing. Ali says my actions today will be heard the world over. It'll spur the Irish and hence the Americans into change. It'll reunite Ali with his brother. The reasoning behind the bomb that killed Shadia hasn't left me. It strengthens my belief and sends me on a straight path to here. A small Irish flag hanging from the side of a horse and cart reminds me of where I'm headed.

I try to pray to Allah, my eyes closed, concentrating. My thoughts are flying around in my head and I can't focus. I hug my clammy hands around my bag and dig my fingers in tight.

I open my eyes to look once more at my mobile to check the time. I've been on for just four minutes but it feels much longer. The next few hours will be torturous. I look around and a colourful butterfly catches my attention. It's flapping around madly trying to find a way out. I will it to escape and allow myself to be drawn by its flight around the tram as it brushes its wings against closed windows and doors. Its frail body circles a man's head and lands on a woman's lap. There's a stain on her jeans and the butterfly's enjoying the scent.

'Move towards the door,' I will the insect as I follow the wing movement up the body of the woman to her face. My heart races and I swallow hard as I realise who it is.

Shona... but looking so strange. I begin to shake. The nausea in the pit of my stomach that I've dismissed as nerves threatens to spill. My beautiful Shona. What's happened to her? She's drunk. She must have gone straight to a bar after she saw me. I've spent weeks building her back up and in one foul swoop I've left her to wallow in sorrow again. I want to go to her. Pick her up and run.

I look down at the bag on my lap with horror. Then I look around me, at normal people, with normal lives. A man with a tiny baby on his lap sits across from Shona.

In a daze, I stand up. I drop the rucksack, knocking it into the aisle. Then I heave my way through the bodies towards the exit. Once off, I run in the direction of the park. Through the arch and to the right until I reach a flowerbed. I breathe in the heavy scent of roses then breathe out, showering the beautiful flowers with vomit. I feel like I'm coming out of a trance. I stand clinging to the railings, staring at the tram. It'll be leaving in a minute and the crowd continues to push in. I need to get back on. The rucksack. I wonder what Ali will have to say about my cowardice? No, not cowardice. I can't be part of killing those people in that airport.

Men and women. Perhaps there'll be children travelling. How can I explain to Ali that it was seeing Shona that stopped me?

The weirdo's rucksack was on the floor of the aisle. Tommy looked up at the seat the guy had run from. He looked around the carriage, but there was no sign of him.

Tommy picked up the bag and examined it. It looked brand new and it felt very heavy; packed to capacity. The man with the face of thunder had obviously left it. He should have run after him but Tommy was too weary to be curious. His mind was full of this guilty woman, this innocent child, and the burden on his eighteen-year-old shoulders of saving one from the other. Lifting Shona's head, he leaned the bag against her on the empty seat, as a prop to hold her up. There. She didn't look half as bad now. Little Ruby shifted in his arms and Tommy sat back in his seat to relax her.

As she settled back to sleep again he sat and watched her mother. In answer to his disgust, or maybe to confirm it, she sat up and belched loudly. The buzz of conversation in their immediate vicinity went momentarily silent. Tommy could feel his shoulders tense once more. Had she no shame?

He was desperately trying to look away from Shona, who was swaying and smiling, eyes darting, awake but not awake, dreamlike. He leaned forward and shook her to stop her mumbling. This was too strange. It made his skin shiver.

He glanced at the crushed body of the butterfly and back up at Shona. Shaking himself, he pulled his baby close to him. Ruby gurgled in response and Tommy's face crumpled into a smile. If hatred was consuming him then so was love. His feelings for Ruby gave Tommy all the strength he needed.

He reached forward and straightened the bag under Shona but as he did so, the side buckle loosened. Tommy peered in to see what might be inside and immediately froze. He had to be mistaken, but Tommy had watched enough war and crime movies to recognise the wires protruding from inside. He stared over at an elderly lady, then looked at the people around him. Beads of sweat built up on his forehead and he stood up. The man in the suit was standing nearby. He would tell him quietly to get the driver to evacuate. Tommy pushed passed a few people and whispered in the man's ear. He turned and stared at Tommy.

'What are you on about?' he sneered.

Tommy pointed at the bag with the now protruding wire. That got his attention.

'Get the fuck off the tram! There's a bomb on the tram!' the man screamed.

At first everyone stared at him. A few girls giggled noisily by the door until the man pushed past them all and flung himself out onto the street and ran away, roaring at everyone.

Inside the tram there was a momentary quiet while people gave the situation some thought.

'It's true,' Tommy said. 'That bag. There's a bomb inside. Will someone help me with my girlfriend?'

The girls by the door grabbed their shopping bags and walked out fast. Others stared at the rucksack and back at Tommy's frightened face before deciding not to take any chances. People started pushing their way out. The doors of the tram closed as the Luas started to move away, resulting in screams as people pounded on the doors to get out. A lady pressed the emergency button beside the door and shouted to the driver to stop. The Luas stopped moving and the doors opened.

Tommy looked down at Shona.

'Will someone please help me with my girlfriend? She's lyin' against the bomb.'

No one even looked in his direction as the word bomb was roared down through the carriage and on to the next one. Tommy knew he wouldn't manage to carry Shona off as well as hold onto Ruby safely. Could he take Ruby off and get a Garda to help? Shona slipped down towards the ground and the rucksack rolled forward on top of her. Tommy held his breath as those still left on the tram screamed more. A shove from behind caused him to almost drop Ruby so he pulled her close as the crowd dragged him along towards the door of the Luas. Just before he left he glanced back at Shona and knew that he had no choice but to run with Ruby.

Outside the tram there was chaos. Worried looking Gardaí were beginning to move people down towards Grafton Street. A woman was screaming for someone called Sophie. People had dropped belongings that were too cumbersome on the street. Tommy ran to a Garda.

'My girlfriend's on the Luas,' he said. Tears were running down his face. 'She's drunk. She's lyin' under the bag with the bomb.'

The Garda looked at him suspiciously.

'You mean there's still someone on the tram?'

'Yeah, her name's Shona Moran. I can't move her by myself and I have to look after the baby.'

'Did you see a bomb?'

Tommy was nodding. 'She's lyin' under it for God's sake. Someone has to get her.'

'Did you actually see a bomb? Did you see who left it there?'

'Yeah, I saw it and I saw him. Mad lookin' fella, but forget about him. You have to get her out.'

'What's your name?' Tommy stared incredulously at the Garda. There was a bomb on the Luas. A girl's life was in danger and he wanted to know names.

'Tommy Farrell... Shite... There's a bomb that could blow at any minute and you want to...'

'There are more Gardaí on the way. We'll get your girlfriend.' He called a colleague over and gave him orders. 'This fella saw the bomb and he saw the guy who left it there. Get him the hell out of here but don't let him out of your sight! Move that baby out of here now. Go on.' He pushed Tommy and the younger Garda towards Grafton Street. Tommy reluctantly walked, looking once more towards the Luas but when Ruby chose that moment to wake up and wail, he knew that there was no way he could risk her life for her mother's, and he ran.

*

166

I watch as the panicked crowd begin to run away in the direction of Grafton Street. Someone has found the bomb. I know little about the contents of the bag but I still have the detonator in a box in my inside pocket. Surely it can't go off unless that button's pressed. Everyone seems to be off the tram by now anyway. Police are materialising from all corners. They look frightened and confused.

Walking fast towards the large pond in the park, I pull the box with the detonator from my pocket and standing at the water's edge I fling it as far into the pond as I can. I turn and stumble back towards the exit. The police are running into the park now, shouting orders at people to get out. I have to move before someone recognises me from the Luas.

As I exit the park I glance back at the tram, just in time to see Shona falling from the carriage onto the ground and trying to pull herself back up.

'Allah!' My breath catches in the word.

I stare. I'm torn between running away and helping her off. If I go back I'll be seen, but I can't leave her. It's my fault she's in that state. A driverless horse and carriage career past shaking me out of my stupor; the horse's eyes a mirror of mine, wide with fright.

'Get those bloody horse taxis under control!' shouts a policeman waving his arms madly in the direction of a younger colleague who looks like he might be about to cry.

'Move! Everyone move fast! Down to the bottom of the street!' Another screeching policeman is taking no nonsense.

In the name of Allah! Have I really caused all this? No. Not in Allah's name. The screaming, running mass of people brings me back to the other bomb in Riyadh months before and back before that again. Before all the madness. The Allah that I've been brought up to worship would never have wanted this to happen. I look up in the direction of a woman clutching her child to her and crying, *Sophie, Sophie*. I remember a passage in the Qur'an that insists that women and children are not a part of war and should not be harmed. No one at the camp in Chagai Hills ever

167

referred to this passage. What has brought me to this?

I rush towards the Luas, ignoring the shouts to keep clear, and pick Shona up off the ground. I shake her and put my arm under her for support. Dragging her with me down Grafton Street, I don't look back at what I've left behind. The noise gets louder behind me as more sirens arrive. There seems to be hundreds of police now, running like headless chickens, shouting orders. Fire brigades and ambulances pull up in the distance. A helicopter hovers in the sky. The media.

I push and shove my way through the last wave of people, with Shona pulling on my strength, to where I'd left my motorbike earlier. How will I manage Shona on the bike in this state? I sit her on and take her face in my hands to try to get eye contact.

'Shona! Shona! You have to sit up straight. Come on.'

She wobbles a bit, but manages to sit upright while I sit behind her, lean around her and rev the engine.

I turn to the sound of a crying baby. Him. The man sitting near Shona on the Luas. He'll recognise me. I have to get out of here fast. I drive off to the right slowly and hope Shona will stay between my arms.

I was meant to see her on the tram. It was her that woke me up to the craziness of it all so it's up to me now to look after Shona.

Chapter thirty

'THERE is still no sign of the woman known to have been on the Luas during yesterday's evacuation of Stephen's Green. New information has come to light that she was sitting right beside the bag that held the bomb. Shona Moran, eighteen-year-old mother from Dundrum, may be a key witness to...'

Tommy reached for the remote. That was enough. Another newsreader reporting that Shona might have seen the man who left the bomb there. The Gardaí had been crawling over the family all morning. Question after question.

'Where might Shona have gone?'

'I don't know. I didn't see her get off the Luas.'

'When did you last see her?'

'On the Luas. I saw her on the tram. She couldn't get off. I left her there while I brought Ruby out. I couldn't manage her.'

'Mr Farrell. Would Shona have wanted to leave you? To walk out on Ruby?'

'Well, yeah. I suppose she might've.'

Then a change of direction.

'Where was Shona sitting on the Luas Mr Farrell? How was the rucksack on the seat beside her?'

Tommy couldn't push himself to tell the truth about that one so he shrugged. He couldn't get rid of the image of Shona being pillowed by a bag that had held a bomb.

'Why did she not get off the tram with you and the baby?'

'She was drunk,' Tommy confessed.

'Can you describe the man who left the bag in the aisle again for us, Mr Farrell?'

The questions were endless. Tommy answered them without

showing any emotion.

'Yeah. She has a drink problem.'

'Yeah. She slipped down under the seat and the bomb fell on top of her.'

'Yeah. She was still in the Luas when it was empty... I don't know how she got out without attractin' any attention.'

'He was about 19 or 20; Arabic lookin'. Stubbly beard. He wore glasses and a black leather jacket. Looked frightened out of his life.'

Tommy wished his house wasn't full. He longed for Des and Norah to go home. Shona's parents had slept in his room. They only lived ten minutes away for God's sake. They didn't need to stay. His dad had been here since early morning. He wished they'd all leave.

He knew he was being unrealistic. He couldn't hold it together with the baby and the Gardaí all on his own. Nerves would be stretched in a normal situation, without the strain of Shona's absence hanging over them all. He didn't have the strength to look after Ruby and his dad was being his rock.

'Alright, son?' he asked, yet again. They were sitting at opposite ends of the couch. Tommy was afraid to touch his father. His closeness to his dad had the potential to open up the floodgates of his life's wreckage and he wasn't ready to face the deluge right now.

How was he feeling?

Nothing.

He knew that his silence made Stephen uncomfortable, but he wasn't up to a chat.

'You could do with a bit of a clean-up in here, Tommy.' Stephen needed to fill the hush. Tommy glared at him and he shut up immediately.

He looked around the room and wondered what his father really thought about the life that his son had made for himself. This room was rarely clean and tidy. It was the baby room, dining room, TV room and sitting room. Tommy had never been very good at housework. When his mother had died, his dad had

170

fallen apart for a very brief time, but then he had taken over the role of mother and father as soon as he was able. Stephen had managed both roles and a full-time job. Tommy felt inadequate in his shadow.

'That Garda said he'd ring if they had any word on Shona, didn't he? We should've given him a mobile number. We still could. We could ring him. Then we wouldn't have to keep answerin' the phone to all those bloody journalists... but then if someone were to know somethin'... about Shona... then they might phone and...' Stephen couldn't simply sit quietly. He had to fill the room with his nervous chatter.

'Dad. Shut up. Please. Look, I'm sorry. But shut up, alright?'

When Shona was living in the house it felt like she was always absent. Now that she really wasn't there the place was full of her. All around the room she had left her mark. A shoe with the heel broken off, a red lipstick on the floor that someone had walked into the rug, a leftover stain on the carpet where she had thrown up a few weeks back.

If everyone would go away, Tommy thought, he would clean it all up; clean Shona out of their lives. He hated himself for the thought. He had walked away from a tram with a bomb on board, knowing that Shona was still inside. He had left her to her fate. Okay, so the bomb had been diffused and apparently she had somehow managed to get off beforehand, but Tommy had wrapped himself around his baby last night with the guilt of leaving Shona sitting heavily with him; alongside the feelings that he wished she would keep going wherever she was and not come back.

Norah came in wearing a tea towel tucked into her skirt.

'I'm amazed that you can live in a house without an apron,' she said. 'How do you cope in the kitchen?'

Silence.

'Lunch should be ready in a few minutes.' Her voice was excruciatingly sorrowful.

Stephen was on the telephone getting rid of another reporter. Nobody expected Tommy to do anything, or to make any decisions. He liked it like that for now. He had been making all the decisions for too long.

'I've been thinking, Thomas.'

He wished Shona's mother wouldn't always call him by what she considered his proper name. He had given up correcting her, although it made him cringe. Silent words passed between his father and himself.

Leave it, Dad.

Stand up for yourself son.

'I'd like to have the priest visit. I think it would do us all some good to thank God for delivering you all safely from the tram and to pray for Shona. Wherever she is. What do you think?' Norah was looking at the floor wringing her hands back and forth. Tommy knew that her faith had probably kept her sane through all the trials of bringing up Shona and she wasn't about to let go at this hour of absolute need.

He started to pick up toys around him to stop himself shaking while he spoke.

'Whatever you think, Norah,' he replied. 'If you think it might help you and Des, then by all means go ahead.'

It wasn't that Tommy *didn't* believe in God before he met Shona but he had let the church go when he left primary school and these last months of living a Shona-led life had convinced him that prayer was futile. But he let Norah have her rock to lean on.

'He might be able to help us all to decide what to do. We have to do something. We can't hang around here and pretend that there's nothing wrong. I mean… maybe we should even have a mass for Shona to pray for her safe return or should we have… a mass in thanksgiving… or…?'

Then Norah broke down, her face crumpled and the sobs echoed in the house where her daughter should have been.

Tommy's dad had had nothing nice to say about Norah Moran's daughter, and not very many nice things to say about Norah herself since he met them, but now he felt really bad. There was nothing he could change to put that right but he put a hand on Tommy's shoulder and nudged him towards Norah. Tommy gave

Stephen another black look and begrudgingly sat her down and held her hand.

He could think of nothing right to say to Shona's mam, so he held her hand and sat in silence, waiting for her to stop shaking. Beside him, Norah's heart continued to break and his anger at Shona rose another notch.

He wanted to escape from here. He looked at his watch and realised he was due in work in an hour. They would all think he was mad if he went. Completely crazy to go to work when your life's been turned upside down. He wriggled his hand from Norah's grip and tried a compassionate smile at her, but only succeeded in looking as crazy as he felt. He backed into the kitchen.

'Dad. I'm goin' into work.'

'What?!'

'Let me know if anythin' happens here. I have the mobile.'

Shona had left them again, this time helping them to achieve unwanted celebrity status. She had always lived a life of high drama at other people's expense and it was clear that nothing had changed.

*

Tommy could feel the buzz the moment he pushed open the door of *Molly's*. The pub was packed with late lunchtime custom and tourists. The noise was nice and loud so there would be no need to make polite conversation with anybody. The guys behind the bar were a great lot but he knew they'd be at a loss for words. They'd be shocked that he was there at all, as he was himself.

Tommy wondered how long he would end up working in this bar. He had taken Mick's offer of full-time work out of necessity, but it wasn't what he wanted to do with his life. College in the autumn still beckoned but he didn't know how he could work it. Shona had been working in *Molly's* when Tommy first met her so knowing what she was like; Mick was lenient when things went wrong. He knew that Tommy was a hard worker and he was steady too. That counted for a lot in the bar with so many staff coming and going and, for Tommy, the job paid the bills – most of the time.

Mick made a beeline for him before he even made it to the bar.

'Tommy. Jaysus man, I never expected to see you in here today. You're all over the news. What're you doin'?'

'Comin' to work, Mick. What does it look like? My shift is 3pm to 9pm today. Right? So that's what I'm doin'.'

'Eh, come into the back, Tommy. Talk to me.' Mick was looking at Tommy like he'd lost his reason.

'It's too busy. We'll talk later. Who's your man behind the bar?'

'I organised some back up, Tommy. Give you some space to get through all this mess. Come on. Come in the back.'

'You did what?' Tommy could feel his anger rising and stormed after Mick into the small room behind the heaving bar. Followed by a lot of rubbernecking from the staff and some shaking of heads, their eyes burned into the back of his head.

'Sit down, Tom. Do you want a cup o' tea?'

'For fuck's sake Mick, if one more person asks me do I want a cup o' tea I'll...'

'Okay, okay. I get the point. Do you want a beer?'

'We're not allowed drink on duty, Mick.' Tommy threw himself into a chair.

'Yeah, Tommy but you're not on duty. Look at the state o' you for a start! You'd be a health risk behind the bar. Have you even washed since you ran from the bomb? Have they found Shona yet?'

Tommy shook his head, then folded his arms and crossed his legs. The bomb. The one word nobody was mentioning at home. Trust his friend not to pull any punches. If Mick thought that this would trigger something in him to come to his senses he'd be disappointed. Tommy Farrell's *girlfriend* was missing, wanted for questioning following a bomb being left on the Luas, and Tommy Farrell was feeling nothing but relief at her absence. No. That was wrong actually. With every passing hour and no sign of Shona, Tommy's heart was feeling lighter. Who could he tell this to? He couldn't even believe it himself.

Mick put a hand to his shoulder. 'Tom. Shona could be in danger. Ruby's mother. This is not the place for you to be. You should be at home, with Ruby; with Shona's family.'

Tommy shook his head. 'I don't care. I don't give a shit.'

'Come on, Tommy. You care about Ruby and I know deep down you care about Shona too. This is me you're talkin' to now. No messin'. Go home, Tom.'

Tommy stood up and spat out the words. 'Mick. I don't give a shit about Shona. I wish that bomb had blasted her into the middle of next week!'

Mick stared at the madman in front of him.

'Tommy. I've said a lot of horrible things about Shona in the past but she doesn't deserve this. You don't know what you're sayin' pal and I know you don't mean that. You're actin' crazy, Tommy.'

Tommy sat back down and smiled crookedly at his friend. 'So why do I feel better than I have for months then?'

The smile faded fast as Tommy thought about his life with Shona and he stood up once more and shouted into Mick's face.

'I ran, Mick! I ran and left her on the Luas lyin' under the bomb!'

Mick caught his arms around Tommy as his friend fell forward; heaving sobs and punches at the air. All that anger and frustration was too much to hold inside; and the past few months, like waves, flowed out and filled the room around them.

Chapter thirty one

STANDING on the deck of the ferry, Shona felt wretched. Sobering up last night waiting for the morning sailing in Dun Laoghaire; she had been so happy to realise that she was with Jameel. Apologising over and over for hurting her, he swore that he was going to look after her.'

'I can't go back home, Jameel,' she had said. 'I feel I'm right back to where I was before I met you. I'm worthless. You were right to leave me.'

'No, Shona. I'm to blame. I did this to you. If I hadn't pretended to leave Ireland you would never have been drunk. I'm sorry. So sorry. I thought it was the best thing for you. But I was very wrong. In everything. I'm walking aimlessly. I can't forgive myself.'

Then he had explained to her what had happened and why they were there. He had been in Stephen's Green when there was a bomb found on the Luas. He had found Shona almost unconscious on the ground and brought her with him.

'I wanted to bring you home to your parents' house last night but you kept telling me that you wanted to get away from your family, Shona. I think it might be a good idea if we go away for a while together,' he'd said. 'It would give you some time to think. We don't need to make any decisions about the future right now. A couple of weeks away might be good for us both. I'm very confused myself right now. I came here to go to English school. Then I met you... and the way forward for me isn't so clear anymore.'

Shona had grabbed at his words and was filled, once more, with a sense of purpose. She believed he meant everything he said to her.

Since she met Jameel she had felt stronger. She hadn't needed to drink. She could face her family. She had grown to like herself and from there she could see a way forward. Even when he had left her she could still feel him with her. It was enough.

She had agreed to go and he had bought tickets for the ferry. Jameel was here with her. Everything else would come together with time. Shona stood on the deck of the ferry and breathed in the sea air. She could see the Welsh coast in the distance. It was early morning, less than twelve hours since she had woken up in the tram. She was still feeling awful but she knew that her drinking binge was not the only thing to blame now.

Jameel's hand touched her shoulder and turned her round. She allowed herself to be wrapped in his strong arms and felt the safety net catch her once more.

'It'll be alright, Shona. We're doing the right thing. We'll stay away for a while and not get in touch with anyone. We'll go back to your parents when you're stronger. When you're more able to cope. Look at me, Shona.'

Shona looked up into those familiar brown eyes and nodded. He was right. Going away was the only answer for now. He leaned down and pressed his mouth to hers and Shona allowed herself to fall into that world that only kissing Jameel could bring her to.

*

Sometime later the ferry was sailing into Holyhead and leaving everything way behind them. Shona wished that Jameel would hurry back from the shop. She didn't want to be alone for one minute and she kept expecting him to disappear on her again.

'It's going to be another scorcher.'

A voice beside her made Shona jump and, panicking, she mumbled a response as she pulled her cap further over her face and walked quickly towards the back of the boat. Holding tight to the railings, she concentrated on the pattern of the waves in the wake of the ferry. Everyone was near the front looking towards where they were going. Only Shona was viewing what she had left behind. There was no one standing near, nobody to hear her talking wildly to herself and to see the tears fall overboard and into the waves.

'I should have stayed... I can't do this... leave... my baby. Dear God, I can't leave her.'

Her inner voice spoke back to her. She had left her long ago. Ruby was never hers. She never would be. Shona had made sure of that with her actions. Months of crap dished out to her.

'She's better off without you!' she told herself. 'Better off motherless.'

She shook at the railings and cried out loud, her sobs silent against the throb of the engines.

'Shona! Where did you go? I couldn't find you.' Jameel came over to her and she stopped crying.

Jameel reached out and wiped the tears from her face. 'Stop now. It's going to be fine. We're nearly here. Let's get going.'

The sea gave Shona strength. She would always be drawn there. As soon as they disembarked at Holyhead, they took a bus further up the coast. Shona jumped off at a village, liking the curve of its strand and the fall of the waves, and they sat on a rock for the rest of the morning talking. Shona clung to him. Without Jameel she had felt fragile and powerless. Now she let his presence fill her. She reached out and held his hand. Jameel curled his fingers around hers and held on.

'Where do we go from here, Jameel?'

'I don't know, Shona. I guess we find somewhere to sleep for a few days while we look for something a bit more permanent. I like this village you've chosen for now. Nobody would think to look for us here.'

'How long do you think I should leave it, Jameel, before I ring home and speak to my family?'

'I'm not sure, Shona but we should lay low for a while so nobody'll find us.'

Shona looked up at him. He seemed jumpy. She knew that he was looking out for her. He had brought her here as a way of getting away from her family for a while so she could get her head together and sort out her future. Their future? Hers and Jameel's? She couldn't broach that subject yet though. She would go with him for now. Wherever he took her she would stay right by his side. She just hoped that Jameel had already realised that they were supposed to be together. She understood that it was as hard for him to turn his back on his family values as it was for her to leave her family. It was up to Shona to put him at his ease. There would be plenty of time later to tell him about Ruby. She squeezed his hand to reassure him.

'Come on then. Let's find a place to stay.' Shona would take charge a little for now. It felt good to be needed. Picking up her small bag with an air of determination, she headed towards a sign that said *B&B (With sea views)*.

'Mrs Lewis is my name. How many days are you staying for my dears?'

'Two, I think,' replied Shona, trying to hide her face beneath her hat.

'That's a nasty fall you've had. Are you okay?'

'Yes. Thank you. I fell over a dip in the path.' The first thing that came into Shona's head as she remembered the bruises she got on her face from falling when she was drunk.

'You're Irish. Wasn't that incredible the stuff that happened there in Dublin yesterday?'

Shona paled under her bruises. 'I – eh – yes. Terrible.' She began to move towards her room.

'But on the news this afternoon they're saying that they're sure now who the man was who left the bomb on the tram.' The landlady sounded excited. 'I suppose that's something,' she added.

Shona glanced over at Jameel. They had seen her photo on the news on the boat but it was a photo from before she'd had her hair cut. No one would recognise her from that picture. Jameel had told her he had found her wandering around after the tram had been evacuated. He said he'd felt terrible because he had let her get into that state by lying to her.

'They've his picture in all the papers too.' The woman was talking to Shona's back as she followed her down the hall.

'Really? Was he...?' Shona wondered who this man could have been. She shuddered to think that she may have been close to death.

'Gone... He was gone but they found the flat he'd been staying in. They were able to name him. Apparently he was... Oh, are you alright love?' Mrs Lewis reached out to steady Jameel.

Jameel had stopped still in the hallway. He dropped his bag to the floor and started muttering in Arabic. Shona turned and looked puzzled.

'Hey? What's the matter?' she asked him. 'I'm sorry,' she said to Mrs Lewis. 'He's okay. He's tired from the boat and we haven't eaten for a while. We need to lie down.' Shona backed into her room, pulled Jameel with her and shut the door. Leaning against the handle she took Jameel by the hands.

'What is it, Jameel?' Jameel sunk to the floor and was leaning against the wall clutching his knees to his chest and whispering something to himself over and over.

A few minutes later there was a knock on their door and Shona attempted to get Jameel to stand up before she answered it, but Mrs Lewis took the silence as her answer and walked straight in.

'Sorry to intrude, dears but I've brought you some sandwiches left over from earlier and a pot of tea. Make sure you have some sugar in it. You need to keep up your strength to recover from that fall and your friend doesn't look too well. I've made cheese in case you were both vegetarians but I hope you aren't dears because you really need your strength.

'Do you want to read today's paper? I have it in the kitchen. I'm finished with it. I'll bring it in to you. His picture is in it and all.'

By the time Shona tried to thank her she was gone and Jameel had jumped from his place on the floor and ran out the door...

'Jameel!' she shouted. 'Where are you going?' He was acting very strangely and Shona was feeling really upset. The trauma of the last couple of days was wearing her out. She needed to lie down. She was so tired. She pulled back the duvet on the bed and pulled off her shoes. She needed to sleep. Then everything would make more sense.

*

My hands shake as I accept the newspaper from Mrs Lewis. I thank her and walk towards the front door. I need to get away from the house and dispose of this paper before Shona gets to read it. How did I think I could run from this and keep it from her? That's impossible. I sit on the rock where I sat with Shona just an hour before and open the paper out. The picture of me is small. A grainy passport photo that was taken in Pakistan for my language school application. My hair's longer there and I'm clean-shaven. Now I haven't shaved in days and I'm already growing a fluffy stubble around my chin. No wonder the landlady didn't recognise me. There's a picture of Shona too. Her hair is long and she's smiling without the bruising she now has on her face. Could I brave it out for a while? Perhaps if I find us a place to stay a bit further out from the village? If I can keep Shona away from papers... I can tell her she needs to get away from everything.

I need to hide away and think about my next move. I'm frightened. Not of the Irish or Welsh police. Not so much of Shona finding out what I've done, but of Zarrar. I haven't forgotten the look in his eyes when we left Pakistan. Or the look of distain when he handed me the suitcase in Riyadh. This man meant me ill before I messed up in Ireland. If Zarrar finds me he'll do me utmost harm. Will he kill me? Or will he make me suffer first? I close the newspaper and hold it tight around me.

'Omar, what have I done?' I sob into the newsprint. 'Omar, Shadia, help me please.'

Chapter thirty two

TOMMY was taking off his jacket in the hall when the phone rang. He grabbed it and held it to his ear.

'Mr Farrell? My name's Garda Kevin Daly. My colleagues were with you this morning? I'm the Family Liaison Officer from your local Garda Station here in Dundrum. I was wondering if I could come around and speak to you.'

Tommy wondered if Mick had been right. Was he really going mad? Why couldn't he speak?

He tried to push some words out.

'Eh, yeah, sure... you've got some news then?'

'Well, I'd prefer not to talk on the phone. Could I drop around now and it'd be best if Shona's parents were there too.'

Tommy knew that if he were thinking rationally he would insist that the Garda gave him an idea of what was going on but for some reason he seemed to be content to let things happen around him.

'No problem there. They seem to have moved in.'

'Ah. Right. Thanks, Mr Farrell. I'll see you shortly so.'

Tommy couldn't coordinate the telephone receiver back into its cradle. Stephen came up behind him and with one hand on his son's shoulder took the phone from him gently and returned it where it belonged. Norah and Des stood near the doorway expectantly.

'What is it son?' Stephen put his free hand on his other shoulder and turned him around.

'The Gardaí. They didn't say.' Tommy stared at the zip on his father's jacket – anything but eye contact.

'He said he needed to talk to us. He's comin' round now.'

Stephen pulled Tommy towards him.

Des reached out and held Norah's hand, and for once she didn't pull away.

Tommy stood back from his father. 'Where's Ruby? It's awful quiet.'

'Your neighbour that minds her for you... What's her name?'

'Joan.'

'Yeah, Joan. She came by and asked did we want her to take Ruby over to her place for a while. She seems a lovely lady. Not a bit nosy about what's goin' on or anythin'. She said to tell you to call on her anytime you need her.'

'Yeah. She's lovely. Ruby loves her.'

Tommy ignored the quizzical look on Norah's face when Joan was mentioned; at least she knew that this wasn't the time for arguments. He sat down on the couch and waited. The Gardaí obviously had news of Shona, but why could he not talk to them on the phone?

When he let Garda Daly into the house Tommy was ready for him. They sat down, the strain of waiting pulling heavily on each of them.

'I have some news for you.'

Tommy waited.

'Shona was seen on a motorbike leaving town shortly after the Luas was evacuated. She was a passenger on the bike. The girl who saw her was also on the Luas earlier. She says she didn't get a good look at the driver but that she's sure it was the girl who was falling over earlier in the tram. She also said that Shona's face was badly cut and bruised.'

'Oh God.' Des put his other hand in Norah's. Twice in one day. Extraordinary circumstances.

'So where is she?' he asked. 'She hasn't been seen by anyone since yesterday.'

'We don't know for sure but we're continuing to look for her. You say that only you and your girlfriend went to town with the baby yesterday?' The Garda looked at Tommy and he nodded.

'And you said that Shona was so drunk that she couldn't have

183

managed to get herself off the tram.'

'She's been under a lot of stress lately.' Norah was crying. She pulled away from Des's grasp. The look she gave Tommy showed exactly who she blamed for giving the Gardaí that piece of information.

The Garda continued. 'We found this on the ground outside the door of the carriage that held the bomb. Is it Shona's?' The Garda handed Tommy the locket he had given Shona for her birthday. Tommy nodded, unable to say anything. 'There was blood on the ground there beside it. It's being analysed for blood type now. Where she went to on that motorbike is the problem. Nobody's seen her. If she's decided to go away, she's had plenty of time now to cover her tracks.'

'What do you mean *decided to go away?*' Norah was furious.

'Well...' Kevin Daly looked at Tommy as if he was feeling the strain of Norah Moran.

'Tommy told the Gardaí earlier that she might have wanted to leave, Mrs Moran. As you said yourself, she was under a lot of stress lately. She may have thought that this gave her an opportunity to actually go.'

'Go? Go where exactly? And leave her baby on her own? Shona would never do that! She'd never go off and leave her with Thomas. Sure he's the cause of all her problems!'

Stephen stood up to defend his son.

'How bloody dare you? You're nothin' but a...'

Garda Daly interrupted. 'Okay, okay. This is getting us nowhere. Look. It will be announced on the news this evening that we're still looking for Shona to help us with our enquiries. Someone will surely see her. Her face is well-known by now. She won't get very far. Whoever she was with may or may not have hurt her. She's a priority missing person for lots of reasons.'

Kevin Daly looked around the room, the look on his face measuring everyone's differing emotions.

'I'll let myself out,' he said putting his card down on the table. 'We'll be in touch if we find anything more and if she gets in touch, ring me immediately.'

It was a while before Tommy realised that Garda Daly was gone. He hadn't noticed him leaving. The quiet in the room was disconcerting.

Norah was the first to break the silence.

'So what should we do now? Where do we begin to look for her?'

Nobody answered.

'Where could she be, Des? Has she friends that she might stay with, Tommy?'

Still they couldn't respond.

Tommy looked over at Des and knew that they both had the same thought. Shona had gone off into the sunset with some guy on a motorbike. She had no idea that she was wanted for questioning because she was out of her mind somewhere with her drinking friends.

'That's it! We could use the fact that the Gardaí are looking for her. We should appeal to her on television. Tell her that we don't blame her for anything that's happened. We should beg her to come home. It could be a new beginning for her, for all of us. Let's sit down and make some plans,' she said. 'Thomas'll go and fix us all a drink.'

But still they were silent.

'What's the matter with you both? We need to find Shona. For God's sake, if you don't need a drink, well I do. Where do you keep it Thomas?'

'I don't.' Tommy exhaled slowly.

'What do you mean you don't?' Norah moved to open the most likely cupboard, but Tommy stood up and slammed it shut.

'I don't keep alcohol in the house Norah because I'm living with an alcoholic. I don't like to encourage her to get plastered around your grandchild. So she does her drinkin' elsewhere. She's been the model mother for a few weeks but she couldn't hack it for long. She's done what she always does. Disappears for days on end. I don't look for her anymore. She always comes back. Like a bad bloody penny. When she comes home she'll take to the bed for a few days until she feels better. We'll tiptoe round each other for a few more days. Then she'll go away again. She lies to me as a way of life. In turn, I lie to you. That's the way it is. So now you know.'

Norah reached for Des's hand again and he let it sit limply in his. His eyes were fixed on the eighteen-year-old man who carried heaviness on his shoulders; too weighty for his years.

Stephen spoke through the leaden silence.

'Son, the news'll be on the television in a few minutes. Do you think..?'

Tommy reached for the remote and sat down to hear what the media had to say about the girl they referred to as his girlfriend. Tommy wanted to tell them that he wasn't that hard up for a girlfriend; that his only mistake with Shona Moran had happened through a haze of drink.

He remembered sitting down to the news before lunch. It was about the man who sat beside them in the tram. Jameel Al Manhal... Tommy thought he had heard the name somewhere before. Had Shona a friend called Jameel? Not exactly a common name in Ireland.

He was drawn from his thoughts by the voice of the RTE newsreader telling them what they already knew. Shona was seen as a passenger on a motorbike. They wanted to find her as she had been sitting almost opposite the man they were looking for and must have seen him. Now she was missing and possibly injured.

Norah looked away from the television as a picture of Shona filled the screen. This was Shona on the morning of Ruby's Christening, holding her baby lovingly, looking stunning with her long, black curls and above all sober. Tommy looked accusingly at Norah who had given the Gardaí the photo of her daughter. If Shona were living rough at the moment; if she were drinking heavily, she wouldn't look anything like the beautiful, young mother in this picture. There would be no reports of sightings of this ravishing, well-dressed woman.

The news report continued to show images of the Luas and the serious looking Jameel Al Manhal.

Tommy opened his clenched fist and stared down at the locket he had given Shona. The photos of their beautiful daughter meant nothing to her. He clenched his fist up again and with a loud grunt of frustration, he flung the locket into the corner of the room.

'Fucking, useless bitch!' he screamed. 'She better not come back to this house again. Ever. How fucking dare she?' Tommy lifted his foot and with all his strength he began to kick the coffee table in front of him. Over and over. Stephen and Des jumped forward and caught him. Stephen put his arm around his son and Tommy drew his breath in letting it out in an apology.

'I'm sorry. It's just so...' There were no words.

Norah stood up. 'Would you like us to go and pick up Ruby... em, Tommy?' she asked.

Had Norah called him by his name? Was he hearing things?

'Thanks Norah, but I'd like to get her myself.' Tommy needed to hold his baby in his arms to make sense of the madness. Then an afterthought. A compromise. 'You can walk over with me though... if you like.'

They walked in silence across the road and towards the minder's house; each guarding their own painful thoughts. It was only an hour since he had answered the phone to Garda Daly but Tommy hardly recognised himself as the same man who had left for work earlier. He was beginning to come around to all the hurt that Shona had caused and he hoped that her parents would go home now and leave them to it. He needed some time on his own.

'Come here to granny, sweetheart, and we'll get you into your jammies and into bed.' Norah was visibly shaken by the evening's happenings, but she obviously wasn't letting go that easily.

'I'll find your mummy, Ruby love. I'll bring her back to you and that'll make everything right. Until she comes back though, I'll be all the mummy you need.' Norah cooed her way back across the road and, as ever, took over.

Chapter thirty three

SHONA looked over at Jameel's sleeping head peeping out from under the cover. When he was awake he looked older and wiser but when he let sleep take hold of him; which wasn't often; he looked vulnerable. She reached over and gently touched his newly growing, fluffy beard. It looked so out of place on his face, like a child playing dress up. Shona marvelled, not for the first time at how meeting him had changed so much for her.

When they had broken in, to squat in this bungalow two weeks before, she had been confused and afraid of what they were doing. Jameel had convinced her that the house was empty; had been for some time. But she was living on the edge expecting someone to knock on the door at any moment and ask them what the hell they thought they were doing.

It had been empty of everything but the basics and most items were covered in layers of dust. Jameel had heard, from a conversation in the village, how it was a shame that the house had been left to fall apart by the owners since they had moved to the States and thought it ideal for himself and Shona to hide away. There had been curtains on all the windows and Jameel and Shona had kept them constantly closed, as they had found them. Using the back door to come in and out seemed to help in keeping themselves to themselves. Jameel had left most of the clearing up to Shona and he had gone shopping in the village. He had bought her clothes and everything they needed for their little house by the sea; and any shopping since, continued to be done by him. He said it was best and she accepted that.

'It's secluded here and nobody knows or even cares that we're using it. You're here to lead a quiet life for a while, Shona. I want to be the one to look after you. Your family may be looking for you. It's best that we stay away from other people for a while. Let me be the one to go in and out of the village, and I'm the one who has the money to pay for everything anyway. Relax here and go for quiet walks along the beach.'

Living with Jameel was helping her to block out what had gone before. Well some of it. She loved Jameel and that really mattered. Sex with him had turned out to be as wonderful as she had thought it would be. When you really loved someone, and were loved in return, then it all came so naturally. For all his talk before on how wrong they were together, it certainly wasn't stopping him now.

She gently pushed back the cover and put on the clothes she had shed the night before. She thought of Jameel's cross face each time she dropped her clothes to the floor at night and left them there. He could be hard to please at times. She walked down the hallway of the bungalow towards the kitchenette, quietly made tea and put marmalade on some bread. She craved some hot, buttered toast and missed having proper food. A kettle on a one-ringed camping stove was the extent of their kitchen comforts.

She sipped her tea, drinking in its luxury and looked out at the August sea view. She added three spoons of sugar to compensate for her melancholy mood. She tried to push away the thoughts that fed her mind every day as soon as she woke, but the sweetness of the drink couldn't quell the desire to hold her baby.

The empty kitchen was always clean and tidy. Jameel liked everything neat. He joked with Shona that he'd never been taught to do housework but had always lived in a spotlessly clean house. He also laughed that it was women's work but that yarn was wearing thin at the moment. Anyone could do housework, but Shona had always considered it a pain in the backside. Her mother was a stickler for cleanliness and tidiness and Shona felt that this had fed her repugnance of cleaning. But it kept Jameel happy. He was much easier to live with that way and it gave her something to do.

The house was gradually beginning to look a little more lived in, than the empty shell it had been when they found it. The continued good weather meant that lack of electricity and heating didn't matter to them either.

Shona hadn't told Jameel about the four hundred Euro she still had, stashed at the bottom of her backpack. The money should have been for Ruby's buggy. She wasn't sure why but she felt it safer to have it there. Jameel seemed to have an enormous amount of money anyway. She hadn't gone to look in the place where he hid it behind the old mirror but she noticed that there were huge wads of notes and he hadn't mentioned to her that he might run out. Maybe his family were very rich. He hadn't even suggested that they were upset about his leaving Dublin. Even so, she felt it was best to hold on to her own money.

The lies about Ruby had also followed her to Wales. Shona hadn't found a good time to tell Jameel about her precious daughter and the longer she left it the harder it was.

Generally, she tried to keep busy; keep her mind occupied. But the books and puzzles that Jameel brought for her were boring. With no television or internet access, Shona was at a loss as to what to do all day.

The want for a drink was still there but it was weeks since she had left home and she had survived without. With little to do, her thoughts took on a forceful energy. Another sip of sweet and heat, the tea helping to blank out the memories, the longings – her whole being consumed by her loss.

One picture haunted her most, one longing. The feelings that engulfed her felt fresh and raw. She closed her eyes and saw Tommy standing by the water in Stephen's Green holding little Ruby. Shona couldn't bear thinking that might have been the last time she would see her. She had swapped that life for this one? Did she really love Jameel enough to give Ruby up? Because she couldn't see Tommy forgiving her for this latest escapade of hers. She knew she should call home; let them know she was safe but each time she mentioned to Jameel that she wanted to call her parents he would get very angry.

'Why are you torturing yourself like this, Shona? Let them go for now. Not forever. But for now.'

Jameel always watched her as she walked towards the beach, to see which way she went. When she returned he would casually ask her to describe her path and what she had seen on her travels.

'Where did you go? Did you meet anyone? Did you speak to them? How did they look at you? Do you think they knew who you were?'

'Jameel! Relax! Nobody recognises me. I doubt that my family are still looking for me. They know by now that I've done a runner. They know what a waste of space I am.' Shona was beginning to find Jameel's protectiveness as suffocating as she'd found living with her parents, or even Tommy.

Maybe she wasn't cut out for living with someone else. Certainly being with Jameel was nothing like she had envisioned months ago. Another sip of tea. It was cooling now, allowing the memories to flood in like waves on the sand. Their sand. Their beach. Hers and Jameel's. Memories of the July sun rising, lifting Shona out from the depths of her dark nights to days filled with a passion for life she had never felt before.

She stood up and opened the kitchen window, allowing the sounds and the smells of the sea to charge her mind with memories. She filled a jug and watered some dying flowers that Jameel had brought her ten days ago. Back then her time with him was still an exciting adventure, but it was over two months since she had first met Jameel and Shona sensed she was losing the feelings for him that she had back then.

She reached to coil her curls around her finger as she'd done since she was little and the lack of hair shocked her again. She still found it hard to believe that she'd cut her hair so short. She had watched the big, black curls fall to the floor of the hairdressers and felt her old self slipping away. A new Shona had walked out of that salon; confident that she didn't look anything like a dead girl called Shadia.

'Look at me,' she had said to Jameel one night when they were arguing. 'I don't look like your girlfriend now. Is that what has you so upset?' Jameel had done what he always did when they rowed. He walked away. Now Shona wanted to go too.

When she ran from Dublin, she had no idea of how much she would miss her baby. It had seemed scary, but simple. She had to stop clinging to her family, pretending that she was somebody. A daughter. A mother. In these roles, she knew now that she had failed.

Shona turned from the window and flung her mug across the room, its pieces shattering against the beige wall, the empty space. Frustration and anger filled her and she reached for the plate of bread and sent it after the mug. Pieces of pottery, mingled with sticky bread, slid down the wall and covered the floor.

Moments later Jameel came staggering into the kitchen, rubbing sleep from his eyes.

'What are you doing, Shona? What's happened? What's the matter?' One hand was stretched out, questioning, as he struggled to put his glasses on with the other. Shona hit out at him.

'Go away, Jameel. I don't want to talk to you.'

'It's okay, Shona. You miss her. I understand.' Jameel was looking at her with compassion. 'Ruby. You want to see her again. I knew you would eventually.'

'You knew.' Shona felt her heart skip a beat, her face incredulous.

'Yes. I knew, Shona. I'm sorry I didn't tell you. I read it in the newspapers. They're looking for you. It said in the papers that you were a mother. That Ruby was born in May. I know about him, too. About Tommy.' Jameel looked defeated.

'There's no Tommy. There never was. I was drunk and we slept together. We had a baby. That's all.' Shona couldn't believe that the truth was out. 'You knew all this time, Jameel and yet you kept it secret. Why?'

'We all have secrets, Shona.'

'You read about me in the papers and you said nothing!'

'If I told you, you might have wanted to go home and I thought it might be better for you to wait awhile.'

'But why? Why would there be a reference to me in the papers? I'm just missing. Like so many others and I'm not a child.'

192

'The tram, Shona. You were on the tram, sitting near the man with the bomb… and then you disappeared. They want to speak to you about what you might have seen…'

'I saw nothing! I can't remember anything!'

'I know, I know but they don't know that… I didn't want to upset you with all this so I decided to leave it all until we *had* to face it…'

'Which is now! Oh my God, what are we doing here?'

Shona was shaking. Weeks of walking on eggshells around each other were coming to a head. Jameel was looking at her very strangely. She had always known he was hiding from something and facing the truth would change everything.

'What about you, Jameel? What's your secret? Why are you here with me?'

Jameel shook his head slowly and sat at the table. Shona was sorry she had asked him. She didn't want to know. She had to get out.

Leaving the mess in her wake, she made her way out of the house. She walked fast in the direction of the sea, her thoughts still full of her daughter. Her secret. Jameel had known all this time and had played along with it. He ran after her calling her name.

'No! Jameel. Stay there. Let me be on my own. Stop this crazy game.'

Shona ran along the path that led down to the shore. She felt that Jameel was using her for something. She couldn't put her finger on it but she was beginning to feel that this hiding away wasn't just for her benefit. Was Jameel the next in a long line of people queuing up to wreck her life? Her birth mother had given her away. Her parents had used her to replace the children that they would have preferred to have, but couldn't. Tommy had spent six months, tearing her apart while he showed the world how good he was.

Shona was nearing the water's edge. Yesterday's abandoned sandcastles littered the beach as the sun rose higher. Images of Ruby made her smile a little.

She loved Ruby. She would go back. Soon. For her. She would make up for the heartache she had caused her family. They would put it behind them. She was getting stronger. She didn't want a drink every minute. At least Jameel had given her this. The strength to say no. The wisdom to know what was really important in life. Ruby.

She would have to let Jameel go. Touch by touch. Starting with the hardest… that kiss. Would she ever feel that with a man again? Shona rubbed the palm of her right hand with her left thumb, moving around and around, recreating the touch of Jameel as he held her hand on the beach that first time. More tears.

Last week they had sat on the sand together at midnight and Jameel had told her about growing up hearing all about the constellations from his servant. He pointed out three bright stars and told her they were called the Summer Triangle. Shona had listened in awe of his knowledge and got lost in the romance of it all. Jameel knew about lots of things in life but he didn't know much about reality and now even his romantic nature was waning.

She kicked off her shoes and enjoyed the feel of the saltwater splashing at her feet; healing. Kneeling down, she wrote his name in the sand.

JAMEEL

Then the waves came in and washed it away.

Chapter thirty four

I FINISH the last of the sweeping and cleaning and let Shona's mess slide into the bin. Then I wander into the sitting room and sink down into the tattered old chair. I put my head in my hands and breathe, exhaling slowly, letting the reality of the situation lie in the air.

I've let Shona down as well as shaming the memory of my beautiful Shadia. I've failed my family. I can never go back to my parents again. Since Shadia was killed I'd only spoken bad words to Mama and Baba. Those words ring now in my ears as it must in theirs. Do they know by now what I almost did in Ireland? I listen to the waves lapping at the rocks on the beach and think of the miles of water separating me from that beautiful world that I left behind. I yearn to go back there now. To Mama nagging me about my studies, to fights with my brother about possessions and to days when I knew that I would study, marry Shadia, have children and live a good life in the protection of Allah. The day I left Saudi for Pakistan and then Ireland, I left my family and friends behind. It all seemed so perfect back then... so right. I trusted in Ali and I was so sure I was heading in the right direction. The only direction. Allah's straight path.

It's almost three months since I left them all for Ali now. I swallow the tears again. I feel like a child. I'd give anything to be at home with my family. To tease my younger siblings. To hug Mama. To go to the mosque with Baba. I stare at the bare room and instead I see our family room in Riyadh. Shadia and her brother Sa'eed calling in. Friends and family. A place where I belong. Home.

I've nowhere to go. I pace the sitting room. Once. Twice.

195

Three times. I open my mouth and shout NO but there's nobody to hear. I know I have to run from Shona now. I've put her in enough danger. I'll tell her to go back to her baby. That it's for her own good that I'm leaving her. If I'd known then that Shona had a child, would that have made me behave differently? What possessed me to bring her here with me? Love? Yes. That and a need to be with someone, to save myself from going absolutely crazy.

And making love to Shona is addictive. The more we do, the more I want. I'm so lost to Allah at this stage that nothing like this matters anymore. There's no reason to keep myself pure. Allah isn't interested after what I've already done. Even when I realised that Shona was a mother and that by not telling me, she lied to me; I convinced myself that this equalled my own lie, but it comes nothing near. It hasn't worked. I'm lost, not only to Shona but to myself.

Yesterday evening, I heard the woman in the shop talking about a man who'd been in looking for his friend. She described the man to the other lady.

'Such a tall guy he was. Lovely brown eyes though and a beautiful smile. A soft way of speaking and I loved his accent. I had an idea I'd seen the friend in the photo somewhere, though I'm not sure...'

I didn't wait to hear if she'd told Ali about me. I dropped my shopping to the floor and ran back to Shona. I've been awake most of the night and fell into a troubled sleep in the early hours. Then I woke to hear Shona's outburst in the kitchen. She's already reached breaking point. I have to let her go. Shona has to run from here too. Not with me though – In a different direction.

I go into our room where we've shared a love I never thought possible and pack up both our bags. Only what we can carry. I find Shona's little stash of money and smile. She's more resourceful then I give her credit for and I put in another five hundred Euro to keep her going. There's a university town not too far away. We'll get a bus there and that's where I'll leave her. She'll blend in and if someone spots her she won't be connected to me. I'll keep going. Ali's found me. Maybe Zarrar is with him and I need to be as far away from him, as possible, if that's the case.

Chapter thirty five

'MR MORAN?'

'Eh, Yeah?' Des fumbled with the phone beside his bed while he rubbed the sleep out of his eyes.

'Sorry to ring you so early in the morning. It's Kevin here from the Garda station. Em...   We've discovered eh... something... and I was wondering could you come and help to identify that it is your daughter that we're looking at.'

Des froze. What was he saying..? Identify his daughter..? What did he mean..? Was he saying..? A gasp escaped from his mouth causing Norah to sit up in bed in time to hear her husband ask, 'Do you mean... that she's dead..? Are you saying that you think you've found Shona's... body?' The last word was no more than a whisper.

'Jesus, no! Oh my God no. I don't mean that at all.' But Des couldn't hear Kevin's words. All he could hear was Norah's screams as she woke and heard the words dead and body.

'Des, Des can you hear me? Shona's fine. Can you hear me?'

'What the hell are you talking about?' Des shouted. 'You said you wanted me to identify Shona. What do you mean? Jesus, wait a minute.'

Des put the phone aside for the moment.

'Norah... Norah, it's alright; it was a misunderstanding. I'm trying to find out what's happening. Calm down now, love.

'Kevin, are you there? What in God's name is this all about?'

Kevin took a deep breath before he launched into an explanation about the video footage on the boat leaving Dun Laoghaire harbour. The footage wouldn't normally have been played through so thoroughly, but there had been a theft in the shop and the staff on the boat were trying to spot the culprit. The manager thought that he recognised a woman buying water in the shop as the woman who had gone missing from the Luas. He had sent it to the Gardaí. In Kevin's opinion it did look quite like Shona but he wanted them to have a look so that they could be sure.

All the time he was talking, Norah was shouting at her husband. She'd obviously got a scare when she heard Des get the wrong end of the stick earlier in the conversation. It wasn't like Kevin to be tactless with his words when dealing with families but it was the end of a long night for him and he had woken the Morans early with his request. He wished that he had waited for Tommy's phone to be answered, and dealt with him instead. He was much easier to manage. Sometimes the man seemed almost relieved that his girlfriend had disappeared. He couldn't put his finger on it but there was an abnormal kind of detachment there or a kind of acceptance of whatever might happen. Where could Tommy have been at that time of the morning with a baby? But Kevin wanted this dealt with before he went off duty and that meant dealing with the Morans.

'So do you think you could come over then? I'm only on duty for another hour.'

'We're on our way.'

Des put the phone back slowly and, still shaking, he turned to his wife. She had quietened down but was still looking at him accusingly.

He explained the story to her and the mix up in words. He was sorry. How many times had he been *sorry*?

'Come on. Let's get a move on and see if Shona has really jumped ship. Literally.'

'Did he say when the footage was taken?'

'No.'

'Did you ask?'

'No.'

'You really are a waste of space, Des Moran. Do you know that?'

'If you say so.'

There was a silence as they both got ready to leave. Eventually Norah spoke.

'It won't be her you know. I know my daughter. She would never run out on us all like that.'

'Let's just look at the video footage and see. Okay?'

'She wouldn't do that. She has her faults. I admit that but she would never walk out on her family. I know it's not her. This is a totally wasted journey.'

'So where is she then?'

Silence. At last. In fact Norah didn't speak another word all the way to the station.

*

She was still silent later as she gazed at the haunted look on her daughter's face as she paid for a bottle of water on the ferry. These security cameras were never very focussed but there was no mistaking the tiny frame and the striking features of Shona's face.

'What do you think then?' Kevin asked. But he knew the answer by looking at their faces. This was definitely Shona. She had grabbed an opportunity and legged it over to the United Kingdom. That was weeks ago. She could be anywhere.

'What happens now? Where will you look for her?' Des sounded lost as his wife continued to stare at the screen.

Kevin sat down opposite them and cleared his throat. He hated this bit.

'Actually Mr Moran, it's very difficult from here. She's not a missing person now because she wanted to leave. We wanted her in connection with what she might have seen on the Luas but the more we speak to Tommy, the more we realise that if she was as drunk as he says she was, she won't have any recollection of the man. She probably got her injuries from falling over. Because of this the Gardaí won't be searching for her anymore. She has no passport, so she couldn't go further than the United Kingdom. There are so many on the missing persons list in Ireland alone;

God knows how many people in the United Kingdom. I'm really sorry but Shona's no longer a priority for the Gardaí now.'

Kevin looked at Shona's parents. It was at times like this that his job was most difficult. Their faces might not have looked much different if they *had* come in to identify Shona's body. They weren't just experiencing loss but the hurt that comes from the betrayal of someone they loved. His gaze shifted back to Shona's picture. Her face looked disturbing. What troubles had haunted this family over the years? He pressed a key and Shona was gone.

Des stood up awkwardly, helping his wife to her feet. He took a deep breath and reached out to shake hands with the Garda who had been so much a part of their lives these past few weeks.

'Thanks... for all your help', he managed.

Kevin shook hands. There was nothing left to say.

*

'Stupid bitch!' Des skimmed the side of the pillar as he swerved into the driveway. 'Stupid bloody bitch!'

Norah sat in the passenger seat shaking and feeling sick. Des had sped all the way back from the Garda station. Until now he had always been the most careful driver she knew. She froze in her seat as he fumbled his way out of the car and slammed the door. She had never seen her husband so furious. Des, the calming influence in their marriage. Where was he now? Who was this monster? Des never slammed doors. But Bang! He nearly took the front door off its hinges.

She knew she should follow him in but she couldn't move. She should try to calm him but she wouldn't know where to start. Her husband was the one who smoothed things over; the calm person who made the wrongs right. Des was Mr Fixit.

'Des....' Norah whispered her husband's name. Even as she spoke, she knew it was a waste of breath. Des couldn't even help himself right now.

Norah sat in the car and wished she had learned to drive. She wasn't sure whether she wanted to escape to somewhere else

201

or to drive herself off the nearest bridge. She thought of her grandchild. Her need. She was the most important part of her life. When did it stop being Shona and before that when did it stop being Des?

At twenty, Norah had loved Des Moran with all her heart, mind and soul. Her glorious married life stretched out ahead of her with her wonderful husband; father of the cherished children they would have. They shared the same dreams. Des would work really hard and set up his own building business and as soon as Norah got pregnant she would leave her job in the local library and stay at home and bring up their children. She was a woman. Having children was her birth right. When their house outgrew them they would move themselves and their offspring to a bigger house. It was all planned.

Norah did get pregnant and she left her job, but she miscarried and she was too upset to go back to work. So she set out to get pregnant again. No problem. Their love making had been wonderfully intimate and Norah had never said no to the love of her life. Getting pregnant was the easy part. She held on to that one a little longer, but not long enough. Norah's third baby lasted to full term and she would never forget the pain and the elation of bringing her baby girl into the world. Maria Elizabeth Moran had died aged twenty minutes and was buried with all the other little angels in Glasnevin cemetery. Most of Des and Norah Moran died with her. Nothing was ever to equal those first few years of marriage. Going back to work was an admission of failure so Norah stayed at home and became the parish's most willing volunteer.

Des refused to risk another baby. No more love making. No more intimacy. No more babies. Just a great big gaping hole in their lives. They had never made love again in all their years of marriage. A few fumbles after a party sometimes, but one or other of them pulled away before it got too far. Norah had never made love to anyone else since she got married but she had her suspicions about her husband.

It was Des who had first broached the idea of adoption. Norah had nearly fallen in love with him all over again when they had one-year-old Shona screaming her head off in the cot in the spare bedroom that was a nursery at last. They would adopt again and perhaps a third time. They would be a proper family at last. The end of their troubles.

But the nightmare was only beginning. Bringing up Shona, Des and Norah Moran wondered what they had done to deserve all this. They couldn't adopt another child. They wouldn't be able for another. From baby to toddler to child to teenager to adult, Shona took hold of her parents and shook the living daylights out of them.

They were still shaking. Des was right. Shona was a stupid, selfish, first class bitch. She didn't deserve their love and care. She didn't deserve Thomas who, God love him, only ever did his best. Most of all she didn't deserve her beautiful child who had come to her with such ease. From now on Norah would be all the mother that Ruby needed and more.

She opened the car door slowly and followed her husband. Mrs O'Connor's net curtains twitched and Norah was very tempted to stick up her two fingers at the window. That cow must have enough material for a good book on the Morans at this stage. Eighteen years' worth. Norah waved and smiled.

Chapter thirty six

'DAD?' Shona's voice shook as she leaned on the phone booth for strength.

'Shona? My God, where are you? Are you okay?'

'I'm fine, Dad. I'm so sorry. I...' Shona could feel everything that her father had been through in his few short words.

'It's okay, Shona. It's okay. Where are you, love? Are you back?'

Shona clung to the telephone in her hand. Why didn't he shout and scream at her, and hate her for what she had done? It would be easier.

'No, Dad. I'm not back. I wish I was but I can't yet. I'm too scared. Too ashamed.'

'Shona, you're upset. Come home, sweetheart. We'll sort it out. Whatever it is. We will, Shona. We know you. Your mum and me... we'll look after you. Where are you Shona? Come home.'

Shona pictured her dad standing in the hall by the telephone table, polished to gleaming by her mother that morning. The wireless phone meant nothing to Des. He took all his calls standing beside a vase of dried, faded, orange flowers, reflected in the mirror alongside his face. How would he look now? Had her latest madness left a few more wrinkles or were there no more places to crease? He had no idea, as yet, that she had run away with another man. None of them knew.

'You've always looked after me, Dad... and Mum too, before she gave up on me. I don't blame her... and even Tommy at one time, but not now... and they're right, I'm no use. You're all better off if I stay over here.'

'That's not true Shona! But where? Where's over there? Are you in England? Are you in London? Have you somewhere to stay?

Have you money, Shona? And you're wrong, love. Your mum has never given up on you.' Des was falling over all the questions that had been going through his head for weeks. All the bad things he had said about his daughter fading amid the importance of knowing that she was safe.

'Yes, Dad. I've money. I'm okay. Dad, I can't come home yet. I can't... I'm in Wales. In a university town called Aberystwyth. I've moved again...'

'Again Shona? What do you mean? Why? Are you in trouble, Shona? Are you in danger?'

'No, Dad. Nothing like that. I told you... I'm fine, alright?'

'Shona tell me where you are. Give me an address. I want to come and see that you're okay.' He sounded frantic.

Shona stood crying with the telephone in her hand and her backpack over her shoulder. It carried the few things that Jameel had packed for her before he dragged her from the beach and they came to this town. The anonymity of the student town would be much easier to hide away in, he said. Shona knew she could go home and her father would forgive her but she wasn't ready to face her family yet. The confidence that Jameel had built in her had been blasted to pieces when he deserted her... again.

Shona listened to her father's breathing as he struggled to know what to say to her. She should keep on talking; make it easier for him, but she couldn't get her thoughts around the words that she wanted to say, the questions that plagued her.

About the past. Where am I from? Who am I? Why am I the way I am?

About the present. How was Ruby? Some questions she had no right to ask.

Shona made a keening noise. She drew the phone close to her face to feel they were near her.

'I love you, Dad.' She brought her fingers down on the button to cut the connection between them before her father could hear the sobs come gasping up from her chest. Leaning her head against the side of the phone booth, Shona let the sound of her crying work in rhythm with her shaking body. She stayed there

205

long enough to let the grief work its way through her. When the tears lessened, the sea began to come into focus for Shona and she stared out at the waves letting them rock back and forth in her mind as she soaked in their comfort. She had been in this place before. Letting the waves hypnotise her. Seducing her with their softness. Beckoning her. Inviting. It would be so easy…

'Are you alright, dear?' Shona jumped at the woman's voice. The sea breeze circled her feet, wakening her from her reverie and she stared at the face of the woman.

'You seem so upset and… well I saw that you were crying on my way down to the shop and now I'm on my way back and you're still here, and I wondered… I hope you don't think I'm being too nosy but… well I couldn't go home and ignore you… It wouldn't seem right. Have you had some bad news, dear? Do you have someone to go to? Someone who'll listen?' Shona smiled a troubled smile at the warmth of the old lady with the sing-song voice and allowed herself to be filled with her care and kindness.

'You could talk to me, dear, if you needed to. We could sit on this bench over here and talk if you wanted to.'

The woman held out her hand to Shona who then realised that she was still clasping the telephone and replaced it. She felt herself being led slowly to the bench facing out to the sea. They sat quietly for a while, the wrinkled sea-worn woman seeming quite content to hold Shona's hand on her lap and stare out to sea with her. They looked an odd couple if anyone had been bothered to notice. Blue jeans, fleece and trainers holding hands with grey mac, woollen hat and black boots. Backpack and shopping trolley sitting side by side at their feet.

'My name's Bridget, dear. Bridget Jones.' Shona smiled at the familiar name.

'Nice modern name I have all of a sudden, eh? It's like an alias.' Bridget chuckled showing her toothless smile once more and her eyes creased up with mirth.

'Niamh Moran,' replied Shona, deciding her middle name was best for now, and she smiled at Bridget's use of the word alias.

'You're from Ireland?' Bridget let go of her hand and sat back a little more comfortably on the bench. 'My mother was originally from Ireland too. Donegal. She met my father in London and they came back here to his family to live. Eleven of us there were. I'm the youngest. Was. They're all gone now. I didn't get married. Too busy looking after my parents in their old age. By the time my father eventually died at the young age of ninety-eight, it was too late for me. I should've run away from home when I was sixteen. That's what my eldest sister did. Ran to Hollywood no less. Became a movie star. Never knew her. She never came back. Not ever. I would've had a husband and my own family to rear. All I ever wanted was a little baby to hold.'

Suddenly she stopped. 'Honestly, listen to me prattling on and on after me telling you to talk to me. You're shivering, dear. Are you cold? Will we go back to my house? I'll make some tea. You can smile all you like, dear; but it really does cure lots of things does a cup of tea. Will you drag that trolley for me, dear? The wheel's wonky and my back's not great.'

Having listened to Bridget's non-stop chatter, Shona was amazed when they walked back to her house in companionable silence. She thought about Bridget's wish for a baby and wondered what she would think if she knew that Shona had abandoned hers in Dublin – as well as a good man.

She followed the woman home without thought to why she was going or who Bridget was. She wasn't surprised when she was led into a terraced cottage across from the pier. It stood out from the others with its tired façade against their brightly-painted fronts. The inside was no different. Bridget was an extension of her house, or it was an extension of her. Shabby yet comfortable. She threw off her boots at the door and slipped on her elderly house shoes. They could have been her father's before he died. Shona tried to hide her smile and allowed the moment to cheer her. Three or four cats came out of the woodwork to welcome Bridget while eyeing up Shona suspiciously.

'I'll stick on the kettle now and I'll make us a nice omelette.'

Shona was starving but she wasn't sure about the eating and drinking thing. It was quite obvious that cleanliness and hygiene were not really Bridget's strength, but Bridget was already breaking eggs and turning on the radio. A habit probably; a voice to keep her company.

'Right, so. A couple of slices of toast I think and I'll do some beans. You look hungry, Niamh.'

Shona reddened when she realised that she had been staring at the food preparation intently. She hadn't eaten since the small bite of toast that morning, but she had been looking after herself until now and she promised herself she would again. She even thought that she had put on some weight. Without warning Shona felt the rub of fur along her feet.

'How many cats have you got?'

'Well, you see, I had six but two died a few months ago – one in a car accident and his sister died of a broken heart shortly after. I'm in the habit of taking waifs and strays in off the road but you're the first human one.'

Shona looked up. Bridget's eyes were full of mirth once more and she smiled back. Their companionable silence returned while Bridget busied herself with her cuisine and they ate the results with gusto.

'Food always tastes better when you have someone to share it with. So, Niamh. Do you want to tell me what's breaking your heart then or am I going to have to chat away to myself for the rest of the day like I always do?'

Shona put down her knife and fork and pushed the plate to the side. 'That was really delicious, Bridget.' She picked up her tea and wrapped her hands around the mug.

'I've abandoned my baby in Dublin.' As always, Shona went for the shock factor.

Bridget picked up her own mug and hugged it close. It seemed she would need the same armour as her guest to get through this story. She stayed still as Shona spilled her heart out but at certain points of the story, Bridget's body parts moved of their own accord. No doubt she was wondering what she had brought into her house? She stared at Shona as if she was unable to speak.

Shona took Bridget's silence for disapproval. She leaned on the table and pushed herself into a standing position. The telling had drained her.

'I'll leave you then Bridget. Thanks... for listening and thanks for the food and tea. Please don't tell anyone what I've told you. I know it's terrible but I didn't *want* any of it to happen. I wanted to... to be loved, properly. To feel romance, some sort of sense of belonging. I messed up. I know. Big time. I'm sorry. I really am.'

Shona was at the front door now feeling her way through her tears. She looked back towards the stranger in the kitchen who she had overwhelmed with her whole mess and she continued. In for a penny.

'I don't know how to go back. I don't know if I should go back or leave them all in peace. They've been through enough. I'm the worst person I know. I'm not fit to be a mother or a daughter. I *should* stay away from them. It would be easier for everyone.'

She turned again and fumbled for the unfamiliar door handle, but before she could get out she felt Bridget's hand on her shoulder turning her around and pulling her tiny frame into the older woman's great softness.

They both cried for all their empty years and empty hearts and when they had cried it all out, they smiled and laughed at the absurdity of this place they found themselves, and each other.

Shona moved her few belongings into Bridget's spare room and enjoyed being mothered. Bridget sat back and enjoyed being looked after while she waited for Shona to find her feet. She knew that Shona would eventually go back to Dublin, and of course that's what she wanted, but Bridget knew she wouldn't fill that gap again. Each day that Shona stayed was like a gift.

Chapter thirty seven

'JAMEEL... Jameel, wake up. Wake up, Jameel!' I can hear Ali's voice and feel him pushing me, but I'm too weak to respond. I've been waiting days and nights for him, but he never came. I needed food. Water. I screamed my anger at the four walls. I shouted my fear at the window. I talked to myself and told myself over and over that Ali would come. There was no way of getting to the toilet and eventually the smell in the room overpowered me and made me retch. As the days went by and my hunger and thirst grew inside me, clawing at me, I lay on the mattress. This bedroom that was a place of refuge and beauty with Shona has become a prison.

Now here's Ali and I can't answer him. I can't move or open my eyes, but I can hear and remember... Minutes after walking away from Shona, Ali passed me in his car. Those eyes, that smile; stopping me in my tracks and once more Ali led me away. He talked me into it. There was nowhere else to go. There was no one else to help. Only Ali.

We drove back along the road to squat once more in this bungalow by the sea that Shona and I had abandoned. Ali gave me tea and food and I lay on the bed and drifted into a sleep. When I woke up I was tied to the bed and he was gone.

'Jameel. I had to go away. I'm sorry. Zarrar said we had to find her and I had to go with him. I thought it would only be for a day, but there was so much to be resolved. We need to find Shona, Jameel. Where might she be? Where can she have gone?'

What's Ali saying? Zarrar wants Shona? No.

'I'm sorry. I knew you had no food. I knew you'd be in a terrible state, but I couldn't do anything. I couldn't tell Zarrar that you were still alive. He thinks I killed you the day after you messed up in Dublin and that I dumped your body way out in the sea. Jameel... Jameel... I should have let you go then. What am I to do with you? What can we do?'

I hear the words... I should have let you go then... What does Ali mean? He should have let me go free? Or he should have let me die? I can't ask him. My lips are too parched to open. Ali lifts me gently from the mattress and holds a cup to my mouth. I gasp as the wetness fills my mouth. I feel like I'm drowning and then I splutter.

'That's enough for now,' he says. 'We'll try again in a moment.' Then he helps me to lie back down and I close my eyes. I see Omar surrounded by a lovely bright light and I cry out for him... 'Omar...' A hoarse whisper.

Here in the room by the sea, I long for him. My parents sacked Omar and Karima because of me, but Omar never blamed me. Or did he? Did he die hating me for what I did? At least he died at home in his beloved Pakistan, surrounded by the family who loved him, and not in Saudi where he would never be anything more than a servant.

I'm weak and hungry and I let the tears fall now. I can hear the emptiness in Ali's words; feel the uselessness of hanging on. He is untying my hands and feet.

'Try to sit up, Jameel, I'll help you to the bathroom. Lie in the bath for a while. I'll take your clothes out to the garden with this mattress and I'll dump them. I should burn them, but that will only attract attention. I need to deal with these flies too. Then we will eat and drink more. I will help you to recover. After that we will move from here. I feel Zarrar knows that I am hiding something. He has known me all my life. We were school friends. It won't be long before he finds us. If I found you that easily...'

I allow myself to be drawn by Ali. I've no choice. Where's Shona? I'll make Ali go far away from here and far away from Aberystwyth to keep her safe. I pull myself up to sit and cry out with the pain of everything.

Chapter thirty eight

TOMMY was settling into life without Shona with alarming ease. He had woken that Monday morning with a great sense of *joie de vivre*. He knew it was absolutely disgraceful to feel this way when the mother of your child had disappeared off the face of the earth, but if the truth were known, he was absolutely delighted with himself.

The day after the Luas incident, when the Gardaí had said they would be looking for Shona, Tommy had experienced a very scary feeling of something bordering on… regret? He had been disgusted with himself, and apart from his meltdown in the pub with Mick, he had gone out of his way not to let anyone guess at how he was feeling. Over the first few days though, as Shona still hadn't appeared, the Detective Inspector's questions had become more and more probing. He had asked Tommy about their relationship and Tommy had stammered his way through answers that even he didn't believe sounded plausible. Did he think that Tommy had something to do with her disappearance? It had certainly seemed like it. The DI and Garda Daly had played good cop, bad cop with Tommy until he felt like screaming. He was glad it was all over. Though the memories still sat in his stomach at times like a chronic case of indigestion. Those questions…

'Where do you think your girlfriend might be?'

'I don't know'.

'You don't know or you don't care, Mr Farrell?'

'I don't… know!'

'*I* see. So Shona has a problem with drink..? Is that right?'

'We've been through this line of questionin' before. You already know everythin' that there is to know about me and my family.'

'Do you hate her Mr Farrell?'

'No!'

'Do you hope that she doesn't come back?'

'For God's sake no!'

The DI had leaned forward in his chair towards Tommy and asked; 'Has there been any history of violence between the two of you during your time together?'

Tommy's stomach lurched as he remembered all the times that Shona had lashed out at him, both verbally and physically, when she was either drunk or hungover.

'No,' he had lied. 'Shona's never been violent.'

'I meant *you* Mr Farrell. Have you ever shown any violence to Shona before?'

Now, many weeks after the event, Tommy had a good chuckle to himself remembering this question. Imagine anyone attempting to smack Shona. They'd have their work cut out for them. He hadn't felt it was so funny at the time. The question from the DI had sent him fuming. The memory of him sitting on his hands, wanting to smack this fella in the gob, still soured in his stomach. He had felt the anger rising in him; the way it did when Shona would begin to rile him, and Tommy had jumped to his feet and shouted.

'You have some cheek sittin' there and pointin' the finger at me. Shona's gone missin'! It's not unusual for this to happen, you know but she *will* be back. She always is!' Even as he was saying the words he had known it was the wrong response.

Tommy had taken a deep breath to calm himself. 'I'd like you to leave now.' Another breath. 'Look, I know that you've got Shona's welfare at heart and I appreciate that you've done your best to look for her but...you see...Shona'll be back...at some stage. At heart she's a good person. It's the bloody drink that causes all the trouble. She's tried...we've all tried...but it's no use. There isn't any point in all this. Leave us in peace now...eh?'

When Garda Daly's number had flashed up on his phone early the following morning he had let it ring out. Whatever it was he didn't want to deal with it.

As it turned out, if ever there was a call he wished he had answered, it was that one. He would love to have been there when the video footage proved that Shona *had* done a runner. It would have given him great pleasure to see her sailing away from him. He was delighted to hear that the Gardaí were no longer looking for her. He certainly wouldn't be looking for her himself. A perfect break.

Especially for Ruby. She was so young now that it was all for the best. When Shona did return, as she inevitably would, she wasn't coming back to live with him, and if that meant going back to live with his dad then that was fine with him.

The relief he felt at not having Shona around was immeasurable. As far as Tommy was concerned, everything had turned out in everyone's favour. Everyone who knew Shona needed a break from her and she was providing them with exactly that, but Shona would be back. Of that Tommy was sure.

That Monday evening, Tommy was in the kitchen cooking his dinner. He was becoming very proud of his culinary abilities. A selection of cookery books on the shelf in the kitchen had been the basis of his trial and error attempts. He was looking forward to sitting down in the knowledge that nothing would interrupt him. Peace and quiet.

Babies needed routine. That's what everyone was always telling him. From now on that's exactly what Ruby would get. Life would become dull and boring. What bliss.

The doorbell interrupted his thoughts.

'Jesus, if that's Norah Moran come to whinge about her daughter to me again, I'll bloody well send her packin'.'

He took the pasta off the boil before he headed towards the door. It rang again before he got to it.

Definitely Norah. Nobody else would be that rude or impatient.

But for the first time in six months, Tommy was disappointed not to see Shona's mother. Instead there were no less than three Gardaí standing on the doorstep. One was Kevin Daly. One was the Detective Inspector back to haunt him and the third was a newcomer, looking hot off the training ground.

'Mr Farrell, eh… Tommy. Sorry to intrude like this. Can we come in?'

'Is it very important? I'm dishin' up my dinner.'

'Actually, Tommy… we've a warrant to search your house. I'm really sorry.'

Garda Daly took in Tommy's perplexed face. 'If you let us in, the DI will explain, while my colleague and myself look around.'

Tommy stood back speechless.

'Sit down, Tommy.' The DI ushered him into the sitting room.

'What the hell's this all about?'

'This is complicated stuff so I'm going to come right out with it. We've found evidence that links Shona with the terrorist who planted the bomb on the Luas. We think that…'

'Are you completely mad or what? There's no way on earth Shona was remotely involved with that crap.' Tommy found himself laughing then at the absurdity of it all. 'Somebody's made a complete muck up of somethin' here and you're wastin' your time.'

'Tommy, am I right in saying that you and Shona were estranged from each other in many ways?'

Tommy stared at the DI to try and figure out what he was getting at, but he hadn't a clue what was going on.

'We…had our problems…Yeah.'

'Tommy, we've found photographic evidence that your girlfriend was… romantically involved… with Jameel Al Manhal. Shona certainly knew him.'

Tommy was handed a blown up photo of a group of teenagers together in a coffee shop. At a table in the background, Shona was reaching her hand out to touch Jameel Al Manhal's cheek and was looking into his eyes lovingly. She had never looked at Tommy like that. But Shona… and *him*? Tommy felt like he'd been punched in the stomach. He remembered now thinking that he had heard Jameel's name before. Tommy had swallowed this piece of information at the time, not wanting it to have any significance on what had happened. And looking at the smugness on the DI's face now, he was more determined than ever not to divulge what he was thinking, but the sight of the photo made him feel sick.

'Oh, Jesus,' he thought. 'Please don't let this be happening.' He stood up and faced the DI.

'Big deal!'

The DI raised his eyebrows in mock disbelief.

'So she met the man. It's a small town.' Tommy mumbled.

'Too many coincidences Tommy. She was on the Luas that day.'

'I swear to God, she was so drunk that day gettin' on the Luas, she didn't even know her own name.'

'She still managed to get off without you Tommy. Without anybody seeing her. She managed to make her way the very next morning to the ferry, and to the UK, in perfect disguise. No one's seen her since. Except the man who was with her when she sustained those injuries to her face. If Shona's not involved in all this voluntarily, as you say, Tommy; then you have to agree that she's in a hell of a lot of danger if she's still with these fellas.

'She was seen leaving town with a man on a motorbike. We think that must have been Al Manhal. The person who saw her said it could have been the man, but she only saw his back. Jameel had a motorbike and it turns out that a motorbike that was found in a car park in Dun Laoghaire a week after that boat sailed, and is covered with his finger prints. And Shona's.'

Tommy was shaking now. How could this be happening? No. He shook his head. It wasn't true.

'Fellas?' asked Tommy. 'There's more than one?'

'Tommy. We've been following a lead to a suspected planned attack by Islamic fundamentalists on Shannon Airport. We were trailing two men from Pakistan before we found the bomb on the Luas. We think that this bomb was meant to get to Shannon. It's something to do with the American army stopping off to refuel in Ireland.

'You have to help us to find this guy. These other two men… we know their names… or the names that they're using. They've been tracked to Wales as well. We think they're with Al Manhal.

And with Shona. Tommy, we have to stop these mad men in their path before some real damage happens. Before people get killed.'

'You're mistaken.' Tommy put his head in his hands. This crazy nightmare was getting worse. He looked back up at the DI. 'She was in the wrong place at the wrong time. Shona could probably organise a piss up in a brewery, but that'd be the extent of her organisational skills. She couldn't have coordinated anythin' like this. She also has no political opinions, one way or the other, except durin' the budget when they up the price of a pint. She's never even heard of Islamic fundamentalism.'

They were interrupted by the green looking child-Garda holding a plastic bag containing a book, and looking very pleased with himself.

'Sir, we've found a book written in Arabic in Ms Moran's room. It looks like it may be a copy of the Qur'an, but I'm not sure. There are lots of pages where whole chapters are highlighted by hand.'

'Thanks, John. Bag it and keep looking.' The DI shot a look of victory over at Tommy. 'There's definitely a link. I think that Shona knew Jameel well and I think if we find her she'll be able to help us track him down, along with any others that were involved in all this in Ireland and maybe in the UK as well.

'Tommy; we were shadowing something really big with these guys before the Luas and we think there's plenty more to come. Your girlfriend is a bloody goldmine right now. This lot of mad men haven't finished with us here yet, Tommy. Not by a long shot. Their man on the ground mucked up big time as far as they're concerned, but they'll be back to finish the job. We just have to make sure we get to them first. I believe Shona can help us with that. I'm sure that's why she did a runner. It had nothing to do with escaping her family and I'm going to find her if it's the last thing I do.'

Tommy staggered back down into the seat and tried to take it all in.

A few weeks ago they had been playing happy families. Shona had been dry for ages and had decided that she was cured. Again.

She had delighted in the domesticity of organising a picnic for her birthday in Stephen's Green.

Now the same woman had thrown their lives into disarray no less than three times. First they thought she was missing. Then she had breezed off to the UK. Now this. Shona Moran, mother, daughter and dipsomaniac was wanted by the Gardaí for aiding and abetting Islamic terrorists.

I guess that figures about right, thought Tommy. Terrorists come in many shapes and sizes and Shona had been terrorising him since the day he met her. Fuck her this time though. Absolutely. Fuck. Her!

Later that night, Tommy went in to check Ruby. She was in his bed as she hadn't been able to settle in her cot. No doubt she was feeling her daddy's tension. Ruby had wriggled out of the blanket so Tommy slipped it back over her and kissed her forehead, careful not to wake her.

He lay down on the bed now beside her and wondered would Shona ever see her daughter take her first steps? Would she ever come back? She had never gone that far away before but did he even want her to come back? He was afraid to answer that right now. Would Shona be able to prove her innocence? Was she actually innocent? Tommy felt the anxious sleep of their child beside him… and pronounced Shona guilty…of something anyway.

Chapter thirty nine

TOMMY was listening to the radio and slamming the breakfast dishes into the dishwasher. The programme was about Shona. Well it wasn't really about Shona, it just seemed like that as it made him think of her and he didn't want to think about her. In fact he wished that he could erase the name Shona from his whole life. The Irish media had become obsessed with talk of 'the war on terror'...

...The Irish have barely finished with their own war on terror... lasted for hundreds of years and the last thing we need is to take on someone else's war... nothing to do with us...

On it droned. There was a fear that something awful was about to happen. The media fuelled the fire, with their constant talk of what was to come. Arabs, especially students, were looked on suspiciously by people who had never given them a moment's thought beforehand. Occasionally Ms Shona Moran's name would be mentioned as someone who was needed by Gardaí *to help them with their enquiries.* Tommy shivered whenever he heard her name mentioned.

Everything on the television, radio and newspapers reminded him of Shona. Apart from news items, there were discussions on alcoholism. Tommy would listen in fascination as he recalled how much they had all suffered, including Shona.

There were adverts on places of refuge for people who were being abused. Tommy felt abused. Not physically, but mentally he felt that Shona had wrecked his head. Maybe he should get some professional help. He could imagine what his aul' fella'd have to say if he told him he was going to see some quack.

Shona was pounding away in his head as if she had never left.

This woman who, let's face it, he didn't even know very well. They had shared a house and then a kid for a few months, but they had hardly ever had a serious discussion about anything. Screaming verbal abuse had been their chosen method of communication for the first while, followed by a silent indifference later.

This woman that he wanted to deny, was so much a part of his life, she was pulling him down with her. His life and fatherhood had been so scarred by Shona. Six months of bringing home her turbulent struggles had left them reeling. For so long he had wished that she would disappear out of their lives and he had got his wish, but she had left a tidal wave in her wake, which was threatening to engulf them all.

Tommy was telling himself to snap out of it when he noticed a Garda getting out of her car outside his house.

'Jaysus. They're sendin' in the women now', said Tommy. 'The DI's probably tryin' a different approach with me. Softly, softly. See if you can get him to open up and spill the beans. When's he goin' to get the message that there are no beans to spill, or if there are, that I haven't got any of them?'

Tommy thought about not answering the door, but to hell with it. They'd only come back again later.

'Yes?' Tommy stared the woman out.

'Tommy. My name's Chief Superintendent O'Grady from the Special Detective Unit in Harcourt Street.' Tommy shrugged his shoulders. A Garda was a Garda.

'Come in.' Tommy led the way into the kitchen, the only clean room in the house. This was as far as he'd got. He'd probably never get the rest of the house clean now before he had to go into work. 'Sit down.'

'So...Shona Moran...terrorist.' Tommy spoke with an exaggerated stage whisper. Then he held her in a stare until she looked away, uncomfortable in his mockery.

'Before we even start, let me tell you that this whole conversation is a waste of time. Your DI... It's like he's after a bitch-in-heat the way he's goin' on at the moment, but the bitch is actually not hot at all and he's barkin' up the wrong tree.'

Chief Superintendent O'Grady looked back at the mad man sitting at the kitchen table as if she didn't know where to start.

Tommy sighed. 'So, what do you want to know?'

'I know you've told the DI a lot before but why don't you tell me about Shona? Not only about who she is, but why you think that she'd have nothing to do with terrorism?'

'Easy question. Easy answer. She doesn't have the capability. Shona's a very bad mother. She's a crap person to live with. She's a useless daughter. She can't hold a friend. She has no ambition. Does she have views on things that matter in life? I don't know. She never told me.'

That was the crux of the matter. He didn't know. She never told him anything. So she could be everything that the DI thought she was. Or she could be just a screwed up mess of a girl who fell for the wrong man. Where was she? For the first time ever, he wished she was here so that he could bombard her with questions.

'You see… the Shona that I know wouldn't have managed to hide for weeks from everyone who was lookin' for her. The money that she had in her bag to pay for the buggy would've run out by now. Shona has never had a job since the day she met a mug that would keep her. Now don't get me wrong, she's very clever. Whatever brain cells haven't been drowned in alcohol are sharp and inventive enough, but up to now they've only been used to work out where her next drink is comin' from or how to get herself out of the drunken scrapes that she lands herself in.'

Then a thought that scared him. The weeks before the bomb on the Luas, Shona had strived to stay sober. Apart from her pregnancy, it was the longest stretch she had managed since he met her. Why was she that determined? He had been so taken aback with the way things were going that it never occurred to him that she might have had an ulterior motive. Perhaps she was working towards something else.

'Something's dawned on you Tommy. What is it?'

'Ah, nothin'. Sure me head's wrecked with all this crap.'

'Tommy… the Qur'an that was found in Shona's room. How do you figure that got there? Why would she have such a thing? Her

221

finger prints, and that of Al Manhal's, were all over it.'

'I haven't a clue. She probably shoved it in her bag when she was drunk and never gave it a second thought. Maybe your man gave it to her. I don't know. What were the bits that were highlighted anyway?'

'They're well known passages that are learned off by heart by people setting out on a jihad. They're parts of the Qur'an that could be understood to have a different meaning, which could encourage Muslims to believe that certain acts of terrorism would delight Allah and give them an immediate passage to heaven. It's a load of rubbish, of course. Just as Christians can take different meanings from what's written in the Bible, so it is with the Qur'an. Plenty of crimes have been committed in the past where the criminal quoted verses from the Bible as their justification. It's not the Bible, or the Qur'an that's at fault. It's the interpretation of the words, but we can take words from anywhere and put different connotations on them. Jameel's mentor probably zoned in on his fears and aspirations in life and suggested meanings that would motivate him into doing what he did. Jameel, in return, could have worked on Shona in the same way.'

Tommy's brain was in overdrive now. Had Jameel Al Manhal translated these verses to Shona? Had he managed somehow to woo her into believing in his cause? Had Shona needed something like this to lean on? Was this what spurred her into going on the dry with Al Manhal as her hero for being the one who helped her to see the light? Was the fact that it was Shona's birthday anything to do with his choice of timing?

'Tommy? What state of mind was Shona in, leading up to the time that we found the bomb? Was she any different than she had been?'

Oh she's good this one, thought Tommy. She can even read effin' minds. Definitely the expert.

'She was off the drink. It was because our little girl had a bit of an accident. It gave her a fright. That's all it was. Nothin' else. Nothin' sinister. She decided to come off the booze and she was doin' really well until that day. I don't know where she went or who she met that afternoon, but when I found her she was pissed out of her mind.'

'So something or someone must have really upset her that day? To send her over the edge again. When she'd been doing really well. Wouldn't you say?'

Tommy went silent. He had no answers any more. What was this cow trying to do? Make him change his mind, so that he would remember something that might incriminate Shona?

'Look. I have to go to work soon. I know nothin' about Shona that could help you find what you're lookin' for and I certainly know nothin' about your missin' terrorist. Can we finish up here?'

'Of course. I'm really sorry to have taken so much of your time, but there's one more thing that you might help with. We've been looking for Shona for weeks now and apart from the boat there hasn't been any real sighting of her whatsoever… but we also had a sighting of Jameel.'

That got Tommy's attention. 'Where? Where is he?'

'We don't know where he is now, Tommy or I wouldn't be here talking to you, but I know where he was and who he was with. Further investigation on the video footage of Shona leaving on the ferry to Holyhead revealed her to have a fellow passenger.'

Tommy went pale. His worst fears were confirmed. Shona had left them for this mad man.

O'Grady leaned over towards Tommy with her head in her hands and asked the question as if their lives depended on it.

'They're together somewhere, Tommy. Why do you think that we haven't been able to find them? What do you think has happened to her?'

Images of Shona tumbled across Tommy's line of vision.

Shona drunk in a ditch somewhere, but then wouldn't she be found by someone?

Shona trying to stay sober, hiding from everyone, but she'd need people to help her stay on the straight and narrow. She always had.

Shona running from responsibilities; absolutely determined to get clear of Tommy and Ruby, but she'd still need people to help her cover up.

Had she run to some safe house in the UK? Were the Gardaí right all along and he couldn't see it? Sure at the end of the day, he hardly knew the girl. Was she being protected by friends of Al Manhal? They'd soon see her for what she was. She could never be trusted.

Then the worst image, but the one that was pushing out in front of all the other images. Shona murdered? For her part in mucking up the plans in Dublin. Her body disposed of.

For fuck's sake. This woman had really succeeded where the DI had failed. She was getting inside his head and twisting the facts around. She knew how vulnerable he was right now. Tommy was beginning to see things that an hour ago he wouldn't have thought possible. He felt exhausted and he was now in no fit state to face work.

He slammed his fist down on the table.

'I don't know where Shona is! I don't know what's happened to her. I haven't a clue what she's done, if she's done anythin'. I don't understand why you can't find her. I know that for the last six months she messed with our lives pretty bad. But you lot. You're completely destroyin' our family. I know nothin'. I've done nothin'. My baby's done nothin' and we've suffered enough.'

Tommy pushed back his chair and stood up.

'If Shona gets in touch with me, I'll let you know. Now I'm finished talkin' to you. All of you. Please … Go… Leave us in peace.'

When she had left, Tommy rang in sick to work. Then he lay down on the couch with his back to the room.

'You never left, Shona. You're still here. You couldn't even leave us properly. Go. Go on. Get out of here. Leave us in peace. Get out of our lives. Get out of my head.'

Tommy could feel that visit to the shrink creeping up on him.

Chapter forty

I WAKE up at first light and gasp for breath. I'm sweating and shivering at the same time. The nightmare came again. I am in the family room back in Riyadh. Karima's serving us our breakfast and she's smiling. Then Baba says something to her and Karima's face gets angry. Her head gets larger and larger and it becomes Shadia's face until eventually it explodes. Then I wake up. It's a ridiculous dream, but it's what happens in my head now every time I close my eyes. It's horrific, but not as bad as the thoughts I have when I'm awake. I think of what I almost did in Ireland. I imagine the carnage that my actions would have caused, the grief within so many families, the aftermath of my life if, no when, I was caught.

There are times when I know I should get up and walk out of here. Turning myself in might atone, in some way, for what I've done. I know this house. I would find a way to escape from Ali. But he's here now. I can hear him in the sitting room, praying. He admonishes me each prayer time for my lack of words. He says my bad dreams are Allah's response to my abandonment of him. But there's nothing that I can say to Allah to make better the sins I've committed. I close my ears to the sound of Ali's verses. The familiarity of them sits in my stomach with the urge to turn back time. So I shut them out. Ali and Allah.

'I prayed for you this morning.' Ali's back in the room with me. The door's unlocked. If I had the energy I could run now. But I'm so tired. 'And for your girlfriend too.' There is malice in his voice whenever he refers to Shona. 'I prayed that I find her before Zarrar, Jameel. What do you want for her? To die by my hand, swiftly and painlessly, or to die with Zarrar who is so angry now there is no saying what he would be capable of if he gets his hands on her.' Ali puts his face in front of mine. 'It will be slow. You may be sure of that. And painful. Very painful.' He moves back towards the door. 'I am leaving you now. If I don't find Shona Moran before I get back to you again then... we are finished... all of us.'

I sit up and stare at the door after he leaves. It's open as if he's willing me to get out. His face when he spoke of Zarrar's anger was terrifying. I move to stand and dizziness pulls me down again. There's no use in trying to go. I've no force left in me.

The shivering I woke up with hasn't left me yet. Ali says there's food in the kitchen but I haven't gone there to eat for some time. I don't even know how long. I choke on anything I put in my mouth. I can hear the waves crash on the beach outside. Each loud splash reminds me of Shona and the danger she's in. What if Zarrar were to torture me? Would I be able to keep her whereabouts a secret or would I scream the name of the town where I left her?

I drag myself to stand with the aid of a nearby chair. I can't help Shona, but I won't be a part of her downfall anymore. It's time to put a permanent end to all this madness. Shadia died because I told her to have one more ride on a carousel. Omar is dead as a result of the stress caused by my actions in Pakistan. Ali hates me because I failed to help him to speed up the release of his brother in Guantanamo Bay.

Shona is all that is left, but I'm a constant danger to her. The best thing I can do now is to find something in this house that will help me to leave the pain behind. To let go.

It's only when I reach the bathroom that I'm aware that I'm sobbing. The hurt that's built up inside me is flowing over. I remember Omar's beautiful mother and her words of wisdom to me in the aftermath of my grief for Shadia. That day I thought that life could never hurt me more. I was wrong.

I rummage in the cabinet for something that might have been left behind by the owners. Paracetamol, or sleeping tablets.

There's nothing here except some very old indigestion pills. I pull at my short beard and regret my decision not to shave. There are no blades that I might use.

Stumbling towards the kitchen I know that I may find a knife or something that I can use. I'm no longer sobbing but wailing as I reach into the drawer and pull out a small chopping knife. That's all I need but how to make it quick, and as painless as possible.

'You coward!' I scream at myself. 'You deserve all the pain you can inflict on yourself you unworthy piece of...'

'Jameel...' I turn and Ali is there.

'You're supposed to be gone,' I say. I try to swallow the sobs but they escape in gasps.

'Jameel...'

'Majid!' I shout at him. 'My name is Majid Al Faisal! Jameel Al Manhal can go to hell!'

'Majid Al Faisal will also go straight to hell if he takes his own life.' Ali reaches out towards me and holds his hand out for the knife.

'He will have good company there with you and Zarrar, and all who are like you. I went to hell the day I saw Shadia die on a carousel and I revisit it each time I have anything to do with you and your crazy ideas. Jameel Al Manhal never existed and Majid Al Faisal is ready to face death on his own terms. Not yours or Zarrar's. Now go wherever it was you were going and leave me in peace to do what I have to do.'

'Jameel... Majid... I was talking on the telephone outside and Zarrar asked me what the noise was in the background. Your crying. I tried to lie it away, but he wasn't fooled. He says he is on his way to find me. He knows you are still alive. If you ever loved me, give me the knife, Majid. It can't end this way. We have to leave here before Zarrar finds out the truth about the lies. And we need to find Shona before he does.'

I sit on the floor of the kitchen. My short burst of energy in trying to find a weapon is spent. I fling the knife across the floor towards the man I once called my only true friend.

'Take it, Ali. But go away and leave me here.'

Ali picks up the knife and places it slowly back in the drawer.

'We're leaving here together, Majid. I have known Zarrar all my life and he has always been a live wire. But now he has completely lost the plot. Tomorrow you can show me where you last saw Shona. We have to get to her before Zarrar does. You owe it to her to keep her from his crazy hands.'

Chapter forty one

'DID you lock the back door?'

'Yes.'

'Did you check the gas?'

'Yes.'

'Did you check all the windows?'

Des glanced up at the front windows. They were closed but Norah caught his glance.

'You didn't, did you? Go back and check the back windows. It's always the back windows they use anyway. Do you know how many burglaries there have been, this year, in this estate alone?'

He didn't, but no doubt his wife could give him the statistics verbatim.

He got out of the car, un-double-locked the front door, turned off the alarm, un-double-locked the back door and went round the back to check the windows. They were all shut. Back in the house, he double-locked the back door, reset the alarm, double-locked the front door and got back into the car.

'Of course, I forgot, the alarm won't set in the first place if all the windows are not shut properly. So they must have been.' Norah busied herself with her seatbelt.

Des took a deep breath to steady his nerves. 'Is that a fact?'

'Yes. So there was probably no need to go back in at all… Come on Des. Let's get a move on. We're late enough as it is… Imagine it's September already. She's been gone almost a month now. Wherever she is she must be broken-hearted missing her baby.' Norah sighed her *woe is me* sigh.

Des wanted to ask how they could be late for an informal cup of tea with Tommy but he knew better than to ask such a question in Norah's present mood. He knew it was only because she was on a huge guilt trip that she was behaving this way. It was really only herself she was angry with. For a week now she had been impossible to live with. Ever since she had lost her temper with Tommy about his lack of interest in finding Shona. All this time, Des knew that Shona was in a university town in Wales. He could go over at any time and have a bash at finding her himself, but he knew the Gardaí would be straight after him. Please God she was safe.

They continued the rest of the journey in silence. This was the bit that Des couldn't stand. Norah would blow the quiet away every now and then with a gale force sigh. At least with her nagging and temper there was some sort of communication but this silence was driving him mad. He thought he'd give her one last try before they arrived in Tommy's house.

'What's in the bag?'

'A present. For Ruby. A singing musical train thingy.'

Jesus. God help poor Tommy's head.

'Lovely… Are you going to say anything to Tommy? About… ye know?'

Silence.

'It wouldn't be good to spoil the lovely present by having an atmosphere about the place.'

'We'll see has he anything to say for himself first. It's not like I'm a difficult person to talk to.'

'Not at all.'

Silence again, for a time, but interrupted by Des.

'Only where Shona is concerned.'

'I beg your pardon?'

'I *said*, only where Shona is concerned. Then you could say… that lately… you were a very difficult person to talk to.'

'You're welcome to your opinion.'

Another few minutes passed while the quiet of their voices screamed inside his mind. Des knew that his wife was not as sure about her daughter's innocence as she insisted she was. He knew that Norah's mind, like his own, was strewn with the debris of their lives since Shona had left. Now there was the evidence of the relationship between Al Manhal and Shona. Hadn't they done a bloody fabulous job bringing her up to know the difference between right and wrong? What wonderful parents they had turned out to be.

As they approached the front door of Tommy's house, they noticed a print he'd hung of little Ruby's footprints on the inside of the porch window.

'You have to hand it to that fella. For a young man of eighteen he really puts a lot of effort into that baby of his. Don't you think so Norah..? Norah?'

'It was probably done at the childminder's.'

Ruby was fast asleep in her new buggy when they went in but despite that, Norah lifted her up into her arms and wrapped her in cuddles.

'I have a pressie for you, my angel.' Ruby rewarded her with a wail for the disturbance.

'Hiya, Des.' Tommy shook Shona's dad's hand, clutching him for support while he banished thoughts of what he'd do to Norah if she didn't put her granddaughter straight back into the buggy to finish the sleep that he'd spent such a long time bringing about.

'Norah.' Tommy nodded in her direction.

Ruby continued to squeal which meant that Norah didn't have to make the decision whether or not to speak to Tommy.

Stephen was there to greet them as well. When Norah and Ruby had gone into the kitchen to *help* Tommy with the tea, Des spoke to Tommy's father.

'Did Tommy bring you along to act as referee?'

'What is it between those two?' Stephen asked. 'They're never of the same opinion as each other on anythin'. You'd think they'd try a little harder when they're around the baby.'

The afternoon continued in this vein, with Norah finding something to do every time Tommy threatened to speak to her.

'I'll put the kettle on again.' Tommy was eager to absent himself from the room. His father followed him into the kitchen.

'What's goin' on now, son? What's all this messin' between you and Norah? Do you not think you could make a bit of an effort for a change?'

'Don't start on at me, Da. That woman is a prize bitch. Always was and always will be. There's nothin' I could ever do to please her, so I've given up tryin'. Okay?'

'So what's the latest then?'

'Norah thinks that I should be the one to go traipsin' around askin' after Shona in different places in the UK. She says no one's goin' to give any information to the police and if Des goes over people will clam up when they see someone his age askin' after her. She reckons that because of my age I'd get a much better response, that I would be able to find her precious princess.'

'She has a point you know, Tommy. Whenever Shona's gone missin' before, you've often been the one to know where she might be hidin'.'

'Thanks for your wonderful support, Da. Sure. I'll abandon my baby and my job and off I'll go so. Never mind that the Gardaí would be after me like a shot. Oh… and get this. She thinks that if I make the effort to find Shona that the Gardaí will think that Shona might actually be innocent, and here's the best bit, that Shona will love me so much that we can all go back to playin' happy families again. As if we ever did.'

'Well do you know what Tommy? I know you'll think I'm mad for sayin' this but I actually admire Norah Moran for the way she is about her daughter. You get your kids for better or for worse and you have to make the best of it all. No matter what's thrown in your face, they're your kids for life. Now from what I can make out, Norah left it very late to adopt a child and too late probably to adopt a second one. So Shona's everythin' to her. Like myself she has one shot at it and she's givin' it her best. As I blame Shona for the mess of your relationship, she needs to blame you.'

'What've I done, Da, except to stand by my responsibilities for the last six months? I've tried my best.'

'You don't really believe that Shona had anythin' to do with all that malarkey? Do you?'

'No... I don't know. All I know is that I've no more left to give Shona. Anythin' I have from now on I'm givin' to Ruby; with or without the help of Norah po-faced Moran.'

Tommy looked over his shoulder to see what his Da was staring at and his heart sank at the sight of Norah standing in the doorway, gripping the handle, the leftover cake from earlier wobbling in her other hand. Tommy knew by the look on her face that she'd overheard the whole conversation.

'Let me take that from you Norah.' Stephen rescued the cake before it ended up on the floor. 'Sit down there now. Tommy has the coffee nearly made.' He noticed that it had gone quiet in the sitting room. 'Where's Ruby?'

'Des has taken her out into the garden for a few minutes. He said they both needed some fresh air... Thanks.' She took the cup offered to her and took her time with the milk and the sugar.

'I suppose you can add nosy auld cow now to my list of attributes. For listening into conversations.'

'And you can add mouth almighty to his.' Stephen gave Tommy an admonishing look and Tommy, in turn, looked suitably embarrassed.

'Norah, part of me is sorry that you overheard all that and part of me isn't.' Tommy wrapped his hands around his coffee for comfort. 'We couldn't keep goin' the way we were. It's no use to any of us. You can't hide that kind of tension away from Ruby anymore. She's still only young, but she reacts to it all badly.

'You have to face it Norah that Shona and I've come to the end of our time together. Movin' in with each other was the wrong thing to do. We weren't in love. We didn't even know one another. I don't regret it for a minute because we went on to have Ruby and I love her to bits. I wouldn't change havin' her for the world. You and Des and Da are fantastic grandparents. If it wasn't for the three of you we'd never have managed as well as we have. I'll never deprive you of seein' your grandchild as much as you want. She loves you Norah like she *should* love her mother... Which brings me back to Shona. I think that Shona's realised that her place isn't with Ruby. Before she went away she'd stopped drinkin' for a while, but she couldn't keep it up. So until she gets control of her alcoholism, 'cause let's face it, that's what it is, then she's not fit to be a mother. I'm sorry, Norah.'

Tommy reached out and touched Norah's hand. She was crying softly, but snatched her hand away.

'I'm really sorry.' He repeated.

'So when she comes back? What will she do?'

'I don't know, Norah. That's up to you and Des and Shona. I'm puttin' Shona behind me now. I'm movin' on. I owe it to Ruby and myself. A bit of routine for her and a slice of normality for me. I'm eighteen years old. I don't want to be a barman for the rest of my life. I want to start my teacher trainin' in two weeks' time. There're lots of mothers who go to college after they've had children. No reason why I can't too.'

'So you're pushing Shona from your life, like she never existed?' Norah had dried her tears and was preparing herself for battle once more.

Stephen stepped in. 'No Norah. Give the lad a break. Of course Shona exists in his life. She's the mother of his child and no breakup between the two of them'll ever change that. If she comes back and all this business with the Gardaí is over, then it'll be time to make plans for their future with Ruby, but Tommy's right. They can't put their life on hold indefinitely. He has to move on. I think his idea of goin' to college is a great one. In the long-term he has to have a dependable job with more suitable workin' hours. Teachin' will be perfect. He's never goin' to achieve that with bar work and I'll give him as much help with the baby as is necessary to get him through. It's not easy bein' a father on your own. I know that myself, but he's doin' a great job so far.'

'He hasn't been a father on his own. Ruby's had a mother and she will do again. All this rubbish about *if Shona comes back*... Of course Shona's coming back and when she does, all this madness will be over.' Norah gave a loud sniff and continued. 'But, I suppose... until it's all sorted out... until her mummy comes back... well, you know where we are... if you need a hand... or whatever. Not that I condone your idea about going to college so soon. I don't. But I'm a grandmother to that child and I won't stand by and see her stuck for anything.'

Tommy thought that if Des and Ruby hadn't come in right then that he might have ended up doing time for grandmatricide. Was there such a thing? There must be.

Norah went rushing into the hall to greet her grandchild.

'Hello, my angel. How's Granny's favourite child? Did Granddad sing you lovely songs, Ruby? Come and sit on Granny's lap, my little princess.'

Stephen looked across the kitchen table at his son and smiled an amused smirk at the antics of this incredible woman. Tommy knew he was telling him that where Shona was concerned, Norah's head was so far buried in the sand that she might never surface.

So Tommy decided to see the funny side of it all and smiled back at him, shaking his head. He shrugged his shoulders and raised his hands in the air in a gesture that said *okay I give up. I'll call a truce.*

Des, walking into the kitchen, realised that their amusement was at the expense of his wife and wasn't sure how he felt about that. Mind you, it was a hell of a lot better than the feud that had been reaching boiling point before he had left. So, he decided to leave well enough alone, sit down and help himself to coffee.

Other people's attitudes to his wife often got Des' back up. He wanted to shout at them sometimes.

She wasn't always like this you know. She used to be the most beautiful, intelligent, caring, fun-loving woman that God had ever put on this earth.

When Des first married Norah he thought he was the luckiest man in the world. She was the key to the door of everything he ever wanted in life, but losing the babies had changed her beyond recognition and bringing up Shona had finished the job.

Des was feeling more than his age these days. Shona had brought the world's troubles down on them this time. Being the wrong kind of celebrity was taking its toll on them all.

Des decided to change the subject.

'You know something, Tommy?' He shook his head as he spoke. 'I'm amazed Shona hasn't come crawling back by now. It's so unlike her. So she walked off into the great unknown in a gesture of self-sacrifice, but normally she'd have got over all that by now and want to come home and drive us demented. This disappearance doesn't fit the Shona that I know.'

Des looked over at Tommy for a reaction.

'I've been Shona's father for over seventeen years and I'm not sure I know who she is. Who knows what she's up to? I'd never say it outside this kitchen but Shona springs no surprises on me anymore.'

An uncomfortable silence bounced off the walls of the room.

'So what're you sayin', Des?' Stephen's voice sounded nervous. 'That Shona could have somethin' to do with all this terrorist stuff?'

Des stood and put his cup in the sink. His face wore an uncharacteristic look of anger in defeat.

'No, Stephen! Ah, I don't know. Shona is capable of wrecking the lives of those she's supposed to love. She's able to walk out on a little baby. God knows what else she's bent on doing.'

Tommy knew it was time to come clean with his family. The Chief Superintendent had said it would be on the news soon, to get the public fired up once more in helping to look for Al Manhal.

'Des.' Tommy put his hand on Des' shoulder. 'The Gardaí have new information. It's pretty damning. The video footage on the ferry where Shona was seen… Well, she had a travelling companion…'

Des dropped his head and made a strangled sound. 'No... Not him! She can't have.' But his face showed that he knew it was true.

Chapter forty two

'MARGARET. Nice to see you.' Des stood back from his front door to let his sister-in-law in. 'Norah's not in at the moment. She'll be sorry she missed you.'

'Yeah. I can imagine. I knew she'd be around at the church now. That's why I came. I wanted to talk to you. Have you the kettle boiled?'

'Come on into the kitchen. We'll even have mugs and put the carton of milk out instead of the jug! Rebels we are.' The two laughed together.

Five minutes later, Des and Margaret were settled with their mugs of tea, eating biscuits straight from the packet.

'If she comes in and sees this, Des, I wouldn't like to be you.' They giggled like teenagers. Des knew what Margaret had come to talk about and they needed to lighten the mood.

'So Shona?' Margaret raised her eyebrows questioningly. 'Excuse my intrusion here but it's all getting a bit out of hand. Have you heard anything at all from her?'

Des looked around the kitchen, thought about the consequences and eventually nodded his head.

'What? When?!'

'I'll tell you in a minute. First tell me this. What do you think of the whole thing?'

Margaret put down her cup. 'I met him you know.'

Now it was Des' turn to look horrified.

'We met up in Bewleys on Grafton Street in July. When I got there a guy got up from the table where Shona was sitting and left. Then I came and took his seat. It was him... Jameel. Shona looked... wonderful. Better than I'd ever seen her. Sort of full of herself... I don't know how to describe it. Confident. Happy. And you see, well, she confided in me. She begged me not to tell anyone because of Tommy and I know I should've before now, but I was sure it would all blow over. I presumed that the Gardaí would realise it was a stupid mistake and that Shona couldn't possibly have known about the man's real motives for being in Ireland.'

'How do you *know*, Margaret? Even I don't *know* she wasn't involved, but my gut feeling tells me she couldn't be.'

'Well, when she spoke to me that day she told me about how much she was in love with this guy. The man she described... the boy... sounded absolutely wonderful. She swore it was because of him she'd given up drinking. She was convinced that she would prove to Tommy, and all of you, that she was capable of being a really good mother. Shona said that her baby would always be her number one priority. She wanted to have a life around Jameel with Ruby at the centre.

'Des, in July, Shona was in love and in her head she was building a life for herself and this guy. Obviously this man had no intention of staying around, but Shona didn't know this. Not long after he was trying to blow up half the country. I'm telling you that Shona Moran had *nothing* to do with it. My guess is... and it's probably rambling thoughts to be honest... but I think Shona found out the day of the bomb, that Jameel wasn't going to have anything to do with her. If she ended up getting out of her head on drink, then that's what we know the old Shona would do when she was upset. She somehow made it off that tram and she ran. Ran away to hide and to lick her wounds. Then maybe she found out what Jameel had done, and later, that she was wanted for questioning herself. God knows how he persuaded her to go with him. I don't know where Shona could be, Des but when she makes her mind up about something she can be as stubborn as hell.

She continued. 'Shona has always had a problem with being confident. She lacks self-assurance most of the time. She thinks the worst of herself and presumes others share the same feelings.

In July she was building up a new idea of herself. Somehow Jameel had managed to achieve this. But if he swiped it away from her again by dumping her and then by showing her that he was never what he had said he was, then she would have hit an all-time low. Wherever Shona is; even if she's with Jameel, in fact particularly if she's with him, she's convinced herself that she's no use to anyone; that nobody loves her and everyone she knows is better off without her. Including her child. Especially her child. She hasn't left us all because she doesn't love us. She's left us because she loves us so much that she doesn't want to drag us all down with her.'

Margaret looked over at Des. His face was crumpled as if he was going to cry.

'I'm sorry, Des. As I said, I know I'm intruding here, but I'm finding it very hard to stand back and let it happen. The longer it goes on the harder it will be to prove to everyone that Shona is the victim here. Not the culprit.'

Des shook his head vigorously and answered. 'You recognise things in Shona that those of us who should know her well, only hope to see. I love her very much, Margaret but Shona isn't the saint that you take her to be. I think you're right, though, in saying that she has become some sort of victim.'

Des and Margaret sat in silence for a while each staring at separate parts of the kitchen wondering what else there was to say. Des knew he should say nothing. He had made a promise to Shona, but he had to do something and he had to tell someone the truth. Shona had trusted Margaret enough to tell her about Jameel. So he would take his cue from his daughter.

'Margaret... if you knew all this... about Shona being innocent, why did you not go to the Gardaí about it?'

'Because I hoped that Shona would get in touch with me. I thought she would, but if the Gardaí knew that Shona had my trust then they might be watching my actions. I wanted Shona to call me. Then I'd be able to go to her... to talk her through all this... without the Gardaí following me...'

'I know where she is, Margaret. I've known for ages. She called and she let slip the name of the place where she was. I only have the name of the town but I would imagine that I'd find her easily enough if I went there. When she first told me, I thought it would be a good idea to leave her for a while, to lick her wounds so to speak. To be honest, I thought she'd be back within a week at the most. By the time I'd decided to go over there, the Gardaí had found the connection between her and Al Manhal. I knew they'd be watching my every move. I'm quite sure that this thing is so big that they'd bug our phones and intercept our mail and email. I don't know, but I'm not prepared to take the risk.'

'Tell me where she is Des.'

'Why?'

'Because the Gardaí are not watching me the way they're watching you. I could go to her. I just want to talk to her, Des. I want to convince myself that she's alright. That she hasn't come to any harm... Please. I'll go today. I'll take unpaid leave if I have to.'

'Okay. I'll tell you because I can't see any other way out of this stalemate. Shona may never speak to me again as a result. I've messed with her trust in me before and I know I haven't that many chances left.'

'Do you mean with her adoption?'

Des nodded and sighed. He was right to trust her. It could be a risk for Margaret if Shona was still with this guy, but they had to do something. He grabbed a piece of paper and wrote the name of the university town that Shona had mentioned. He then pushed the piece of paper towards Margaret.

Margaret read the note. 'I've been to this town once before. My friend went to university there. It's a big enough place to get lost in if you wanted to, but I'll try.'

'At least you'll know your way around.'

Margaret pushed her chair back and stood up in the kitchen. She walked over to the fridge and picked up a recent photo of Shona. 'I'll need this if I have to go looking for her. I'll get the next flight today. I'll just go home and pack a few things first.'

Des took out his wallet and handed her the silver locket he had retrieved from the corner of Tommy's sitting room. 'If you find her give her this. It's got photos of her baby in it. If Ruby doesn't bring Shona back then nothing will.'

'I'll be in touch with you whether I find her or not. But I will find her, Des and I'll do my best to bring her back. Before things get any worse.'

Des reached over and gave Margaret an awkward hug as he wondered how things could possibly get any worse.

Chapter forty three

SHONA and Bridget were holding hands. This was their second visit to the maternity wing of the hospital in as many days. Yesterday a doctor with a kind face had told Shona that she was having a baby. Another, with a face that wished she could be kind, but knew it wouldn't make any difference, had told her very matter-of-factly, that her baby was dead. In one day she had been given monumental news by two different people.

'Congratulations. You're having a baby.'

'I'm sorry, your baby's dead.'

Today Shona's baby was leaving her. The doctor was calling it a delayed miscarriage. Two nurses were standing by and letting it happen. She was stretched on a trolley in a room that was eight foot by twelve foot. A coffin of ghosts. She felt the walls caving in, the floor rising, the ceiling hanging low. Crushed. Her free hand was gripping the side of the bed, her knuckles protruding from the backs of her hands with the strength of her hold. A nurse wrung her own hands and smiled without moving her eyes. The other talked of happier days to come. Shona wanted to smack them. To lash out.

She felt her birth mother in this room, giving *her* away. She felt Norah in the room, before Shona was born, giving up her dead babies. She felt Bridget's dream babies being snatched from her. She screamed words of indignation. She heard her mother's words and Norah's words and Bridget's words and the words of a thousand mothers, whose pain filled the room. As their babies left them they shed their tears in silence.

A surge of pain and the last of her baby left her.

'It's over now, dear. When you go back to the ward, we'll bring you something for the pain.'

Shona felt that years later, she would still be waiting.

*

Aberystwyth hadn't seemed so big when Margaret had visited for her friend's graduation. She had hardly spent twenty-four hours there that time. B&B. Conferring hall. Restaurant. Nightclub. B&B. Back to Dublin the next day. But now she was seeing it as the large student town that it was.

She wondered now how she would possibly find a young, pretty female, who may well be drunk; when half the town's population was young, pretty females; often drunk. Would Shona have a job? Where might she work? Margaret knew that Shona hadn't had a job since she left school but that her last part-time job had been in a pub. She had to be working. How else would she keep herself?

Margaret had started with the bars. If Shona wasn't working in one, then she might be drinking in one, but when that drew a blank she had moved on to the shops. She had to buy food. Had she changed her appearance from the photo that Margaret was carrying? Margaret had been here three days and had found nothing. In her spare time, she walked the beaches. She found some peace from her frustration with the rise and fall of the waves and the feel of the stones at her feet. Her eyes were on the lookout all the time for a small young woman walking lost along the sands.

'Shona!' she shouted into the sea. 'Shona...'

Eventually she struck gold, but it led her to the last place she wanted to find Shona – in a hospital.

*

The girl on the street who had recognised Shona's picture said she lived next door to an elderly lady whose new lodger had had some medical emergency the day before. The girl's brother had given them a lift to the hospital. She said the girl's name was Niamh Moran, not Shona, but it was definitely the same girl. Margaret had latched onto the surname.

When she enquired at the hospital she was shocked to hear that there was a Niamh Moran in the maternity wing and her faith, that she had come to the right place, waned. Shona? Pregnant? No it couldn't be her. With whose child? She got the impression that Tommy and Shona were not even on speaking terms, never mind anything else. Margaret thought of the relationship with Jameel and she shivered.

It wouldn't be Shona. It would be somebody else with the name. When she had seen this girl she would go back home to Dublin. To her job. Put her life back the way it was before she got mixed up with all this madness. She had done her best.

Margaret walked into the ward where the receptionist had told her Niamh would be. The bed she had mentioned was over beside the window. An old woman was holding the small hand of a girl in the bed, a look of deep concern on her face. Shona wouldn't know this woman. It wasn't her.

Margaret pulled back the curtain that was half shielding the girl. As she looked down at her, the old woman looked up at Margaret and both spoke out together.

'Jesus, who are you..?'

'My God, it's...'

Then they looked down at Shona who opened her eyes for a moment.

Waking in her hospital bed, Shona looked up and saw that Bridget's hand had become Margaret's hand. Why was Margaret holding her hand? This was a crazy dream. The pain killers were overpowering.

'Bridget,' she called out. 'Bridget,' she whispered as she closed her eyes again and let the drugs do their work.

Bridget came back into the ward clutching two polystyrene cups of tea. The cure for all shocks.

'Is she still asleep?' she whispered.

'She woke up briefly. She seemed to get very agitated when she saw me. She called for you. Then she went back to sleep.' Margaret spoke in a quiet voice and accepted the cup that was offered with a gentle smile. She sighed for the girl in the bed who had suffered so much that day and for all that she would suffer. Margaret remembered her sister Norah crying in her kitchen after each miscarriage.

Bridget's voice broke into her thoughts. 'I'm not surprised she was agitated. She must have nearly died of shock when she saw you standing there. She told me that nobody except me knew where she was. You must've moved mountains to try to find her.'

'It's been a bit of a struggle alright, but I just followed my instinct until I got here and it paid off. So how do you know Shona?'

'I've only known her a short while but I've loved her company. She's been through a lot of struggles.' Bridget reached out her hand and stroked the side of Shona's cheek, smiling a motherly smile. 'I think you might be able to help her, Margaret. She's talked about you. She was tempted to call you a few times but she was afraid to drag you into her mess. You know I think that you might be exactly what Shona needs in her life to make sense of it all.'

Margaret nodded.

'There's something else, though Margaret.' Bridget continued with a grave face. 'My house, where Shona's staying, was broken into last night while I was here in the hospital. I don't know yet if anything was taken. Shona will have to check herself because they only went through her things. You say you know all about what's happened to her. Well I haven't reported the burglary yet but really, Shona needs to go home and sort out this sorry mess... She could be in danger, through no fault of her own, of course. But I'd better hush now. Firstly you're going to take a lot of explaining.'

Chapter forty four

SHONA woke to the quiet of the afternoon with a jolt. She reminded herself why she was in a hospital bed and her hands drifted down to her lower stomach. Empty. Hollow. Her head and her heart, and her womb. Nothing.

The tears came again. The nurse had told her earlier that the doctor would be in to discuss her aftercare and then she would be discharged. She longed to go back to Bridget's house where she could hibernate in her room and speak to nobody. Was Margaret here? Why did she think that?

Light footsteps broke the quiet behind her bedside curtains and the tall figure of a doctor stood over Shona, smiling through his dark beard. His eyes shone and Shona felt his kindness.

'Hello, Shona,' he said. 'I'm sorry about what has happened to you. Your beautiful baby... gone.' He dragged the curtain around her bed and pulled a chair closer before sitting down.

'It hurts, Doctor,' Shona replied. 'The pain is still bad. Will it hurt for long?' Useless words she thought. Of course it would hurt. For a lifetime.

'I've nothing to ease your pain, Shona,' the man said in a hushed voice. 'The only healing I can give you is in words. You know that losing this baby was the work of Allah, don't you? It's your punishment. What you and Jameel did... it was evil. You were bad and you got what you deserved. Both of you.'

Shona stared at the man in the chair beside her. The drugs the nurse had given her began to churn in her stomach and she swallowed. How could this man know about Jameel?

'Who are you?' She was frightened.

He ignored the question and let it hang in the air. Staring at her and smiling. No longer the friendly doctor she had mistaken him for.

Beads of sweat began to drip down her forehead and her throat ran dry.

She took in the smile, the brown eyes, the thin curls and the soft beard and remembered Jameel's words when he spoke about his friend… *Ali is the only man that I could ever call my brother. I would trust him with my life. He is my only true friend.* Shona had been hurt by the words.

'Ali Al Aziz…' she said. 'Jameel's friend. He spoke about you.' Ali's smile faded and his face darkened.

'So you know me already? What exactly did our friend Jameel tell you about me and more importantly, how did you manage to persuade him to call off his plans?' Ali moved his face closer to her. 'In his bed? Was that it?'

Shona hardly heard what the man said. She could only stare at the face that clearly meant to do her harm. Bridget had informed her previously of everything that Jameel was supposed to have been involved with. She had found it impossible to believe and felt there must be something behind it all that would explain Jameel's innocence. She had managed to stall Bridget from going to the police while she tried to get her head around all that was being reported in the papers and the television.

Looking towards the gap in the curtains, she opened her mouth to call out, but without hesitation Ali produced a knife from his sleeve and held it to her throat.

'Tell me what you know!' Ali spat the words at her in a loud whisper.

'Nothing…' Shona's voice was barely audible. 'About what? Jameel told me your name. He said you were the only true friend he'd ever had. He spoke your name out loud once and made me swear that I'd never repeat it.' Shona barely managed to get the last words from her mouth it was so dry.

Ali's arms relaxed slightly and he sat back in his chair slowly, the knife still sitting in his hand. He sat silently, contemplating. This man was not as Jameel said he was. He was crazy. Why was the doctor not coming? It was so quiet…

The man's face became reflective. Shona thought for a moment that this might be a good time to try to run but his words kept her still. 'If it wasn't for you, Shona Moran, Jameel would have had a chance to become a great man. We would have remembered him with respect and spoken his name with awe.'

Outside the curtain, Shona could hear the noise of the tea trolley entering the ward and the chirpy voice of the attendant asking 'one sugar or two?' Within minutes she would be at Shona's bed and she thanked God as she watched Ali's horrified face. He was in danger of being caught and he knew it.

'I suppose I always knew that ladies would be a problem for Jameel and look how right I was. Now the time has come for me to say goodbye to him. For good.' Ali's words were hurried now and he closed the knife before it disappeared back up his sleeve. He leaned forward then and spoke his parting words quietly.

'Your Jameel Al Manhal will be with Allah soon. When I leave you I will do this. Even though he failed in his mission he will turn this around at the end of his life. I will persuade him that taking his own life to protect our jihad is the only thing he can do. To protect us all from the authorities. To protect himself. I will tell him that you killed yourself from grief when I told you the truth about him. It will be easy to persuade him that there is nothing left for him.'

The creaking wheels on the trolley were fast approaching.

Shona couldn't speak. She lay completely still as the tears slid down her cheeks. She knew now. Jameel had been brainwashed by this madman, and from here he was going to persuade Jameel to kill himself in the name of some crazy scheme.

Ali stood, towering above the bed and shook his head as if to erase the thoughts of his friend as his face became business-like once more. The rattle of the teacups was getting closer.

'You are lucky to be leaving here alive Shona, but when you do I want you to remember this. Do not say anything of our conversation to anyone. Do not leave this bed until I have gone well away from you, and if ever you are tempted to open that mouth of yours just close your eyes and think of each member of your family. Think about how you would feel if they were lying in a hospital bed as you are now – or somewhere even worse. There now... Close your eyes... and lie silently in wait for me.

'*Ma'a Salama.* Goodbye. May Allah guide your thoughts.'

And with that he was gone.

'*One sugar or two dear?*' It was all too much for Shona and despite the warm and welcoming face before her she couldn't help herself as she leaned over and vomited all over the tea lady's shoes.

*

Two days later, Shona had become great friends with her pillow. In this room in Bridget's house, she felt safe. Outside the room she had lost a baby that she hadn't known she was carrying and she had met a man who was from Jameel's world, who she never wanted to see again. Ali Al Aziz had given her a scare that she knew she would never recover from. It was all too weird. Her life had been crazy enough before last week but now it had gone completely haywire. She wrapped her arms around the pillow and snuggled her face to its tear-dampened warmth.

Was Jameel dead? Had Ali killed him? Margaret had filled her in on all the things that she and Bridget didn't know about Jameel.

Shona would never trust anyone again.

'Jameel, Jameel...' The tears kept coming. She had loved him so much.

The only thing that kept Shona's interest was the news headlines. Bridget had fixed up the old television in her room and again and again the police had pleaded for information on Jameel's whereabouts. Shona could have saved them time and effort. He was probably gone. She waited to see his face come up on the screen. Shona knew she should have given herself up the minute she found out that they suspected her of being connected to the bomb, but Ali's visit had scared her too much and she

249

was staying right here in an attempt to lay low. No amount of persuading by Bridget could push her to do what she knew in her heart was right. She hated Ali Al Aziz. Hated and feared him. In the meantime the media would move on. Jameel and Shona would become old news. Maybe it would all just go away... but Ali never would.

Shona rubbed her hands over the empty part of her body. Could she have loved this baby as much as Ruby? How had she not realised that she was three months pregnant? Because she didn't *want* to acknowledge it? When she thought about it there were signs, but she had put it down to the general stress of her messed up life.

Shona wanted to get up right now and go out... Maybe she could go looking for a drink...

But a knock on the door interrupted her thoughts and she feigned sleep, as she always did, when Bridget or Margaret came to *talk to her.*

'Shona...' Margaret went over to the bed and gently shook her. 'I know you're not asleep, Shona. I need to speak to you.' Margaret sat on the edge of the bed and Shona reluctantly pulled herself up into a sitting position. Margaret would tell her to get up and get washed and get dressed and to talk about the baby. Talk and talk and talk.

But she wasn't interested.

'Okay, Margaret but talk about something else other than the baby. I know you mean well and I appreciate you making the baby such an important thing. And it is, but there are other things that you and I should discuss. Like you going home and getting away from this mess.'

'I know, Shona, but we can't ignore what's happened...'

'Margaret...'

'No really, Shona. You're right. We need to talk about where you go from here.'

'In a few days, Margaret. Not now. Not yet.'

'I need to go home, Shona. I need to go back to work.'

Shona looked at Margaret and swallowed, remembering that

her aunt had put her life on hold to come and find her.

'You go back Margaret, and sort out everything that you have to sort. I understand, but I have to stay here.'

'I'm not going back without you, Shona. I've turned my life upside down looking for you. Now I've found you I'm staying with you. You have to come back too.'

'You seem to have disregarded a few major stumbling blocks, Margaret. I'm wanted by the Gardaí in Dublin, so as soon as I set foot there I'll be arrested.'

'At least you'll be safe though. I'm worried about who it was that broke into your room here when you were in the hospital. To be truthful, I'm worried for all of us. It's getting completely out of hand. We don't know what these guys are like... what they're capable of. You've done nothing wrong, really, Shona. You didn't know anything about that mad man's plans.'

Shona sent Margaret one of her most withering looks.

'Right. Though you've overlooked that Tommy never wants to set eyes on me again. I ran out on my child and my parents. What about them? I can't look my father in the eye after what I've done to all of them. My mother hates me and she has every right to. I've given her a crap life. No, Margaret. You go home. I'll stay with Bridget.'

'Firstly, your mother doesn't hate you. Norah Moran has been standing up for your antics for as long as I can remember. The woman is a saint, and secondly, Shona, Bridget and I've been talking and she wants to come back with me. You know the way her mother was from Ireland; well she's thinking of going and finding her relations and that. But she says that she'll only come back if you come with us. So if you insist on staying here she'll have to stay too and look after you – and she wants to go, Shona. She really does...'

Shona said nothing so Margaret continued.

'You'll have to face them sometime, Shona. You can't hide away here forever. They'll catch up with you and the sooner you deal with it the easier it'll be. Honestly. And if the police don't find you then Jameel's lot will... It's not safe here. What do you say,

Shona? Will you at least think about it?'

'I can't do it, Margaret.' Shona lay back down and put her arms around her pillow and held on tight. 'I'm not like you. I really can't.'

'I've something for you, Shona. I wanted to give it to you when you came out of hospital but I didn't think you were up to it.' Shona didn't move.

'I'll leave it here on the bed, then.'

It was her last chance to convince so she put the locket down on the bed and left the images of Ruby with her mother.

Chapter forty five

ALI and I sit side by side on the floor. I've eaten very little, my mind now sickened by weeks lying in this room surrounded by memories of Shona. I stare ahead at nothing, not catching much of what he's saying. Something about going to Allah... Yes... that's the best... There's no life for me between these walls and no life outside either. Ali's going back to Pakistan? Is that what he's saying? Yes... best to let go now... Go to Allah... To protect the *jihad*... To protect his brothers in Pakistan...

He offers me some more food.

'Eat, my friend. We're leaving here today and I need you to build up your strength. I have found Shona and she's planning on going back to Dublin. We need to get rid of her before Zarrar or the police get to her. I need your help in this. I think that if she sees you, she will come to you. You are my bait. So eat and drink. I will come back soon.'

Eventually I turn around to look for Ali... but he's gone. He's coming back soon... and he'll help me to let go of the pain... All I want now is to let go of life. To be with Shadia... Life was so good before Shadia was taken away... I should've known that I couldn't live then without her... can't live now without Shona...

What did Ali say about Shona? ... She's going back..? If Ali's found Shona then she's in danger. A sudden jolt of fear for her energises me slightly and I try to stand up, but I fall back almost straight away. I'm weak from hunger. I've let my body slip away. There was nothing else to do. I needed to let go, but now Ali's saying that he's going to get rid of Shona and he's bringing me to see her.

I reach over and pull the box of food towards me. I must eat.

Shona needs me.

I think about the times I made love to Shona in this house. She's the only girl I've ever known in that way. She smiled at me and said over and over that she loved me. I'll never forget the angry look on her face in Aberystwyth when I told her I'd never see her again. Even in her sadness she looked beautiful. Now she's in danger. I'll make it up to her for all the trouble I've caused her. I'll do this for Omar. For all the values he instilled in me growing up. I'll do this for Shadia. For the way she taught me to love as we grew up together in Riyadh.

Shona needs me now. I have to build up my strength. I don't know where Ali's taking me but any place in the world is better than lying on this mattress waiting to die and I really have been waiting to go. To Shadia and to Omar. Now though, I have reason to hang on. I push myself up and drag my feet to the bathroom to try to wash. My clothes are filthy. The only other clothes in the bungalow are the jeans and hoodie I was wearing when I came here with Ali. When was that? I throw some water on my face. I take off the dirty clothes and stand shivering in the freezing room. I pick up an already filthy towel and use it to scrub away some of the grime. It'll take more than one wash, but I do the best I can with such little energy. Using the bathmat as a towel I dry myself as quickly as possible. If the temperature's anything to go by, we are well into the fall. I'm freezing.

The short beard I've grown on my face feels itchy and dirty and my hair's grown. How long have I been here?

I grab some bread from the kitchen and go to the sitting room. Picking up a throw from a chair, I wrap it around me. It's soft with pictures of butterflies. I'd bought it for Shona when we first moved in here. I imagine the smell of her is still woven through the fabric and I breathe in the familiarity of her. I feel a little better, but exhausted from my efforts. What is it Shona says about a quick wash? *A lick and a promise.* That's it. I promise now I'll clean myself… well as soon as I'm stronger. I take a bite of the stale bread. I don't feel like eating, but I know I've to eat to get strong. I automatically promise Allah that I'll build up my strength. Is he listening to my promises? My pleas? Am I ready to pray again?

Ali says that he needs to get rid of Shona? That's just Ali's madness creeping through but what about that guy Zarrar? Well maybe he's gone back to Pakistan. If I can persuade Ali to let Shona be... If I can give myself up to the Irish authorities. Explain about Shadia... about what had happened since then... perhaps I can make them understand that I was simply going through some temporary madness after Shadia's death. I didn't detonate the bomb.

I'm going to pretend to help Ali find Shona and then I'll run with her. It can still work out. It might be alright. Ali's going through some terrible trauma. He'll get better. He's a good, holy man. I have to make him see that there's a better way to free his brother from Guantanamo Bay. A peaceful way in which no more people have to be hurt. I'll be Ali's bait to find Shona. Shona's the way out of all this. She saved me once and now we can save each other.

Today, I'll eat and drink, exercise and wash. I'll quiz Ali about Shona when he comes back to see me and then I'll make a plan.

Chapter forty six

I FALL over the step on the way out the door. I straighten myself and look around me. The sheets of rain coming down make it impossible to see far and the wind makes it hard to walk forward. It feels wonderful after weeks of being indoors. The fresh smell of autumn is exhilarating. Ali pushes me on towards a silver four-wheel drive that's parked on the road beside the beach. The sea and the sand make me think of Shona and my mind is focused on what's ahead of me. My hands are tied but Ali helps me into the car, wrapping the seatbelt around me, I'm going nowhere without him.

He reaches over and pulls the hood of my fleece up over my head before walking around towards the driver's side of the car. I close my eyes. This is for the best. It's the only way... Wherever Ali brings me, that's okay with me. Coming out into the world after weeks of captivity's a dizzying feeling so I sit and allow myself to simply be...

A familiar voice makes my eyes shoot open within seconds though. Zarrar's standing behind Ali. Where has he come from? I watch in horror as he leans forward with a knife and holds it to Ali's throat.

'Where exactly do you think you are going with this apparently dead man, my friend?' Zarrar speaks in a voice that makes me want to run, and keep running for my life. Ali opens his mouth to speak but the only noise that comes out is a gurgling sound as his throat is cut. Blood spurts out and I want to scream, but I'm rooted to the seat with fear. Zarrar has killed his own childhood friend. He'll have no qualms about sending me in the same direction.

I watch as the life blood drains from the man I once called my best friend, and Zarrar looks over at me, holding the bloody knife up to make his point clearer.

'Stay there.'

I'm locked in. I've no choice but to stay absolutely still. I begin to cry. Then I force myself to look at Ali and I start to scream.

'Scream as much as you like, dead man. There's nobody to hear you. Get it all out.' Then Zarrar puts his arms under Ali's arms and drags him, from the car, all the way down to the seashore. I wriggle in my seat, my screaming quieter now as I try in vain to reach the seatbelt release.

'Ali,' I cry. 'Ali, Ali,' over and over. I look down towards the shore as Zarrar rolls Ali's body into the sea, heading in after him and swimming in an effort to drag his friend further out. The wild winds will carry Ali elsewhere and the rain will quickly wash the blood away. For a moment I imagine Zarrar might be pulled under the waves and not be able to come back up but I know this is a false hope. This monster grew up surrounded by the sea. I watch him now as he surfaces, swims into the shore with ease and walks along the beach back towards the car.

'You'll pay for his death, you useless piece of shit!' he roars.

He's heading for the house now. I can run from here but then Zarrar will probably find Shona before I do. At least if I stay, I might be able to help her. That's all that matters now.

A few minutes later, Zarrar emerges wearing some of Ali's dry clothes from the house. He walks away leaving the front door wide open and jumps into the driver's seat. The knife lies across his lap; all traces of Ali's blood washed away while the rain cleans the splattered blood from the outside of the car. Soon there'll be nothing to show that Ali was here, just moments before.

'Shut up,' Zarrar responds to my whimpering. 'No more noise. Now let us get rid of your girlfriend, dead man. She is heading for Dublin tomorrow morning and we are sailing there this evening to act as her welcome committee.' He turns the ignition and drives along the road and I look back at the house for long enough to see the flames lap around the windows and the open door, winning the battle against the rain and leaving no evidence that Shona, me or Ali had ever been there.

So Zarrar knows that Shona's alive and he's taking Ali's place in using me as the bait to reel her in. Ali was supposed to have killed me and he's paid for his failure with his life. As soon as Zarrar has Shona in his sight he'll have no problem getting rid of both of us, and then he'll disappear having all loose ends from Ireland tied up.

I sit up in my seat and it all makes sense now. Ali's long absences and ramblings about Shona. He's been with Zarrar all this time. Zarrar's going to use me to find Shona. This man's not going back to Pakistan until he's able to report that although the mission's failed, there's not a trace of evidence left alive. I wish I'd asked Ali more about where Shona was. I look back towards the shore, where his body can no longer be seen, and I hope that my own death will be as swift as his has been. I weep in silence as the car speeds away, tears of fear mingled with those of grief. Another loss. *Ali...*

Zarrar drives a few kilometres down the road and pulls in. I watch him get out and open the trunk of the car. He then comes around the passenger side and opens the door.

'You can spend the rest of our trip in the trunk. I can't bear to have to look at you. I will keep you alive until I have the girl with me. Then you can have the pleasure of watching her go. One word from you in there though and I'll have no problems with disposing of you immediately.'

I climb in without a fuss, determined to be quiet. I'll do nothing to bring attention to myself. There might still be a way to help Shona. Zarrar looks down on me and smiles. His broken teeth adding to the ugliness of his sneer. I'm thinking of how much I hate this man when he speaks to me again.

'When I planted that bomb on the carousel in Riyadh, Jameel I never meant to kill any good Muslims with my efforts. It was only meant for the Irish on their ridiculous celebration in a land that was never meant for them. I was angry at first when I heard about Shadia. But now? I look at you and I'm filled with delight that I caused you such pain, and I will enjoy doing so again with another woman that you hold so dear.' Then he leans his fat hand on the door of the trunk and laughs. I stare at the man whose confession makes me relive so much grief and as if he can read my thoughts he clears up the matter screaming in my head. 'Yes it was me,' he says, 'and your beloved Ali too. He was the mastermind behind the action. All I did was press his buttons for him.'

I wriggle and roar at this evil man who's taken everything from me and I try to sit up, but Zarrar brings the door down on me with a thump. The first nail in my coffin.

Chapter forty seven

SHONA knew that going back to Dublin meant she was facing arrest for all sorts of weird things that she didn't even understand, but Bridget and Margaret were right. She couldn't run forever and since Ali's hospital visit she had been waiting for some horrific news of something terrible happening to her family. If she could give herself up in Dublin and say nothing about Ali... if she could prove to Ali that she would never put her family at risk...

The ferry journey was happening in slow motion with all the details of the last few weeks swirling around in Shona's head. They were sitting up on deck, waiting for instructions to disembark. Margaret kept reaching over and squeezing her hand and smiling in that reassured manner that was beginning to make Shona want to go straight to the bar and order a vodka on ice. That would set her up nicely. The wind was picking up now and it was beginning to rain, but they stayed where they were.

'You're definitely doing the right thing, love. I promise you. You'll be glad you came back.' If Margaret nodded her head like that once more Shona was going to sock her one.

'Margaret, how the hell would you know what the right thing is for me?' Shona's voice was full of resentment. 'I bet you've never done a *wrong* thing in all your days. You don't have any idea what it's like to have to face this. Well I've been singing out of tune forever, but I've never quite hit as bad a note as this one. I've never felt this bad; so angry with myself. I'm so bloody afraid of what's going to meet me at the other side.' Shona felt the tears coming and blinked. She was never very far from tears since she had the miscarriage.

'I'm off. Come on.' Shona stood up and grabbed her bag.

'Where are you going? We're just about to get off,' asked her aunt.

'The pub.'

Margaret stood up and faced her niece full on.

'Sit the fuck down this minute.'

Margaret had used the f word. Things were obviously that bad. Shona sat.

As if Shona had said nothing, Margaret continued lightly, 'I wish Bridget didn't have to go and collect all that baggage. Looking at her house, you'd wonder where she'd even kept all the stuff that she's brought. I hope she hurries back. I'd prefer if the three of us had stayed together.' Margaret looked uneasily at Shona. 'She's probably fretting over her cats and whether her neighbour will remember to feed them.' Eventually, with an angry look at Shona's sulky face, Margaret slumped down on the bench, leaving a few feet between them. For the next ten minutes they said nothing to each other. Margaret turned towards the sea and Shona stared at the deck.

She swallowed the lump in her throat. It was all bloody Margaret's fault and that bloody father of hers for telling Margaret where she was. When she got hold of him, she'd kill him.

She'd trusted him to be quiet about her whereabouts. He had always been on her side when it mattered. Her dad was the only one who had ever managed to discipline her; the one who did *not* make allowances for her when she messed up. He was the one person in the world to whom she showed respect…except she hadn't shown it very much over the last few months. She had taken her father's betrayal, his lies about her parentage, very badly. Of all people, she couldn't believe that he had done that to her and now he had let her down again. Shona stopped blinking and let the tears fall. It was the only way to release the emotions clogging up her brain.

She missed her father and deep down she knew that his sending Margaret to look for her was his way of reaching out. Des knew that talking to Margaret was exactly what Shona needed to make sense of everything, and he was right.

261

Bridget knew that too. When Margaret eventually tracked Shona down, Bridget took them both under her wing. Over the days that followed, Bridget was the driving force behind bringing Shona around to Margaret's way of thinking. She pushed and pulled and moulded and twisted and turned things to make Shona's life make sense. For someone who claimed to have no experience of life, Bridget had an awful lot of wisdom. Shona smiled at the thought. If Bridget really knew how troubled Shona's years had been up to now, she might not have committed herself so much, but Shona was sure that Bridget was to play a part in her future. They had become close. She was so glad that Bridget was coming back with them. She would help to shield her against the firing squad that Shona was about to face.

Margaret had also made her see how much her parents loved her. It was for them that Shona was coming back. Especially for her father.

Not to mention the beautiful baby she had left. She had been walking out on her almost from the day she was born. Shona had spent hours bawling over the photo of Ruby in the locket. Tommy's lovely birthday present. Ruby had looked so beautiful and innocent. So trusting. So absolutely amazing. She wanted to hold her. Her child. Ruby owed her nothing. No more than any of her family did. She shivered that she might have put them in some sort of danger and looked around nervously at her fellow travellers for the umpteenth time. Where was he? Was he in Dublin already? Did he know she was on her way home?

Shona had called Tommy that morning to explain about her coming back but he had put the phone down as soon as he heard her voice. She had called back a second time.

'Tommy, please listen. Listen to me and then hang up.'

'What could you possibly have to say, Shona that I'd want to hear?'

'I'm coming back, Tommy...'

'Like shite you are!'

'No, Tommy, hear me out. I'm coming back to give myself up to the Gardaí. No matter what happens after that, I want you to know that I never had anything to do with what Jameel did. I've been involved with a lot of crap this year, Tommy but never that. I knew nothing about it. I swear to you.

'I'm really scared Tommy. I don't know how to prove to them that I knew nothing. They're bound to believe that I'm guilty because I did a runner straight after. It looks so bad.'

'That's because it is, Shona. So, what made you decide to come back? Why are you really comin' back? Because the Shona Moran I know doesn't do sensible.'

'Margaret made me realise a lot of home truths.'

'Yeah... well... the one good thing your mother did was to choose Margaret to be your Godmother.'

'Yes...' Shona couldn't explain everything that had happened to her yet. Would she ever be able to tell Tommy about the ordeal that she had been through? That they had lost their second child. Probably not. Would he blame her as she did herself?

'Yeah, Margaret's great,' she said. 'I couldn't have managed coming back without her.'

His last words had been cruel, but justified.

'Shona. There's no point beatin' about the bush here. I'm not goin' to lie to you and pretend we're somethin' we're not. I wish I'd never met you. You've fucked up my life since the day we first slept together but that brought us Ruby. So you gave birth to her, but as far as I'm concerned that was it. Right now, today, I don't want to have anythin' to do with you. I've spoken to Margaret and she's told me she believes you had no idea about Jameel's true identity. Maybe I'm gone completely mad here, but I have to try to believe that too. For Ruby's sake.'

'It's true, Tommy, I...'

'Enough, Shona. I'm just not interested. Listen. And this is for your family's sake, not yours. Try to get out of Dun Laoghaire port. Go to Dundrum Garda Station and ask for Garda Kevin Daly. He's their family liaison officer and a good man. He'll do his best for you. If you're arrested at the port it'll all get out of hand.' Then he hung up.

Shona knew she deserved every last bit of his anger.

Maybe at some stage in the future, she and Tommy could be friends. When all this settled down, when the nightmare was over, Shona was going to work hard on getting him to forgive her. To try really hard to make him a friend, she'd had so few of those.

The ferry lifted suddenly and fell, and with it Shona's stomach turned. She barely made it over the side of the railings before vomiting.

'Oh, shit.' Margaret wiped the spray from her coat.

'I'm sorry, Margaret. Oh God. So sorry.' Shona took some deep breaths to help the nausea subside, willing her body to behave.

Margaret reached into her bag to pull out a packet of tissues and wiped herself down as best she could, until she was looking, and smelling, vaguely normal again. Shona had a mangled packet of mints in her bag from bygone days so they downed the lot between them.

'Okay, Shona. So you go out by yourself and I'll follow after. Bridget will meet us by the taxi rank as soon as she's collected her bags. Keep that cap on and your face neutral. It'll be fine. We'll be in a cab and heading for Dundrum Garda Station before we know it. We'll see that Garda Tommy mentioned in no time, and we'll get the whole sorry mess sorted.' Margaret pulled Shona in for a hug and stood back and smiled.

'I don't know which of us smells worse. Go on. Get out of here. See you in a few minutes.'

Chapter forty eight

MOVING slowly towards the exit, Shona's nerves were shattered. Thanks to Margaret's ingenious planning, she knew she'd probably have no trouble if she was stopped. She clutched her age ID card in one hand and her boarding pass in the other. Due to a misprint, her ID card had been issued with her middle name of Niamh and not Shona and as her boarding pass read Niamh Moran too, she'd have no problems.

Shona watched Margaret go towards the bathroom, so that they wouldn't be passing through together in case they were being followed. Her aunt had thought of everything.

Bridget was the only one of the three who had to collect suitcases. When she was through the passenger terminal, Shona would wait for the others outside at the taxi rank. She looked ahead of her to the front of the queue of people. They were rushing all the UK and Irish passengers through and, as a consequence, seemed to be looking at nobody. So much for security. Shona couldn't believe her luck. She gripped her bag and headed towards the exit. She had no intention of declaring herself as yet. With every step she waited for a hand on her shoulder to stop her, but she walked fast, willing herself to look straight ahead and not search the crowd for Ali.

Pulling the straps of her rucksack up over her shoulder, Shona walked outside the passenger terminal to see that there wasn't much of a queue at the taxi rank. She looked around but, as yet, there was no sign of Margaret or Bridget. She leaned against a wall and breathed a sigh of relief. She was through. Nobody had stopped her. She wasn't sure if the dizziness she felt was from giddy relief or the fear of what she was about to do. She walked across to the taxis to wait for the others to come out, willing them to hurry.

She was almost next in line when she heard him. A man was shouting in Arabic at the passenger in a four-wheel drive behind the short line of taxis... The language and volume caught her attention and as she looked back her eyes filled with terror as they locked with Jameel's.

'Jameel!' She called out before clamping her mouth shut as soon as the name had left her lips. But it was enough for the man sitting in the driver's seat beside Jameel to look her way. He stopped shouting, looked up and smiled. Jameel was screaming something at her. She looked at the man beside him and was filled with fear. Not Ali, but another man. There were probably lots of them. All out to do her and her family harm. The man began to shout at the wriggling Jameel again and pushed him back against his seat to keep him from getting out. Shona could hear Jameel telling her to run, to get away. But she wanted to run to him.

'Shona! Stop, Shona!' Another male voice calling behind her sounded familiar, but she couldn't look. She jumped into the taxi and closed the door.

'Where to, love?'

'Can you just drive for a minute; quickly!' Shona could barely speak. She looked briefly back over her shoulder. Jameel was still screaming at the man. He was causing a scene and a security man was heading towards the illegally parked silver car. 'Eh, I'm thinking... em, drive towards Dundrum and I'll make up my mind along the way.' She should do as Tommy said and go straight to Dundrum Garda Station, but what if the man saw her go in and headed straight for her family? Shona felt the familiar tightness in her stomach again.

Margaret headed out of the passenger terminal in time to see Shona taking off by herself in a taxi with Tommy running after it. She called after Shona's taxi to stop, but it was too late. She caught up with Tommy.

'What are you doing here? Not that I'm not delighted to see you, Tommy, but it looks like we have a problem.'

'What's she doin' goin' off on her own?'

Margaret looked panicked. 'I don't know Tommy, we had a plan. I don't know what she's playing at.'

'Neither do I, but come on. Let's hop into the next taxi and try to catch her up. I don't know what's the matter with her. Maybe the silly bitch has decided not to give herself up after all and do another runner.'

'What about Bridget?' Margaret was running back to the taxi rank with Tommy, but looking hopefully for signs of their friend at the terminal.

'Who's Bridget?' Tommy wasn't waiting for anyone.

'Shona was staying with Bridget in Wales and she came back to Ireland with us.'

'Well we'll have to find her later. Right now I'm goin' to catch that stupid cow just so as I can shake the fuckin' daylights out of her.'

'I have to say, I'm surprised you came to meet her, Tommy. She's really put you through the wringer this time.'

'Des thought it'd be a good idea for me to get a taxi out here and go with her to the Garda Station. Show them that we're all on her side. Moral support. I'll give her bleedin' moral support when I get hold of her.' Margaret recognised Tommy's breaking point so she jumped the queue and spoke to the people in front.

'It's my sister you see. We travelled to the port together, but I'm travelling on to France and she has my passport and... well, she's not answering her mobile...'

The crowd stepped back to let Tommy and Margaret in and the taxi driver put the pedal right down to the ground and raced out of the port after the other taxi. They reached for their seatbelts and Tommy looked over at Margaret. He could see she was nervous and on edge. A week of living with Shona would have that effect on you.

Tommy thought back to the events of the day so far and

267

wondered could they get any stranger. Never a dull moment in his life since the day he had woken up in bed with Shona Moran. After her call that morning, Tommy had contemplated what she had told him. He believed what she said about coming back and facing up to everything. It didn't sound like the Shona he knew, but maybe Margaret had managed to get through to her.

He had called Des. Always a good bet in an emergency. Having spent seventeen years bringing up Shona, Des was now an expert at emergencies.

'If she's stopped at Dun Laoghaire before giving herself in, if the media catch hold of it, it'll end up a right mess,' Des had explained.

Tommy wondered, not for the first time, how Des Moran had stayed sane living with Shona all those years. Tommy'd only done a six-month stretch and had lost the plot completely. Mind you, Des had had a few years of living with Norah before that. The man was a complete saint.

Tommy was afraid to make conversation with Margaret as the driver would most definitely cop on to them and drive a little slower than he was travelling at the moment. Considering the rain that was pelting down on them, and the approaching night, they were making good headway on the taxi in front of them and there was plenty of time for explanations later. He smiled over at her and she put a finger to her lips as if she had read his mind.

Tommy screwed up his nose suddenly at the smell in the car. 'What the hell is that?'

Margaret smiled. 'Your girlfriend puked and I caught the backlash. Sorry.'

His girlfriend? Tommy didn't like this one bit, but he would have to deal with all that later.

'Has she still got her mobile, Margaret?' Margaret shook her head. Tommy wanted all this over with. 'Can you get a bit nearer to the car?' he asked the driver. 'We're eh, runnin' out of time.'

The two cars came close to each other as they were approaching *The Goat Grill*. The taxi driver behind started to flash Shona's driver ahead and beeped his horn at him to stop. Shona's driver drove through the staggered crossroads, pulled in just past the traffic lights and got out of his car. Shona stayed in the taxi, petrified as to who might be behind them.

Presuming the worst, she closed her eyes and waited for what was to come. The man in the four-wheel drive had caught up with her. This was it.

She heard the crash like a series of muffled thumps followed by a screech of brakes. The sound of metal being crushed and glass smashing made her eyes fly open. Shona took off her seatbelt and leaned over to look out the window. She gasped at the sight of a lorry turned sideways across the crossroads.

She had to get out of the taxi. She couldn't sit and watch. Others had got out of their cars too, oblivious to the weather and the emerging dusk.

Shona pulled back out of sight as a silver four-wheel drive swerved and shifted out of the traffic. Jameel's car. The side of it was badly damaged. Had his driver caused the accident? Had he meant to hit her taxi and somehow the lorry had got in the way? Now he was trying to get away. He reversed back, stopped and looked around as if he was looking for a way out.

People were making their way towards the other side of the lorry. There was shouting and screams as they rounded the back. Shona stood unnoticed, hidden by the crowd. She knew it was callous of her but she thought she could probably run from this. Jameel and that man were backing away. Tommy had told her to go to the Gardaí, but if the man saw her... Ali had meant what he said. She needed some thinking space. There was no doubting that the man with Jameel had looked like he meant to harm her.

Shona began to move indecisively, wondering which way would be the best to go. She would have to leave her bag in the taxi. She couldn't carry it on foot. Getting away was more important.

Bending down to tie the lace she feared would trip her up when she ran, Shona was able to see under the huge wheels of the lorry. Another taxi was half crushed underneath. A mess of twisted metal; its hazard lights still strangely flashing, as if the warning of danger could help them now. 'Jesus,' whispered Shona. The driver was slumped over the steering wheel. Dead or unconscious? There was a woman too, her hair covering her face, trying desperately to get out from the back seat, arms flaying, terrified screams – but the doors were stuck.

That could have been me thought Shona. *It was supposed to be me. It was him.* Shona stood up quickly and the blood rushed to her head. She clung onto the bonnet of the taxi, while she steadied herself. When she felt a bit more stable she looked left and right for the car with Jameel. Moving away from her own taxi she heard the hushed conversation from the watching crowd.

'The man in the back is in trouble. Could he even make it out of that?'

'There're ambulances on the way.'

There was something about the woman in the back of the taxi. It was as if she had been shouting straight at Shona. She knew she needed to move soon, before police and others arrived, but she just couldn't pull away from what she knew to be her fault. The nightmare of Ali's words was turning into a reality. Shona bent back down to look again, this time letting out a piercing scream. They were Margaret's arms looking for a way out. Her *family and friends*. That's what Ali had said.

The crowd turned and watched her run, pushing her way towards the car.

'Margaret! Jesus, Margaret!'

Shona could hear the sirens in the distance. She watched Margaret moving around and hoped that meant she was alright.

'Please let her be okay.'

Margaret was frantically pointing at the man beside her, and horrified once again Shona put a hand to her mouth when she recognised the crushed body in the other seat. Tommy... How had he come to be there? She scrambled around to the front of the lorry to get to the other side of the car. The sound of sirens was getting nearer.

But walking in front of the lorry, Shona heard a loud revving sound and turned towards the noise. The silver four-wheel drive was now in front of her and the man behind the wheel was staring straight at her. She froze, standing with her back to the lorry, the palms of her hands stretched out behind her, reaching for something to grip. The driver, a menacing look on his face, smiled and began to reverse slowly away from her down Goatstown Road. Jameel was still in the passenger seat, writhing and twisting, shouting at her. Shona held her breath. Where was he going? Had the sirens frightened them into leaving? Her realisation that he had indeed caused this crash, hurt the people she loved made her feel weak. They had found out that she was coming home to face the Gardaí and they wanted her silenced. Had he seen Margaret with Tommy and decided to hurt the people she loved? These men would never go away. As long as Shona was alive, they would be a danger to her family. They had already shown this today. It would never stop.

Shona began to shake. When the car had reached as far back as it could go, it stopped and began revving once more. She cried out as she watched the man began to drive towards her with speed. She should run or duck back under the lorry, but she stood still and waited. This was for the best. So many times in the last few months she had wanted this. Total oblivion. An end. The car got nearer and she saw Jameel scream and struggle with his seatbelt. Shona stopped hearing the sirens then and felt her ears whoosh with dizziness as her legs gave way underneath her.

*

I throw myself around the passenger seat and roar at Zarrar as he races towards her.

'No! Shona, No!'

My anger fills me with strength. Allah's worked through Shona to protect others before. Now he will work through me to save her. My own death's imminent and no doubt Zarrar has something horrific planned for me, but I'll die in my own way. This is Allah's plan. And I'll take this mad man with me. With both Ali and Zarrar gone, Shona'll be safe. Powered with

271

determination, I manage to pull my seatbelt from its socket and in the same swift movement, I fling myself across the car on top of Zarrar, redirecting the steering wheel and shouting one last prayer.

'Allah Akbur!'

*

When Shona came round, it took time for her to focus on the sight of Jameel slumped across the silver bonnet in front of the driver, on a bed of broken glass. Sitting up slowly, she grimaced at the driver's slashed face. The paramedic was holding his wrist and shaking his head. Jameel lay on his side, his head lolled over the edge; his eyes wide open. Shona saw the bloodied hands tied in front of him. A prisoner. He hadn't been part of this. She closed her own eyes and willed his to do the same.

Another paramedic was by her side within seconds and she sat up. She tried to take in everything that had happened around her. 'No, I'm fine,' she said and pointed at the taxi under the lorry.

'They need you.'

'Another ambulance crew is with them,' said the man. 'Are you hurt?'

Shona shook her head and pulled herself up in time to see the driver's body being stretchered into an ambulance. She pushed away the yearning to run to Jameel and hold him; to close his eyes.

'He's dead. Oh God, he's dead.'

'They both are,' the man by her side was nodding gravely.

She fought the tears and tore her face away. She knew she had to drag herself around to the side of the lorry where Tommy and Margaret were still trapped.

Tommy's eyes were open; looking terrified. He blinked. Shona stared incomprehensibly at him. What was he doing in a taxi with Margaret? Where was Bridget? Only Tommy's head and shoulders were visible, twisted at an angle. One hand was raised up over his shoulder.

'Not you, Tommy. Oh, God. I'm so sorry.'

There was a gap in the wreckage where Shona could squeeze her fingers through and she held Tommy's hand. She told him that the paramedics would help him. To hang on. Shona talked. About anything that would keep Tommy with her until the ambulance or fire brigade could get him out. She spoke across to Margaret. Calmed her. The driver came round and Shona spoke to them all. She said all the right things.

It took almost half an hour to break away their metal cell. Piece by piece. So slowly. All the time Shona held Tommy's hand. She never noticed the Gardaí moving everyone back into their cars and away from the area. She heard the conversation behind the lorry about Jameel's hands being tied and the need to let the Gardaí take photos before they removed the body. The rain softened and stopped, then sprinkled and built momentum until it was howling around them again. Firemen and paramedics worked on around her. The dusk became darkness, lit up by the flashing of ambulances, fire brigades and Garda cars, and still Shona talked.

First Margaret was free and Shona watched her walk almost unscathed to an ambulance. Jim the taxi driver was carried out; the blow to his head didn't seem to be too bad. Sirens announced their departure to hospital.

When the car was unwrapped from Tommy's body, Shona stopped talking. He was screaming about the pain in his leg and Shona looked at the paramedic in panic.

'The pain is a good thing, love,' he said. 'It means he can still feel everything. I wouldn't be surprised if he's right as rain in no time.'

When they eventually lifted him from the car to the stretcher, Tommy passed out. Shona wondered how he had stayed conscious for so long anyway.

She was heading for the ambulance to go with Tommy when she felt a tap on her shoulder and she turned around. A Garda was looking at her curiously.

'Did you see what happened?' he asked.

By the light of the moon in the newly cleared sky, Shona could see the door of Tommy's ambulance closing without her. She looked back at the Garda and nodded. This was it. Any minute now she would be surrounded by Gardaí, all waiting for a slice of the Shona Moran who was wanted for crimes of terrorism.

Chapter forty nine

'WAS that your boyfriend taken away in the ambulance?' The Garda asked.

Shona wondered if he meant Jameel or Tommy? It didn't matter. Jameel was dead and Ali had organised someone to carry out his threat to hurt her family.

'Yes,' she said.

'Did you witness the accidents? Were you here when the cars crashed?'

'Accidents?' Shona stared at the Garda. They still didn't know who was dead in the other car. They had no idea, as yet, who she was. She could still run. Show Ali that she had no intention of telling anything.

'The crashes. They were separate, yeah? Terrible business with the foreigners and the guy whose hands were tied. Did you see it happen?' The Garda was getting impatient now and turned his eyes upwards as another Garda joined him. Shona looked back at the crushed taxi, then over at the four-wheel drive that had held Jameel prisoner minutes before. There was no point in running. She would have to take her chances with the Gardaí.

'Yes,' she whispered.

'Will you come down to Dundrum Garda Station and give a statement?'

She looked after Tommy's ambulance driving away.

'We'll give you a lift up to the hospital straight after.' The second Garda was heading towards their squad car and beckoning her to follow him.

Dundrum? She might make it there yet. This was for the best. It was the only thing that she could do. She found herself floating

275

towards the Garda car and allowing him to usher her into the back seat. She wasn't being arrested. It was okay. She had done nothing wrong, but that didn't stop her shaking. Both Gardaí got into the front of the car and didn't lock the doors. She could still leg it out at the traffic lights if she wanted to.

'Are you hurt yourself? Were you in the car?' The female Garda motioned her to put on her seatbelt.

'No.' The less said, the better for now.

'But you know the people in the car? It's your boyfriend?'

'Yes.'

'And who else?'

This was tricky. Which car was she talking about? Shona shrugged her shoulders and let the tears come. Only a little. She couldn't give in to the grief yet. She had to hold back. The driver shook his head and tutted.

'Leave her alone now, Jenny until we get her into the station and give her a cup of sweet tea. She's been through a terrible trauma.'

Shona was thankful for the quiet. Her head was bursting with thoughts that were threatening to overpower her. She tried to overcome the rush by imagining she was holding her child in her arms, the soft baby smell filling her nostrils. Thinking of her daughter helped to settle her and whatever happened from here she would get to see Ruby again. She knew she would have a fight on her hands getting Tommy to let her back into her baby's life, and she didn't blame him, but it was a fight she wouldn't back down from. She knew her parents and Margaret would be there to help too.

They pulled into the station car park a few moments later. Getting out of the car, Shona leaned against it again for support, as another Garda rushed out of the station.

'Daly.' Her driver nodded at the man coming towards them.

Lifting her head very slowly, Shona made full eye contact with him. Was this the man who had been working with her family to find her? The Garda who had gained Tommy's trust. He said his name was Daly didn't he? Kevin Daly. Did he recognise her? Yes.

His eyes were wider now; his jaw dropped slightly. She should say her name quickly. Give herself up before he said anything. It would be better.

'Jesus. You're…'

'Yes… I'm Shona.'

He turned then to the other Gardaí. 'Why is she here? You should have brought her to Harcourt Street. And why is she not handcuffed?'

The relief of being here at last flooded through her, but the other two Gardaí looked from one to the other, confused.

Suddenly the door of the Garda station burst open again and a shout made them all turn around.

'Shona!' Bridget came running towards her, breathless. 'Shona, you just tell them the truth. Like I told you. The truth is the only thing worth having. I've been telling them that you were on your way here. I came looking for you. It's going to be fine, Shona. Just you wait and see.'

Garda Daly took out his handcuffs and motioned for Shona to turn around, but she let out a yelp and ran towards Bridget's open arms.

'Bridget… they did it!' she spluttered. 'What they said about getting my family… Tommy's hurt badly and Margaret's in hospital too. You have to get out of here. He'll get you too. Jameel's dead, Bridget. He was tied up and the man who had him is dead too. You have to get out of here.'

Garda Daly tried to reach for her again, but this time he was rougher and swung her around using the other Gardaí to hold her while he handcuffed her.

'You have to go and mind them! Mum and Dad and Ruby! He'll be there already. It's already happened… What he said about hurting my family…'

'Shona Moran. I'm arresting you for aiding and abetting a terrorist…'

'No!' said Bridget. ''She didn't do anything. She didn't even know that…'

'Ali will get my family if I tell you anything. You have to send

277

someone to protect them. Please...'

'Ali?' Garda Daly was all ears now. 'Do you know his full name?'

Shona looked around her warily in the dark of the car park. She expected to see him, hiding in the shadows, ready to attack her as soon as he could.

'Ali Al Asiz,' she whispered.

'Was he a part of Jameel Al Manhal's group?' asked Kevin. Shona nodded.

'Well, Shona. We'll send a unit around to your parents' house but... the man you're worried about? ...There was a body washed up on a beach in Wales this morning. That of a man in his mid-twenties. Welsh police have identified him as wanted terrorist, Ali Al Asiz. Police in Ireland and the UK have been searching for this man for months, in connection with the bomb scare in Dublin on the 8th of August... So I doubt he poses any more of a threat to you.'

Shona took a deep breath. She could barely hear what the Garda was saying, but she had got the essence of it. Ali was dead. The other two Gardaí were chatting excitedly about what they had just heard. They were beginning to realise who she was and why their colleague was so stressed about her being there. She continued to breathe heavily, in and out. If Ali was dead and that other man who was with Jameel was also gone, then maybe she was out of danger. Perhaps the worst of this was over and there would be nobody left to hurt her family. Ruby would be safe.

'So... we'll try that again.' Garda Daly looked at Bridget, daring her to interrupt again. But Bridget stood back, knowing that it was time to let Shona do what she should have done weeks ago. 'Shona Moran. I'm arresting you for aiding and abetting a terrorist. You are not obliged to say anything unless you wish to do so, but...'

She didn't wish to say anything and Shona heard nothing more. With her hands behind her, she looked up now at the clear night sky and saw three stars shining brightly. Jameel's stars. The Summer Triangle. She couldn't remember their names, but she knew they were important to Jameel in some way. The sight of them filled her now, not with the grief she would have expected, but with a gift. The gift of hope. Jameel had said that the constellation was first visible in the East in the spring and could be seen in the West into the autumn.

And there it was.

'Let's go, Shona.' Garda Daly turned her now towards the station door, but she looked back once more at the Summer Triangle. Jameel, Shona and Tommy. Or was it Shadia, Jameel and Shona? Either way they were Jameel's stars now and he was part of them, following a different path.

Well Shona would follow hers. She wouldn't let the past ruin her future.

She nodded then at the Garda and for the first time in months, maybe years, Shona Moran moved a step forward in the right direction.

"Because sometimes you have to do something bad to do something good."
– Oscar Wilde, *The Complete Fairy Tales*